Reckless

Copyright © 2023 by Becca Steele

All rights reserved. No part of this book may be reproduced or transmitted in any form or by any means, electronic or mechanical, including photocopying, recording or by any information storage and retrieval system, without written permission from the author, except for the use of brief quotations in a book review.

Editing by One Love Editing

Becca Steele

www.authorbeccasteele.com

This is a work of fiction. Names, characters, businesses, places, events, locales, and incidents are either the products of the author's crazy imagination or used in a fictitious manner. Any resemblance to actual persons, living or dead, or actual events is purely coincidental.

AUTHOR'S NOTE

The author is British, and this story contains British English spellings and phrases. The football referred to in this story is known as soccer in some countries.

Please note that this book may contain triggers for some readers. Please view the content warnings page below for details:
https://authorbeccasteele.com/trigger-warnings/

For those who love the beautiful game

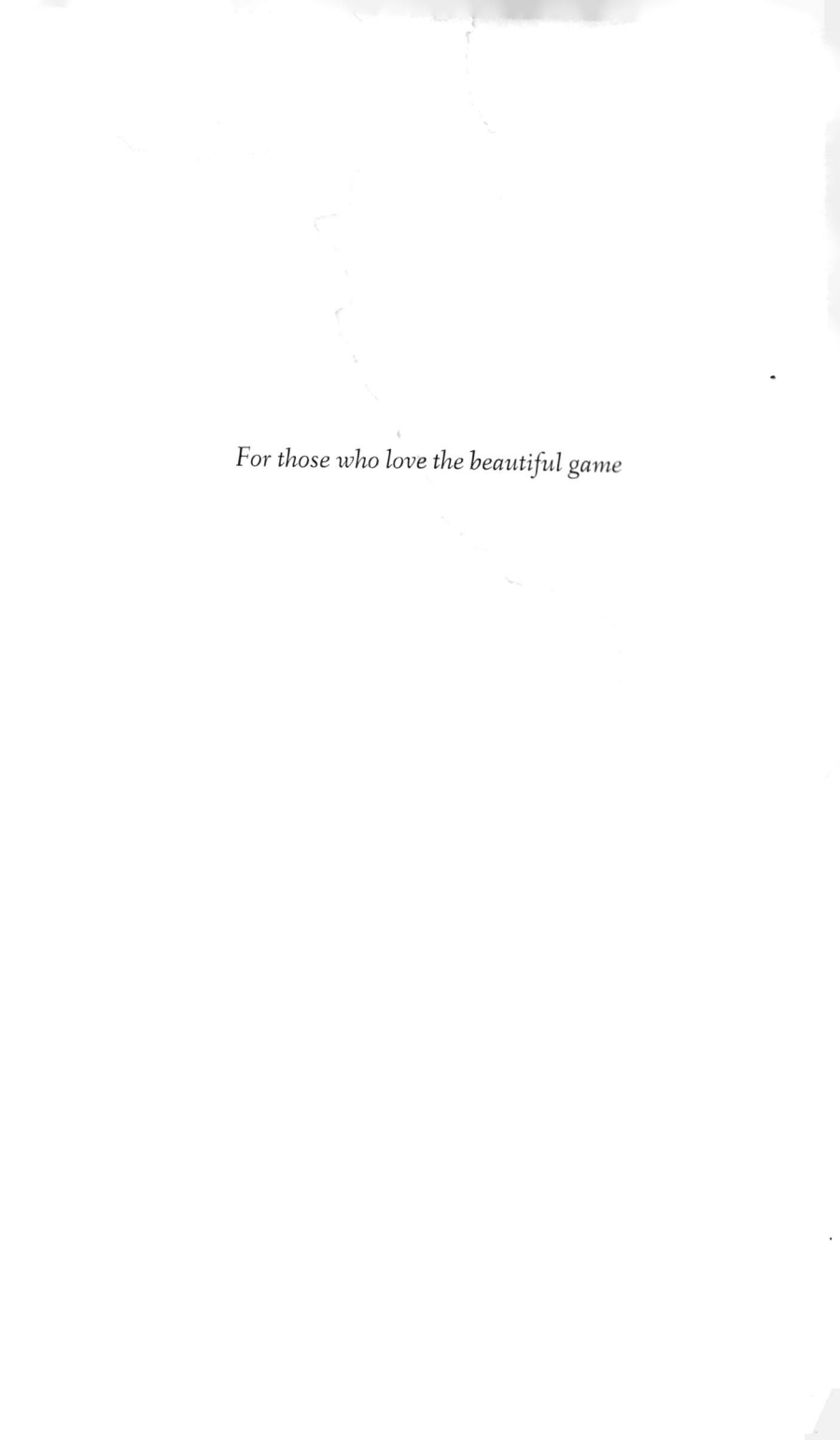

The more difficult the victory, the greater the happiness in winning.

PELÉ

JORDAN

PROLOGUE

How was this my life? On a plane to fuck-knows-where, with the one person I really, truly hated, forced to spend the next however long cooped up with the miserable bastard?

What had I done to deserve this?

Okay. There were one or two...or three or four events that had led up to this drastic "intervention," as my agent called it. As if giving it a name would make it any better.

I guess I should rewind time a bit to work out just how I'd managed to arrive at this point...

The first time I met Theodore Lewin, aka Theo, aka fuckface twatwank, we were both thirteen years old, on the first day of youth academy training. For prospective footballers, getting into a youth academy was a chance to break into the pros. For the academy we both joined, Cotswold Elite Football Youth Academy, aka CEFYA, we got to be mentored by professionals as we grew up, and scouts regularly visited us. And for those lucky few exceptionally talented members, they might get a shot at a place on the youth team of a Premier League club.

Theodore, or Theo, as most people called him, was an arrogant, haughty little shit. My first memory of him was him swaggering onto the training pitch where I was doing drills with cones, wearing a perfectly pressed football kit and the Adidas boots that I'd been coveting for almost a year but couldn't afford. He looked around him with a sneer on his full lips and his nose in the air. His light blue eyes scanned over me as he ran his hand through his sleek black hair, and for some reason, I lost my concentration and tripped over the cone I was about to run around.

The stupid stuck-up brat laughed, pointing in my direction, his voice easily carrying to where I lay, sprawled on the grass.

"Mother said this was the number one academy, but honestly, if they let clowns like that in, I'm not sure I want to waste my time here."

I glared at him. Rude, posh bastard.

Leaping to my feet, I placed my hands on my hips, staring him down. "Got lost on the way to the opera, did ya? Or was it afternoon tea?"

His lip curled into a sneer again. "It may surprise you, Trip, but there are those of us with breeding that do have the ability to kick an inflated pig's bladder around a field with some measure of skill."

My mouth dropped open, totally against my will. What thirteen-year-old kid talked like this? No one else I knew, that was for sure.

Wait a minute. *"Trip?"*

"Well, I did see your rather spectacular fall just now. Seemed fitting."

"Don't ever call me that again," I growled, stepping right

up to him and shoving my chest against his, full of the reckless bravado of a teenage boy.

Before he could respond, a whistle blew, and we were being pulled apart by one of the members of staff.

That day was just the beginning.

The months, and then the years, went by, and as we honed our skills, it became apparent that we were both suited to the same position of right-winger. Which meant that when we played other academies and youth teams, we were in constant competition with each other. And Lewin was good. Really fucking good. He was the arrogant thorn in my side, always there, ready to take my place on the right wing. Maybe he thought the same about me—we were pretty evenly matched—but if he did, he didn't show it. He just liked to taunt me in private and keep his untouchable, icy persona in public.

I'd never hated anyone until I met him. But from the age of thirteen, we were enemies. It was an indisputable fact. The sun rose in the east. The moon orbited the earth. Jordan Emery and Theodore Lewin hated each other.

When we both went pro, I had another reason to resent him. When he was seventeen, he managed to land a coveted spot on Glevum FC's youth team, and from there, he was offered a place on the main pro team. Glevum FC had always been my preferred choice. Not only were they in the Premier League, arguably one of the best and most elite football leagues in the world, if not *the* best, but they were also my local team growing up in my home county of Gloucestershire. I'd spent many happy Saturday afternoons in the stands with my dad, draped in the team's scarf in red and gold, cheering on the players alongside the other Glevum Gladiators—the nickname for Glevum FC's fans due to our local Roman history and the Roman helmet on the club's badge. I'd always dreamed of playing there, and I knew I was good enough. But for whatever reason, they bypassed me in favour of Lewin. The contract I ended up being offered was for another local club, Forest Green Rovers, but while I was really fucking happy to be offered a contract with a professional club, and one in the same county at that, they were in League Two, and from the moment I was signed, the Premier League seemed like a pipe dream.

Forest Green Rovers were amazing. I couldn't fault them. The staff, the team, the ethics of the club...they ticked so many of my boxes. I threw myself into the game, concentrating on honing my skills, and did my best to ignore the ball of resentment in my stomach that seemed to grow bigger every time Theodore Lewin was mentioned. The ball that grew bigger every time the pundits spoke of Glevum's league chances for the season and how Lewin could play a major part in the club's success.

I did my best, but my best wasn't good enough.

My resentment grew.

Then, something happened to change the trajectory of my career, and while it should have been a dream come true for me, it ended up as a nightmare.

One pivotal moment in my career led to a chain of events that put me on the plane to tropical hell with my rival...

PART 1

ONE

THEO

"Thanks for coming in today on such short notice." Glevum FC's manager, aka the gaffer, aka Harvey Raines, steepled his fingers as he stared at me impassively from across the table. The overhead lights gleamed on his bald head, giving it a shine as if he'd polished it. He gave a slight nod to the left, and I swallowed, lowering myself into the indicated chair, and surreptitiously wiped my sweating palms on my perfectly pressed trousers. Next to me, Amir, my agent, sighed. He couldn't even tell me what today's emergency meeting was about.

Couldn't...or wouldn't. I shot him a suspicious look out of the corner of my eye, and he just sighed again, taking his own seat and busying himself with opening up his iPad, the keyboard lighting up as he input his password.

Returning my attention to Harvey, I folded my hands neatly in my lap and waited.

I didn't have to wait long.

"As you know, Knowles sustained a hamstring injury against Liverpool last Saturday. Unfortunately, it's worse than we anticipated. He's going to be out for the rest of the season."

"Shit," I muttered under my breath before inwardly cursing myself. Years of being around football players meant that some of their bad habits had rubbed off on me. Still, I supposed swearing was one of the more harmless vices I'd adopted. I doubted my parents would agree, but then again...they'd have to take an interest in me in the first place to be in a position to agree or disagree. That was highly unlikely to happen, based on their track record ever since I'd diverted from their chosen path to become a professional footballer. It had been harmless when it was only a "hobby," but to choose it as a career? It was unheard of in their circles. Not to mention the fact that I had chosen to play instead of attending a prestigious university. But in the world of professional football, most started young. While there were a select few who had been able to complete a degree alongside the rigorous training schedule that made up our day-to-day lives, for those in the English Premier League, they were few and far between.

"Indeed. Here's where I find myself in a bind." Harvey leaned forwards, planting his hands on the table. "I have the chance to sign another player in the January transfer window. His club doesn't seem to realise what a talent they have on their hands, so it looks like we'll be able to get him for a steal."

"That's good, isn't it?" I glanced over at Amir again, but he was tapping away on his iPad, studiously ignoring me, frowning at the screen through his chunky, black-framed glasses, with his mouth pulled into a thin line. I wasn't going to get any help from my agent, that was for sure.

"It's good...but it has repercussions for you."

Wonderful.

"We'll need to move you from the right-wing position to the left wing. He's almost hopeless on the left. I've watched hours of footage and studied him in person, and it's the only conclusion I can come to. By moving you to the left, Glevum FC have a good shot at finishing in the top ten of the table this season, maybe even higher. If we could actually get a shot at Europe...it would be unprecedented for the club. To achieve that as the manager..." Trailing off, Harvey shook his head with a small huff of laughter. "I'd be fulfilling a lifelong dream."

"I don't play on the left." My words came out steady, but my hands were trembling beneath the table. There was a reason I was building up a reputation as a solid, dependable, talented right-winger. *Because I was fucking good at it.* And not only that, but I loved it.

Harvey exhaled heavily. "I know you don't, but you and I both know you can. You've done it before when Knowles has been injured. You're good, Lewin. Very good. I wouldn't ask you to do this if I didn't believe you were capable."

I was actually going to have to do this, wasn't I? It wasn't as if I had any other choice.

Harvey was still speaking. "I've arranged for some additional training sessions to get you used to playing on the left. Once the transfer is complete, we'll get you doing drills with Emery. He's going to be thrown in at the deep end, coming to a Premier League team from League Two, and he won't have much time to get used to the team before we need him out there on the pitch."

Emery. *Emery?* No. No, no, *no.*

"Jordan Emery?" His name was ground out between gritted teeth, and my hands were no longer shaking with nerves but with rage.

Harvey smiled, the gold cap on his left incisor flashing

at me. "That's him. You were at CEFYA together, weren't you? He doesn't know anyone else on the team, as far as I'm aware, so I'm expecting you to be the one to show him the ropes."

What was this hellhole my life had suddenly descended into?

Jordan fucking Emery. That brown-haired, grey-eyed, golden-skinned bane of my existence ever since we were thirteen years old was going to be my teammate? And even worse, to take my fucking place on the team? That was a hard-won position. A place that had cost me blood, sweat, and tears.

He thought he could usurp my position as Glevum FC's right-winger?

Absolutely not.

TWO

JORDAN

"I've perused the offer and contracts, and I've had my guy check the paperwork over, as well as Glevum FC's lawyers. Everything looks good, as far as we're concerned. Are you ready to sign? The club won't hold off forever." Rory, my agent, rubbed his hand over his dark, neatly trimmed beard as he eyed me from across his desk. Picking up an expensive-looking silver fountain pen, he tapped the stack of papers in front of him.

"I want to. It's just—"

"Jordan. I'm going to give you some tough love here because you need it." Placing the pen down, he planted his hands on the wooden surface on either side of the paperwork, his dark gaze intent on mine. "Playing in the Premier League is your dream, and you should never lose sight of that. Signing for a top-flight team is something you and I have been working towards since you turned sixteen. You're nineteen now, not too far off from turning twenty, and I'm telling you that it's highly unlikely you'll get another chance like this. Are you man enough to put your petty, childish differences with one person aside and act like the team player I know you are?"

Becoming Theodore Lewin's teammate... Did I want that? Fuck, no, but Rory was right. I'd be a fucking fool to turn this opportunity down. This was my chance to play at elite level, for the team I loved. My dream football club wanted me. *Me.*

"Gimme the pen," I muttered, and I was rewarded with a hint of a smile from my agent.

"Good boy."

"I've told you before not to say that. I don't have a praise kink. It sounds weird coming from you. Why don't you go out and find a hot, willing woman to fuck—preferably one with an actual praise kink and a thing for bossy, bearded men?"

Tutting, Rory shook his head, his small smile widening into an amused grin as he handed me the pen. "The mouth on you. I think I liked you better when you were a sweet, innocent teenager."

"You *thought* I was sweet and innocent." Uncapping the pen, I began scrawling my signature at the tabbed places. I also had an electronic copy to sign, as requested by the club, but Rory liked to keep things old-school and definitely less environmentally friendly than he should.

"Look at all the trees and squids that died for this." I waved my hand over the never-ending pile of printed pages. "What's your problem with technology, grandad?"

"Brat. That ink does not come from squids, I'll have you know. You should be more concerned about the information you have online, Jord. AI is in danger of taking over the world one day."

"When that day comes, I'll bow down to our evil robot overlords."

"Jordan. This isn't a joking matter."

Glancing up at him, I noticed the serious look on his face, and I immediately nodded, in complete agreement. "I know. I fucking hate that AI shit. But I'd like to see them try to replace me with a robot. The fucker wouldn't have a clue what to do."

He shook his head again, huffing out a laugh. "No one could ever replace you. Who else would grind my gears like you do?"

"Yeah, you're right. No one could replace me because I'm one of a kind." Reaching the final page, I signed with a flourish. "Done."

"Right." He was all business again, gathering the papers into a neat stack and setting them aside before sliding his laptop across the desk to me. "Now you need to do the same thing with the electronic version. Once everything's signed and Glevum confirms receipt, we'll liaise with them to arrange a press conference or whatever they want to do to announce you as the club's new right-winger."

A smirk tugged at my lips as I imagined how pissed off Theo was going to be at the news that I was taking his position. If only I could have been there to see his face when the gaffer told him. Equally, if the shoe had been on the other foot, I knew he would've taken great pleasure in gloating about how he'd taken my place.

Rory was still talking, and I tuned back in to find him saying something about money. Time to concentrate.

"...While your initial wages will be low for the Premier League because you're new and need to prove yourself, we can boost them with sponsorship deals, and there's a clause in your contract that allows us to renegotiate your wage if you make enough of an impression. That means regular games, scoring goals, you know the drill."

"What are the sponsorship deals?"

He picked up his briefcase, laying it on the table and unclipping the catches. "Let me see... I've rejected a couple already. The supplements, no. The energy drinks, no again—"

"But I like energy drinks!"

"Yes, but the club already has an endorsement deal with another brand. You won't be allowed to drink anything but that brand. Not in public, at least."

"No more Pacific Punch?" I pouted, earning an eye roll from Rory.

"I'm sure you'll survive. Now, here's a sponsorship deal that I think might interest you. It's an underwear brand aimed at the eighteen-to-twenty-something market. Guys who are seriously into working out and looking good. The social media posers like you that enjoy flaunting their six-packs everywhere they go." He patted his own slightly soft middle. "Unlike me."

I laughed. "You've still got it. You're a daddy. A zaddy, in fact. Women go crazy for that shit, trust me."

He gave a long-suffering sigh, pinching his brow. He loved me, really. "I don't even want to know what a 'zaddy' is, and aside from that, how would you know that women go crazy for it?"

"Because." Pulling my phone from my pocket, I scrolled through my social media until I found the picture of Rory I'd posted earlier today. Dressed in his smartly tailored suit, with his neatly trimmed beard and styled hair, he was walking through the car park towards me, briefcase in one hand and a takeaway coffee cup in the other. The sun was gleaming on his dark hair, and I'd caught him at a flattering angle, if I did say so myself.

I grinned. "Look at the comments and likes on this post."

I'd captioned the image, "Big things are coming... Meeting my agent @rorynashagent," and about twenty seconds after I'd posted it, I'd received a huge flood of likes and comments. The image now had over twelve thousand likes, and as for the comments... I handed Rory my phone, watching with a grin as he scanned the screen, a flush appearing on his cheeks.

The minds of some women...and some gay men...they could be really fucking dirty at times. Some of the comments even made *me* blush. Well, not really. I was used to that shit. Half of my social media was me posing, because let's face it, if you've got it, you might as well fucking flaunt it. The other half was all related to football. The number of propositions I'd had in my DMs—I'd need at least two dicks and two lifetimes to service every woman that wanted a piece of me.

I wasn't exaggerating. Much.

Rory handed the phone back to me, his mouth in a flat line, and I couldn't stop the laugh bursting from my lips. "See? They want you, bro. They'll be hitting up your DMs, I guarantee."

"I'm not your bro," he clipped out. "And I would appreciate you not posting my image without permission."

"It's an expression for friends. Like dude. Or mate. Or bruv. Get with the times, grandad. Or should I call you 'zaddy'?" He gave me a warning look when I tapped my chin, pretending to think about it, and I relented. "Alright, I'm sorry I posted your photo without asking you first, but look at it this way. Thanks to me, you might actually get laid this century."

"I don't get paid enough for this," he muttered darkly, but I could see him trying to bite back a smile.

I pasted on my best innocent smile. "None of your other clients care for your well-being as much as I do. Here I am, thinking of your poor, neglected di—"

"Jordan Emery. Enough." He used what I called his "teacher" voice, which he brought out when he needed me to be serious. "Now, do you want this underwear brand endorsement or not?"

Playtime was over. "How much are they offering, and are they using any other sports personalities? What's their ethical stance?"

Pulling up their company info on my phone, Rory and I went over the offer they'd sent me, and just under an hour later, he'd composed an email to say that we were interested and would like to see the full contract. As he sent the email, his inbox pinged with an alert, and he glanced up at me with a smile.

"Glevum FC just confirmed receipt of your contract. You're officially a professional footballer in the Premier League."

A wide grin split my face, and I jumped up from my chair, rounding the desk and throwing my arms around my agent. "I couldn't have done it without you. Thanks, Ror. I know you put up with a lot of shit from me."

He ruffled my hair, and I made a mental note to check a mirror before I stepped outside again. "Ah, you're worth it, I suppose. Want to celebrate with champagne? I have a bottle on ice."

"You were that confident I'd sign?" Hopping up onto the desktop next to his chair, I grinned down at him.

"Yes. You're not the type to let a petty feud stand in the

way of your dreams. You just needed me to remind you of that fact."

As he called his assistant, Sunita, to bring the champagne in, popping the cork and pouring three brimming glasses, I lost myself in imagining Theo's reaction to my signing and ousting him of his position.

I couldn't wait to see his face. In fact... While Rory and Sunita were occupied with the champagne, I quickly pulled up my social media messaging app. While I didn't have Theo's phone number, I had his social media details. The fucker had more followers than me, but that would soon change once the news of my signing came out.

> @JORDANEMERY_OFFICIAL:
> Heard the news yet? Looking forward to your new position on the left???

A reply came through almost straight away, but I had to wait until Rory's attention was diverted again before I checked my messages. He would most definitely not approve of me antagonising my future teammate.

When I finally got a second to myself, I opened the app, a grin pulling at my lips as I read Theo's response.

> @THEOLEWIN_OFFICIAL:
> Do me a favour and block me, Emery

> @JORDANEMERY_OFFICIAL:
> That's no way to greet your new teammate

> @THEOLEWIN_OFFICIAL:
> Don't get used to it. Harvey will soon see he's made a mistake

> @JORDANEMERY_OFFICIAL:
> Haha I wouldn't be so sure

@THEOLEWIN_OFFICIAL:

> I would. I've been here since the beginning of the season. Where were you? Oh yes, you were playing for a sub-par team in league 2

@JORDANEMERY_OFFICIAL:

> Fuck right off. FGR are not a sub-par team you egotistical wanker

@THEOLEWIN_OFFICIAL:

> Regardless, the fact remains that I was the one signed to a top-tier team and you're only here because Knowles was injured, and you were dirt cheap. As soon as he's back to full fitness, you'll be relegated to the sidelines where you belong

My grin disappeared. Fucking bastard. He wasn't wrong about most of it, which left a bitter taste in my mouth, but I wouldn't let him rain on my parade. Whatever the reasons were, the fact was that there were other good wingers available for transfer, but Glevum FC had chosen *me* out of everyone. My dream was coming true, and I wouldn't let one asshole ruin it for me. And I was going to fight to keep my place, even if Knowles came back—which might not even happen because he was one of the oldest players in the league, and there had already been talk of retirement before he was injured. I'd just have to prove to everyone that I had the talent and the drive to succeed. I'd make myself indispensable to the team, and then they'd have no choice but to keep me on.

@JORDANEMERY_OFFICIAL:

> Say what you want but I'm the one taking your position. Remember that. Have a good evening bestie

I added a couple of kiss emojis and then pocketed my phone so I wouldn't be tempted to continue the conversation. I'd riled Theo up enough.

For now.

THREE

THEO

I was living in a nightmare. From my vantage point in the back corner of the room, I watched the cameras flash in quick succession, making the cluster of microphones that had been thrust under Jordan Emery's nose stand out in sharp relief. This was supposed to have been a low-key event—who cared if a Premier League club signed a virtually unknown player?—but the reporters had done their due diligence, and someone, somewhere, had found out about our supposed "feud." My money was on that slimy git Greaves—he'd been at CEFYA with us both, and he'd always resented us for being more talented than him. The last I'd heard, he was playing for a non-league club, but it looked like he'd had a career change since he was sitting amongst the other journalists. From the smug, satisfied smile on his face that I could easily see from my position, it didn't take a genius to put two and two together. The jealousy radiating from him as he reclined in his third-row seat was almost palpable, despite his obvious glee.

Thanks to Greaves, Harvey had asked me to come along today, even though I'd rather poke out my own eyeballs with a fork than endure this farce of a press conference. He'd laughed off the rumours, but he wanted to make a point of showing the press that there was no animosity between myself and my new teammate.

The reporter from Sky Sports cleared her throat, glancing over her shoulder at me before returning her gaze to Emery. "Do you think you'll be able to put your differences with Theo Lewin aside and do what's best for the club?"

I sucked in a breath, my body stiffening as a significant number of the press in the small conference room turned their attention to me. I'd never been more thankful for my breeding, which allowed me to smile graciously while I internally cursed Jordan Emery for putting me in this position.

"Helping Glevum FC to go as far as they can in the league is my one and only goal. Yeah, Theodore and I clashed in the past, but we were children back then, and we didn't know any better. You know what kids are like. Now, we're teammates and professionals, and we've put the past behind us. We both have the same goal." Jordan laughed lightly as his gaze flicked to Greaves and then back to the Sky Sports reporter. "I hope none of you have been listening to rumours from unreliable sources."

My smile felt brittle, but I held it for as long as I could, nodding to indicate that I agreed with the liar at the front of the room. He gave me a thumbs up with a wide, fake smile, flashing his straight, white teeth. The press seemed to eat it up, and as they returned their attention to Jordan and his agent, who had taken a seat next to him, I closed my eyes and let my head fall back against the wall behind me.

We hadn't put the past behind us at all. We hadn't even spoken in person since we were seventeen.

I heard Harvey announce that they'd be taking a few photos, and when I opened my eyes again, Jordan Emery was holding up a deep red football shirt with his surname and his new number—22—emblazoned across the back in gold. His fake smile had been wiped away, replaced with a beaming grin, and I immediately slammed my eyes shut again. Seeing him with his new shirt made things far too real for me.

What I needed was a distraction to help me temporarily forget this nightmare. Preferably one in the form of a beautiful brunette woman.

We were due to play an away game against Arsenal next weekend. Perhaps I could get myself on the guest list at Sanctuary after we'd played the match. It was one of London's hottest, most elite nightclubs, and as well as the main club and highly regulated VIP section, there was supposedly a brand-new secret basement area that could only be accessed by those who needed absolute privacy. From the rumours I'd heard, phones were banned there. Anything that could capture footage was banned, in fact. Everyone who was allowed access was thoroughly scanned for electronic devices.

It meant that I could party without worrying that the paparazzi would get a photo of me or if someone would sell me out.

I made a mental note to speak to Amir later to see if I could get on the list. Nothing was guaranteed, not even for top-flight football players. But even if I couldn't get on the list, Sanctuary's VIP area would most likely afford me enough privacy. I'd heard that the owner of Sanctuary didn't take too kindly to negative publicity, and paparazzi were barred from photographing inside the venue. As yet,

I'd never seen any leaked photos from the club. Not even from the main dance floor.

"Lewin."

My head flew up at the low hiss, close to my ear, my eyes widening when I saw Jordan Emery standing in front of me. During the time I'd been lost in thought, it appeared that the impromptu press conference had finished, and the room had emptied out.

"Jordan Emery. To what do I owe the pleasure?"

"Pleasure?" His brows rose, and I rolled my eyes. Of course he wouldn't understand the phrase. Or...he did, and he was trying to get under my skin. Either option was just as likely. He continued before I could form an appropriately cutting response, jerking his head towards the door. "Can we talk? In private."

I noticed his gaze dart to his agent, who gave him a short nod, motioning with his hand, and it suddenly became clear to me. Whatever Jordan wanted to speak to me about, his agent had clearly put him up to it. I momentarily wished that Amir had been here to talk me out of what was most likely going to be an inadvisable conversation, but he was my agent, not my minder. He could have been here—in fact, he'd offered to come, but I'd insisted he take the evening off. The man worked harder than anyone I knew. Although he was London-based, he owned a small flat in Gloucestershire, and he'd come up this weekend for our home game against Chelsea. He was currently enjoying a meal at a Michelin-starred restaurant in the local town of Cheltenham with his wife, courtesy of yours truly.

"I suppose so, if we must," I drawled, pushing off from the wall, bringing me closer to him. My jaw clenched when I noticed that he was now almost the same height as me. He must've had a late growth spurt.

"I wanna do this even less than you." This close, I could see the brown and gold flecks in his light eyes. It might have been the lighting in the room, but his grey eyes looked green today. Of course he couldn't be normal. No, he had to have ridiculous colour-changing eyes.

"Let's get this over with." Having this conversation was the last thing I wanted to do, but he was right. We did have the same goal—to help our team go as far as they could. And despite the fact that I abhorred the man standing in front of me, he was my teammate, and there was nothing I could do to change that fact. For now.

When we were alone, safely behind a closed door in a small side room, Jordan's neutral look faded, replaced with a smirk that I immediately wanted to smack from his face. "It must be killing you to have me here."

I stepped up to him. I'd never let him push me around before, and he had to know that nothing was going to change in that respect. "It must be killing you to know that I've been here since the beginning of the season, playing against some of the best teams in the world, and you—"

He lunged at me, getting his hand around my throat and pressing me into the wall. The smirk was finally wiped from his face as his eyes darkened with anger, now a stormy blueish grey.

I swallowed around his grip, throwing my arms around him in a grappling move. His grip tightened on my throat, and I wanted to hurt him so badly, but I also didn't want to be sued for being the one to break his bones. Or even worse, mine. "What the fuck are your eyes doing?" I rasped around his hand.

His grip loosened, and I took in a much-needed gulp of air before releasing him suddenly and giving his chest a hard shove, which made him stagger backwards. With a growl, he came at me again, but this time, I was prepared, and I sidestepped him, twisting around and coming up behind him. This time, I was the one pressing him into the wall, my hand covering the back of his skull, mashing his face into the hard surface. Hopefully, it would bruise.

"You fucking wanker," he ground out, his words muffled as his face was up against the wall. "What the fuck are you saying about my eyes?"

Pulling back a little but still holding him in place, I attempted to gather my thoughts. It was difficult—he'd always had a talent for annoying me so much I'd forget the original reason I was upset with him. The temptation to get under his skin, the way he got under mine, was always there. Every time I saw him.

"Never mind. Do you have to be such an attention-seeker?" I whispered harshly. "I'm already sick and tired of seeing your poser photos appearing all over my socials."

He barked out a laugh, and I pressed his face harder against the wall. "For you to see my photos, that must mean you've been stalking me. I'm flattered, really, but you need to stop. You'll only give yourself a complex, wishing you could measure up to me and knowing that you'll always fall short."

"You're such a fucking brat." With one final push at the back of his head, I stepped away.

"Why does everyone keep calling me a brat?" he muttered to himself, rubbing at his face. When he turned around, I noticed that his cheek was red, and I couldn't help smiling. My smile soon dropped when he stood there, silently glaring at me.

"Are we going to get to the point of this conversation? I have places to be."

"More tea parties to attend? Or do you have tickets to

the croquet?" Folding his arms across his chest, he leaned back against the wall, a challenging look in his eyes. This bastard lived to get under my skin.

"I thought you might have grown out of your childish taunts, but I should've known better. Has anyone told you that you have the emotional maturity of a thirteen-year-old?"

"I was thirteen when I met you."

I rolled my eyes. "I suppose you want to blame me for that, too?"

"That was the worst day of my life."

"Really? Not the day when my team beat yours 9–0, and I scored five of those goals? And what was it that happened? Oh, yes. You got a red card because you couldn't control your temper." I laughed as his eyes darkened, his brows lowering and his mouth flattening into a thin line. "It was quite amusing to see you kicking that chair over and then tripping over the legs. You really did earn the nickname 'Trip,' didn't you?"

"I hate you so fucking much," he spat between gritted teeth. "You were an asshole then, and you're an asshole now."

"Likewise."

"Fuck." Rubbing his hand over his face, he exhaled sharply. "Enough. Let me say what I was forced to come here and say, and then we can go our separate ways. I'm sick to the back teeth of seeing your face, and I'm not the one stalking the other on social media."

I didn't bother to mention the fact that he'd messaged me via his social media, so he was clearly lying. That would only lead to another argument, and I wanted to spend as little time as possible in his obnoxious presence.

"Go ahead." Spreading my arms wide, I gave him an expectant look. "I'm all ears."

"Fine. All I brought you here to say was that we need to act civil with each other in public. I have to look good for my brand endorsements, and I don't want to fuck things up with the club, either. As much as I know you hate it, Glevum needs me. I don't want them thinking they made a mistake in signing me. It won't look good for you, either."

Of course he'd focus on his brand endorsements before anything else. I'd expect nothing less from someone so self-centred.

Hold on, he *already* had brand endorsements? "Brand endorsements?"

He gave me a smug grin. "Yep. A big one with an underwear company. Guess they appreciate my pictures more than you do."

Underwear. More excuses for him to show off his body. I shouldn't have expected anything less from someone whose social media was filled with half-naked mirror selfies.

"What a surprise. You're such a poser. You just love to show your body at every opportunity, don't you?"

"I'm not a prude like you," he shot back, raking his gaze over me in a disdainful way that made my blood boil.

"It's called having a sense of decorum, something you'd know nothing about." I smiled internally when he glared at me. "But to get back to the point, because I have far better things to do than discuss your lack of clothing, I agree to your terms. I don't want to ruin anything for the team, and I'm prepared to act civil to you around the team and the wider public. Outside of that, you'd better stay as far away from me as possible."

"Believe me, I don't want to be around you any more than you want to be around me."

Good. Then we were done here.

Without another word, I turned on my heel and left the room.

As I walked, I tapped out a quick message to the group chat I had with some of the footballers in the team.

ME:

> Does anyone fancy going to a club after our away game at Arsenal?

Reuben Mendy was the first to respond. He was our best striker and currently the fifth-highest goalscorer in the league. His message was closely followed by a reply from Ainsley Shaw, one of our defenders.

REUBEN:

> Drinks, women and a VIP area? Sign me the fuck up!

AINSLEY:

> Time to initiate our new team member

No. The last thing I wanted was to invite Jordan fucking Emery.

ME:

> We don't want to scare him away

REUBEN:

> Team bonding night innit. It'll be good for him!

AINSLEY:

> Let's show him how the Glevum team party

He added a row of emojis—champagne bottles, a person dancing, a face being sick. I sighed. I had no one to blame but myself for this.

LARS:

> A team party? I will join you. Is everyone invited?

Great, even Lars Nielsen was in on it now. Our Danish goalie was generally quiet, and he didn't often come out with us, but if even he was making the effort, then there was no getting out of this.

I'd just have to stay well away from Jordan. I supposed that at least with several team members there as a buffer, it would be a relatively easy job.

ME:

> We may as well open it up to the entire team

REUBEN:

> Yes! Fucking get in!!!!!! TEAM BONDING NIGHT!

The man had a love of exclamation marks that I could never understand.

LARS:

> Will we add our new teammate to the group chat?

No. Never, ever.

ME:

> No, not yet. We don't know him well enough

AINSLEY:

> Heard about your feud ahaha. That real?

REUBEN:

> Man's got jokes innit

LARS:

Sometimes I think my English is better than yours, Reuben

REUBEN:

Hahahaha!!!!!

ME:

There's no feud, it's just a ridiculous rumour

The last thing I wanted to do was to make them nervous. We needed to focus, to prepare for not only tomorrow's home game against Chelsea but next week's game against Arsenal because it was going to be a tough one and Jordan's first time in the spotlight. There would be enough eyes on us as it was—I wasn't going to do anything to jeopardise the game.

ME:

You'll meet him tomorrow

I'll book the club for us all

GRANT:

Sign me up. Yes to team bonding. I was going to suggest golf at Nottswood Country Club but this is better

There was our final group chat member. Grant Evans, our team captain and midfielder. He was the most sensible of us all, but he still liked to party hard, and he could drink almost all of us under the table.

REUBEN:

I'm shit at golf so I vote this

Pocketing my phone, I left them arguing about the merits of golf, climbing into my Aston Martin to make the drive home. As I drove, my mind kept replaying the conversation I'd had with Jordan earlier. Could we really manage to stay civil? Was there any way I could get my position on the right wing back and, preferably, get rid of him in the process? Why, of all the people in the world, did he have to be the one to join my team?

Taking slow, measured breaths, I reminded myself of what was important. I'd come this far, and I wasn't going to let Jordan Emery ruin things for me.

I closed my fingers around the small blister pack in my pocket. At least I had a guaranteed way to forget about him tonight. I'd be able to forget about everything that was troubling me and sink into blissful oblivion once again.

FOUR

JORDAN

I'd survived my first week of training, and my body ached all over. Prodding one of the bruises on my arm, I winced, deciding that maybe it wasn't the best idea to touch it.

I couldn't complain too much, though. Going from League Two to the Premier League hadn't been as much of a learning curve as I'd thought it would be training-wise—mostly, the difference was in the size and quality of the facilities. But because the gaffer wanted me to gel with the team as quickly as possible, that had meant hardcore training all week, and my body was feeling it. Lucky for me, the team physio had been on hand, along with the ice baths that I hated but helped more than anything.

I still couldn't believe I was here. About to play my first Premier League game, at Arsenal's Emirates stadium, in front of over sixty thousand people, with millions more watching on screens around the world. I knew my dad was out there somewhere in the crowd with the contingent of Glevum supporters that had come down in the fan coaches. He was probably bursting with pride that his son was playing for the team we'd both supported all our lives, and I'd do my best to make him proud. I'd make the team proud. And...I'd remind Theodore Lewin just how fucking good I really was.

Eyeing my reflection in the away team bathroom mirrors, I grinned. I definitely looked the part. My brand-new kit was crisp and clean, and damn, I made it look good.

Glevum FC's home kit consisted of a deep red shirt with gold trim around the collar and the club's golden Roman helmet badge positioned in the top left corner, black shorts, and red football socks.

But today, since Arsenal's home kit was also red, we were wearing our away kit. My gaze lowered, scanning over the white shirt with the same gold trim and badge as the home kit, then over the black shorts, down past the white socks covering my shin pads, and stopping at my new custom black football boots with a golden swoosh. Fucking gorgeous. And underneath? My new underwear sponsors had come up with the goods. A jockstrap. Black, some fucking soft and silky material, breathable and moisture-wicking, ethically made, with my name embroidered in gold around the top band. They'd even added the Roman helmet of the club's logo next to my name. Before this deal had happened, I'd always worn boxer briefs or compression shorts underneath my football shorts, but I was already a convert to the jockstrap. I now understood why so many athletes wore them for support, and as a bonus, they made my ass look fucking *amazing*. The way the straps framed it...women were going to go fucking feral when I posted a photo—which I planned to do right after we won the match. Which we were going to do.

Spinning around, I craned my neck to view the back of

my shirt in the mirror. My surname, in gold block lettering rimmed with black, above my number. 22.

Yesssss. This was quite possibly the best moment of my life, and it needed to be documented. I strode over to the bank of sinks where I'd left my phone, and when I retrieved it, I turned on the camera and moved back in front of the mirrors, this time facing away from them. Snapping a photo over my shoulder, I quickly posted it to my social media. About thirty seconds after the photo had gone live, I had a message from my agent.

@RORYNASHAGENT:

TURN YOUR PHONE OFF, JORDAN! THIS IS THE BIGGEST MOMENT OF YOUR CAREER

@JORDANEMERY_OFFICIAL:

All those shouty caps make me think you need a hearing aid grandad

@RORYNASHAGENT:

JORDAN. Do not make me come down there

@JORDANEMERY_OFFICIAL:

Sorry this place is off limits to agents before a match

@RORYNASHAGENT:

Brat. Good luck out there though. I'll be cheering for you

@JORDANEMERY_OFFICIAL:

Thanks. Really. I appreciate your support

@RORYNASHAGENT:

Good. Phone off. Head in the game. Show everyone how amazing you are

Warmth filled me. I was so fucking lucky to have Rory

as my agent. Having people in your corner was something that was never guaranteed, and I knew I was one of the lucky ones. Between him and my dad, I had all the support I needed. My dad was a real man's man. It was probably a stereotype to say that, but it was true for him. He was in the building trade, a single dad, constantly surrounded by men who were very traditional in their actions. He rarely, if ever, showed his emotions, but although I never knew what he was feeling, he never left me with any doubt that he was behind my career every step of the way. As for Rory—he had other clients, but when he was with me, he always made sure that his full focus was on me, and I never felt like I was competing for his attention with anyone else.

@JORDANEMERY_OFFICIAL:

> Thanks R. Get ready to see me making headlines!

I powered my phone down and rejoined my teammates in the dressing room, chucking my phone into the cubby beneath my seat. Across the other side of the room, I could feel the heavy weight of someone's stare. I knew that if I turned my head, I'd see blue eyes burning with hate and resentment, and the thought made a smile curve over my lips.

The satisfaction that I was pissing off the posh wanker whose position I'd stolen was forgotten as soon as Harvey Raines entered the dressing room. The atmosphere immediately thickened, tension and excitement mounting in the air.

"Alright, lads." He clapped his hands together just once, a resounding smack that echoed around the space, rebounding off the walls. "Focus time. They'll try and walk it in, but we're not gonna let them. Don't let anyone get past you. Defenders, push forward. Let's get them on the back foot from kick-off and get this win in the bag in the first five minutes."

His statement was concluded with the players slapping hands and backs, and then we were filing out of the dressing room and down the tunnel that led out onto the pitch. Cameras were everywhere—something I wasn't used to in League Two, and it was the first thing that highlighted just how different this match was. My heart rate kicked up, my palms sweating as I concentrated on breathing, forcing myself to stay focused.

But then I stepped out onto the pitch and heard the roars of sixty thousand people echoing around the stadium. My breaths were suddenly loud and shaky, even with the noise of the crowd, and I swallowed hard. *Fucking keep it together, Jordan. This is the biggest moment of your career.*

"Good day for a win, innit?" A voice sounded in my ear, and I turned to see Reuben Mendy's grinning face. I'd never admit it under pain of death, but playing alongside one of the best strikers in the league was a dream, and I was a little bit intimidated and a whole lot starstruck.

"Uh, yeah." I cleared my throat to get rid of the scratchiness. "Yeah," I said again, this time with more conviction.

There was a flash of empathy in Reuben's eyes as he briefly squeezed my shoulder. "The gaffer wouldn't have you here if you weren't up to it, man. Let's show the Gunners that they can't fucking walk it in, like he said."

"Yeah." I straightened my shoulders. "Let's win this."

"Good man." He jogged over to his starting position, and I took up mine, finding it easier to tune out the crowd after his little pep talk. The excitement I'd originally felt was back, and I savoured it. This was my time to shine. For the whole team to shine. Except for Theo Lewin.

Oh, fuck. That wasn't even true, was it? If he fucked up, that would fuck us all.

Focus, Jordan.

The whistle blew, and then my nerves suddenly disappeared. I was caught up in the game I loved. Nothing else mattered. Only working with my team to score as many goals as possible.

And we did.

Walker or Sinclair passed the ball down the pitch to me whenever they could, and I did my best to get it to Reuben Mendy. He was one of the top strikers in the league for a reason.

All our hard work paid off. We fucking smashed it, 3-0. I got two assists, and even better, Theo Lewin did nothing memorable.

My entire body was buzzing, on a high I'd never experienced before. This was the life I'd always dreamed of.

Finally, I'd be recognised for my talent.

I could see the headlines now.

FIVE

THEO

That fucking bastard. Jordan had the press and, even worse, the team wrapped around his finger. Everyone loved him.

Apart from me.

The early headlines were grating. Everyone was quick to shower praise on our new "saviour," conveniently forgetting that the rest of the team was doing their best to fill the hole that Knowles had left. With or without the bratty fucking poser Jordan Emery.

My life had become a nightmare. When I'd read today's editorial on the website of a well-respected newspaper, not even one of the tabloids, it made me sick to my stomach. It mentioned that Emery had been born to play on the right wing, and I was apparently "not as indispensable as Harvey Raines had insinuated."

My hands were shaking as I popped a tablet from the blister pack. I'd started taking sleeping pills when I first joined the team, when it was almost encouraged to do so before a match... Who didn't have trouble sleeping, after all?

I'd had problems with sleeping through the night for a lot longer, though. If I could trace it back, it had probably started when I was thirteen, when I'd joined CEFYA. Possibly even before that. No...not possibly. Certainly. Then when I'd transferred to Glevum FC and one of the players had dropped sleeping pills into the conversation as if it were a normal occurrence before a match, I'd been intrigued.

I'd been more than intrigued, if I were honest. For the first time in years, I was finally able to sleep through the night. I was finally able to calm that jittery rush that sent my heart rate spiking.

Now, I... I took one or two pills. Or three. Every day. The club doctor had given me a prescription, but it wasn't enough to fulfil my needs. If you were a Premier League player, though, you could get whatever you wanted, whenever you wanted, and I had more than enough.

As I swallowed the tablet with a chaser of vodka, the thought crossed my mind that I probably shouldn't have taken it before I went out. But the fact was my body was used to the effect, and therefore, I needed a head start tonight if I wanted to actually sleep. I had to spend the evening with Jordan Emery, after all, and I'd need all the help I could get.

I knew that I shouldn't be taking so many pills. I knew that I was relying on them too much. I knew that I had a problem.

But the truth was I didn't know how to stop.

I arrived at Sanctuary amidst the flash of paparazzi cameras. Thankfully, they weren't allowed inside, and the bouncer quickly waved me in, letting me escape them without issues. Amir had informed me that the secret basement either didn't exist or wasn't available for a team night, but he'd arranged for us to have privacy in the VIP area. I hoped that he'd done his job because I hated having to go out and make people sign NDAs. This club was supposedly locked down tightly, which made me breathe a little more easily.

What I needed to do tonight was to drink and forget and preferably bury myself inside a hot, willing body. I never had to apply any effort to get women, but I did have standards. I had no time for the clout chasers that were only interested in sleeping with a pro footballer, and then they'd go on *Love Island* or some other reality show or trashy magazine, claiming that I was their ex, even though we'd only spent a couple of hours together. Yes… this exact scenario had happened to me, and it had left a sour taste in my mouth.

As I made my way through the club towards the VIP section, though, I wasn't thinking about women. I wasn't forgetting. No, my mind was replaying the match in vivid detail.

Playing on the left was foreign to me. I'd done it on occasion, and I knew I had the capability, but I'd never felt at home the way I did playing on the right. I was a professional, though, and so I sucked it up and took my place, determined to give it my all. I wouldn't be the one to let the team down. When the match began, I threw my entire focus into the game.

I soon grew frustrated because it seemed like the ball was always being passed up the right side of the pitch. When Jordan crossed the ball to Reuben, and Reuben tapped it into the net, curving the ball around the Arsenal goalie's outstretched body, I gritted my teeth, even as I automatically ran to join the rest of the team in exuberant celebrations, throwing my arms around my fellow players and pumping my fist in the air. I could almost hear my father berating me in my head for my behaviour, but I'd grown used to tuning that out over the years.

I was elated that we'd scored, but it was overshadowed by the fact that Jordan had set everything up so Reuben could get the goal. If it had been anyone else, I wouldn't have had an issue. But it was him.

My frustration mounted as the match continued. I barely remembered Harvey's half-time pep talk—I was too busy stewing in my own anger and resentment. I should have been happy that we were winning, but when the win came courtesy of Jordan Emery? No.

It was completely fucking unprofessional of me to be so resentful, but I fucking hated him so much.

After the match had concluded and Glevum FC had won 3–0, I watched as the assembled reporters clamoured to interview Jordan. Sweating, out of breath, and with a bright smile on his face, he took their questions as if he'd been answering them all his life.

Then, when he was finally finished, he strode into the dressing room alongside Reuben to be treated like a king. From the congratulations my teammates were giving him, it almost felt as if we'd won the FA Cup, not just one single match against another Premier League team.

Just when I thought my loathing for him was at an all-time high, it got worse. He stalked into the bathroom, tugging his football shirt over his head as he walked, carelessly dropping it to the floor behind him. Before I knew what I was doing, I was pushing my way into the bathroom alongside some of the other players, only to be confronted by the narcissistic poser stripping off his shorts in front of the mirror, a smug, satisfied grin on his face as he stared at his reflection.

All he was left in was a fucking black jockstrap and his white football socks.

I froze in place, my entire body going hot, then cold. This fucking poser—

"Take a picture, it'll last longer!"

"Good job today!"

"Stop eye-fucking yourself and put some clothes on, for fuck's sake!"

"Is that a jockstrap? What the fuck?"

"Hey! I wear jockstraps, dickhead!" Another jockstrap came sailing through the air, glancing off Jordan's calf before landing on the floor. It only made him grin harder.

"Me too! Don't knock them 'til you've tried them, bro."

A loud voice cut through the chatter. "You ready to be initiated into the team, new boy?"

My head flew around to see Reuben grinning at Jordan. He stepped forwards, his hand outstretched. "Good game, bro. Ready to find out how the Glevum team parties?"

The clamour of our assembled teammates died away as Jordan smiled, accepting his handshake. "The question should be, are you ready to find out how I party?"

Reuben laughed and clapped him on the shoulder. "I like you, man. C'mon, get showered, and then we can get out of here and proper celebrate."

Before Jordan could reply, a hush fell over the room. Harvey Raines was here.

"Good game, lads. We'll dissect it in detail on Monday, but for now, enjoy yourselves. You've earned it." He inclined his head, a smile tugging at his lips. "I don't want to jinx *anything. But all I'll say is keep it up, and we might have a shot at Europe. And we have a really good chance of finishing in the top ten, at least."*

A palpable sense of excitement spread through the room. Everyone was in agreement. We were one of the smallest teams in the league, but if we could place high enough to get a spot in one of the European tournaments, we would cement our place among the best teams in the world. Seven English teams qualified for a European tournament each season, either through being one of the top teams in the league or winning a cup tournament.

That was our goal, and although it was a lofty one, the fact that Harvey Raines thought we even had a chance was one hell of a confidence boost.

Harvey's next words sent my stomach dropping. "Emery. Good job today. Keep it up." That was high praise coming from him, and as soon as he'd spoken, Jordan was once again surrounded by my teammates, all congratulating him on a job well done. I was left alone, forgotten.

I needed a drink. There was no getting around the fact that Jordan Emery had been a vital part of our win, as far as my teammates were concerned. If I'd been on the right, we might have won by an even bigger margin... No one would want to hear that now, though. All they wanted was to celebrate.

I needed to do the same. I needed to pretend that it wasn't cutting me up inside that everyone was fawning over the person who'd been my rival growing up. The person who was still so arrogant and obnoxious, who cared about himself above anything else. It was good that we'd won. *I was happy.*

I just had to keep telling myself that until I believed it.

As I ascended the stairs to the VIP section on the mezzanine level of the club, scanning over the booths scattered around the area, my eyes met a pair of grey ones flecked with blues and greens, his expression smug and amused.

Jordan Emery thought that one game had bought him the right to take his place with my teammates? To slide into my world and suction himself onto my life like a leech?

That was not going to happen. Not now, not today, not ever.

I narrowed my gaze, my lip curling as I drew closer.

It was time to teach this narcissistic brat a lesson.

SIX

JORDAN

My eyes widened as I met Theo's. Fuck, he was *really* pissed off. His normally light blue gaze was dark and stormy, and his entire body was tense, completely on edge. I'd thought... I didn't know what I'd expected, but maybe I'd thought that he'd be happy about our win. I was. I was so fucking happy. Buzzing. Lighter than air. My first ever Premier League match, and we'd *won*. Against one of the best teams in the league.

I hadn't had a chance to see my dad or Rory yet, but I'd received congratulatory texts from them both, and I knew they'd be celebrating right along with me, even if we weren't in the same location.

"Emery," Theo ground out as he drew closer to the booth. Shit. It was gonna go down, wasn't it? Grant, our captain, wasn't even here yet to keep the peace, although he was supposed to be turning up at any minute. I didn't want to get a bad rep on my very first night out with the team, so I did what any sensible person would do—I slid out of the booth before Theo could trap me inside and legged it.

I ended up jogging past a stone-faced bouncer into

another room where...fuuuck. One of the hottest women I'd ever seen was sliding down a pole...upside down. Stopping dead, I drank in the sight in front of me, barely taking in my surroundings, my gaze fixed on the blonde under the spotlight in front of the mirrored wall.

"Emery!"

Shit, he'd followed me in here. The woman was instantly forgotten as my gaze darted around the room, looking for a place to hide. It was dark in here—everything was black, including the floors, which sparkled, and there were booths similar in design to those in the main VIP area. Except...were there privacy curtains around them?

Perfect.

I ducked into one of the booths, tugging the curtain shut behind me. Five seconds after I'd collapsed down against the leather, the curtain was yanked open, and a body came crashing into mine.

"You smug fucking bastard," Theo snarled. "Why do you have to be so—"

"So what? So good at everything I do?"

"So fucking smug and arrogant." His harsh pants of breath were hot against my ear. "Everything in my life was perfect until you came back into it."

"Did you see the headlines?" I shoved at him. "Everyone loves me."

"You fucking—"

"I don't know whether to be turned on or call security," a third voice mused from behind us, and we instantly sprang apart.

"Oops. Did I say that out loud?" The newcomer clapped his hands to his mouth, his eyes sparkling with humour. It took me a second to notice anything else about him because Theo's hand was clamped around my thigh, his fingers digging into my leg and squeezing hard, as if he could reduce my circulation with the power of his grip alone.

Two could play that game. I clamped my fingers around his wrist and squeezed just as tightly. Theo immediately yanked his hand away, baring his teeth at me, so I bared mine right back.

"Can I get you guys anything?"

Oh, yeah. I'd forgotten about the newcomer. Wrenching my gaze away from Theo, I eyed the stranger, who was now standing directly in front of me. A body that was even more cut than mine, impossibly tight shorts, tanned skin covered in...was that glitter? and a bright white, professional-looking smile that became a little strained around the edges when the silence stretched.

"Whoa, Jordan, didn't know you swung that way."

"Don't be getting any ideas when we're in the showers."

"Yeah, my ass is off limits. Stay away from me."

For fuck's fucking sake. I caught Theo's visible wince from the corner of my eye as several of our teammates slid into the booth with us, setting bottles of champagne and various other drinks on the table. In front of me, the newcomer's smile was instantly wiped away, his eyes narrowing as he placed his hands on his hips.

"News flash. Just because someone's gay doesn't mean they're interested in every man, and it especially doesn't mean that they're going to try and sexually harass them. That is so fucking—" He broke off with an angry exhale, scrubbing his hand across his face. "This is my place of work, and I like my job, so I'm not going to say anything else. But if you want to come and find me afterwards and say that to my face...all I can say is, I hope you're not feeling too attached to your balls."

"Ouch, man." Reuben's hands instantly went to cover his junk. He glanced around the booth, his gaze lingering on the two players who had made the comments. "Sorry. They—I mean, we were out of line."

"You're *gay*?" Grant whispered to me, his brows raised, surprise clear on his face.

What? The conversation replayed itself through my mind at warp speed, and I groaned. Loudly.

"Listen up." I raised my voice, enough to cut through the chatter. The newcomer, who'd been glaring at James Walker, one of the guys who had made the comments that had him so riled up, turned his attention to me, along with everyone else. "I. Am. Not. Gay. I'm straight. With a capital S. For fuck's sake! Why would you even think I wasn't?"

"You were cosying up to that stripper."

Okay, now James Walker was really fucking starting to piss me off.

"Excuse me, babe." The guy in the shorts spun on his heel, stepping up to James and stabbing his finger into his chest. "I am not a stripper. I'm a dancer."

"Same dif—"

"Walker." Grant's warning tone was enough to cut him off mid-sentence.

"Can I just point out that all he was doing was standing in front of me? You put two and two together and made twenty, dickhead." I bit down on my tongue when Theo jabbed me in the ribs with his elbow.

"Stop talking. You're making it worse," he hissed in my ear, and I turned to him in surprise. Blinking, I stared at him for a long moment before I shook it off.

"Aww. You do care about me. So sweet." I blew him a kiss, making his nostrils flare and his jaw clench. Then, because contrary to popular belief—or Theo's belief, at least, I wasn't a total asshole—I slid out of the booth, jerking my head at the dancer guy. "Can I have a word?"

He rolled his eyes but followed me over to the bar, where I leaned back against the gleaming surface with a sigh.

"Look, I'm, uh, really sorry about all that." I waved my hand in the direction of the booth. "They're probably just giving me shit because I'm new, uh, new to their football team, and you got caught up in it."

His mouth thinned as he shook his head. "It's still not okay. Even if you're not gay, comments like that—"

"I know. Believe me. There's a lot of, uh, casual homophobia in football. Not even casual, I guess. Even if it's unintentional, it's not okay. It's...uh...I dunno." I shrugged, at a loss for words.

The guy gave me a small, tentative smile. "I won't hold it against you personally." He held his hand out to me, his smile widening into something more genuine. "I'm JJ. And you must be the new footballer everyone's getting so excited about."

I took his hand, clasping it in a brief handshake. Glittering specks drifted from his skin to the floor. I hoped it was biodegradable glitter. "Yeah. Jordan Emery. You watch football?" Even though I tried to keep my tone neutral, there was still a note of disbelief that I couldn't quite disguise.

JJ sighed. "What, because I'm gay, I can't be into football?"

"Uh...uh...no," I stammered. "I didn't know you were gay. You never actually said, and anyway, that wasn't it. I just...oh, fuck. You're so...sparkly."

He stared at me for a moment and then doubled over laughing, clutching the bar counter. "I can't be into football because I'm *sparkly*." There were actual tears in his eyes.

Sinking my face into my hands, I shook my head. Thank fuck Theo wasn't close enough to witness this train wreck of a conversation. At least my humiliation seemed to have chased away all traces of his anger. "That isn't what I meant. I meant—I meant—"

His hand patting me on the back made me jump out of my skin. "Calm down." When I lowered my hands from my face, he winked at me. "FYI, I'm not into football. But the staff like to gossip, and I have a housemate who's very into football, and you might have come up in conversation once or twice. Your social media is quite...interesting," he purred.

"I'm straight."

"Mmm, you said. Shame. Keep posting those pretty pictures, though."

"I will." A smile tugged at my lips as I finally relaxed. It wasn't like it was news that a gay man appreciated the hard work I put in to look good. I had plenty of comments and messages from men as well as women. "In return, can you get me an intro with her?" Pointing at the blonde on the pole, I lost myself in watching the sinuous movements of her body.

"Honey Rose? Nope. Sorry. There's one rule here that we all have to abide by. No touching the dancers." Amusement flared in his gaze. "How about you get out of here, back into the VIP area you're *supposed* to be in, and I'll have a word with the bouncers. Honey Rose isn't your only option tonight."

"Yeah, okay." All I wanted was to celebrate. Theo had derailed that as soon as he'd arrived, but now it was time to get this party back on track.

"You owe me. I'll have some bottles of our most

expensive champagne delivered to your table, shall I?" JJ winked at me.

"Deal. Put them on Theo Lewin's tab. He kindly agreed to treat everyone tonight. It's the least we can do after all the disruption."

JJ stared at me for a second and then glanced over to the booth, where I could see Theo's gaze fixed on us, his eyes dark and intent. When he looked back at me, he shook his head. "The two of you are going to be trouble, aren't you?"

"Me? Never. I'll be on my best behaviour tonight. A model citizen."

"We'll see" was all he said.

A few hours later, everything in my world was *so good*. I loved everyone. Everyone loved me. Here I was with my new best friends, having the best time everrrr.

"Fuckin' love you, bro," I slurred into Reuben's ear, slinging my arm around his shoulders.

"Yeah. Love you, too, bro." He gave me a lazy, crooked smile as he tipped the contents of his sixth...or maybe his eighth shot down his throat. Leaning forwards, he pressed his lips to the throat of the girl currently straddling his lap. He repeated his previous words in a slow, drunken drawl. "Love you, too."

"An' me." Ainsley waved his hand in front of my face. He was one of only three people in our booth without a girl all over them. As he'd told me earlier, he had a long-term girlfriend. Then there was Grant, who was married, and the other was...me.

I guessed I was more picky than I thought. None of the girls that had been sent our way had caught my eye, even though they were objectively fucking hot. Honey Rose had been the only one I'd been interested in, and even then, I'd known it was a lost cause without JJ having to tell me. Places like this always had strict rules in place for their dancers.

Avoiding looking at the other end of the booth, where Fuckface McFuckerson was currently trying to extract the tonsils of some poor girl with his tongue, I slumped against Ainsley. "Yeah, yeah. All the love. Hey, Ains? We're gonna win the league, yeah?"

"Yeah, man. Champions." Ainsley fist-bumped me but missed and ended up jabbing my bicep. "Whass that noise?"

Over the thumping beat of the club music, I could hear a tinny sound coming from Ainsley's thigh. I smacked my hand onto it. "Your leg's ringing."

"Wha'?" Staring blearily at me, he joined me in smacking his leg. "Make it stop."

"Your phone is ringing, you…bell end." Lars reached across Ainsley, extracting his phone from his pocket.

"'S'all one word. Bellend," I mumbled while Ainsley jabbed at the screen until the noise stopped.

"Yes. Bellend." Lars nodded, lifting his pint glass into the air. I also lifted my glass, clinking it against his. The girl on his lap giggled, turning her head to kiss his neck. He seemed sober, but I could've sworn that was his sixth or seventh pint. Wait. My gaze narrowed at my own glass, the table tilting in front of my eyes. It was empty. When had that happened? How many had I had?

"I'm going back to the hotel now… No. Haven't been drinking…"

I snorted at Ainsley's slurred words, and he shot me what I thought was supposed to be a glare.

"It's his girlfriend on the phone," Lars whispered. Or shouted. Huh, maybe he was drunker than he looked.

Ending the call, Ainsley staggered to his feet, and immediately, Grant was there, propping him up.

"Not like any of you drunk fuckers care, but I'll get him back to the hotel, and then I'll come back."

It didn't seem as if anyone else was paying attention, other than me, so I made sure I gave Grant a thumbs up. When they were both gone, I collapsed back against the booth, closing my eyes.

Just for a second.

"Oi, Emery!"

The shout made my eyes fly open. Oh, Grant was back.

"Time to go." He made a grab for my arm, but I was perfectly fine. I could get up myself.

Whoa...the world was spinning.

I dropped back down into the booth. In my drunken state, everything seemed to be coming from far away, but I was dimly aware of Grant complaining, something about babysitting players.

Then another person took his place. "Jordan. Get the fuck up. Now."

Those posh, clipped vowels were as effective as a bucket of ice water being thrown over me. Or maybe not, but they had a sobering effect that was equivalent to a shot of caffeine to my veins. I managed to climb to my feet and stood, swaying slightly.

"Theo?"

"Don't fucking speak my name." An arm came around me, yanking me forwards, and I found myself leaning against someone. Someone so fucking warm and solid and fuuuuck...they smelled so fucking good. Like salt and waterfalls and nature-y things.

"Jordan. Fucking stop."

The voice penetrated the haze surrounding me, and I lifted my face from where I'd apparently *buried it in his throat*. "What the *fuck*," I whispered to myself, taking a step back, except I couldn't move because Theo's arm was banded around my waist.

"Yeah. Don't ever do that again."

Even in my drunken state, I could hear the rasp in Theo's voice, and maybe if I'd been more aware, alarm bells would've rung.

Theo manoeuvred me through the club as quickly as possible, and before I knew it, we were outside, the chill in the air making me shiver. "Where's the girl?" It was the only question my brain could latch on to.

"Gone. Thanks for that. Fuck, Emery. Why do you have to ruin everything?"

"Me? I didn't ask you to look after me. That was your decision, Lewin."

He manhandled me along the street in the direction of the hotel. I let him because all I wanted now was my bed.

"You coming to Glevum has ruined everything," he hissed, and I rolled my eyes.

"Yeah? What happened earlier against Arsenal, then?"

A low growl came from his throat, and I fucking relished it. The fresh air had sobered me up enough to appreciate the fact that I still had the ability to piss Theodore Lewin off.

"You're so fucking smug," he spat, and it was as if a dam had burst. He ranted about how much he hated playing on the left, how arrogant I was, how he hated me and my posing and my general looks and personality. Basically, he annihilated me with his words. There wasn't one single thing about me that he liked.

I'd always told myself that I was okay with criticism. Putting yourself out there, not just on social media but as a footballer, meant opening yourself up to the judgement of random strangers. But to hear a complete annihilation of my character come from him, shining a spotlight on my worst parts... Yeah, I knew he hated me...but that point was hammered home right then.

Something cracked inside me. Something fragile that left me exposed and vulnerable.

I *hated* it.

"You think you're so fucking perfect," I said in a low voice. It took everything I had to keep my words even and steady. I'd never let him know how much he affected me.

Now, all I wanted to do was to hurt him, like he'd hurt me.

My words kept coming. "I hate you. You resent me, but guess what? I'm good. I'm so fucking good. That's why I've taken your position. That's why, at the end of the season, I'll be the player everyone's talking about."

An almost inhuman sound came from him as he launched himself at me, sending me staggering into a restaurant front. We grappled, aiming blows at each other, although both of us had drunk too much to do any actual damage.

Distantly, I was aware of the flash of cameras, but it didn't register until I was straddling Theo, pummelling him, while Lars was attempting to drag me off his body.

That was when the headlines really began.

SEVEN

THEO

"What were you thinking?" Harvey slammed his hands down on the table in front of him, his face twisted in a rage I'd never seen directed at me before. "What the fuck possessed two of my players to have a common brawl in the streets in front of the paparazzi?"

"I was—" Jordan started, but our manager cut him off with another slam of his hands, making the table shake.

"I don't want to hear your excuses. You're our new player—your conduct should be fucking exemplary, especially with those rumours that both of you assured me were false." His gaze whipped to mine. "And you. You've never given me cause for concern. Yet now our phones are ringing off the hook, and our PR team are scrambling to explain your actions, which is a bit fucking difficult, given that every media outlet has video footage of you going at each other!" A vein pulsed in his forehead.

"I'm sorry." My voice was low but sincere. It shouldn't have happened, no matter how much Jordan got under my skin.

Harvey shook his head, sinking into his chair. "You'll

both be fined a week's wages. And you'd better be on your best behaviour from now on."

"My client assures me that this was a one-off. It was his first time playing in a Premier League match, and he let himself get carried away. It won't happen again." Jordan's agent, Rory, spoke up, his smooth words clearly rehearsed.

Next to me, Amir sighed. "My client has an impeccable record, and we have plans to remind the media of that. I have a photo op set up for next week with the academy that taught Theo everything he knew and a statement prepared to go along with it. The press will eat it up."

This was the first I'd heard about it, but I kept my mouth shut, smiling internally when Jordan bristled and then shot his agent an expectant glance. Rory rolled his eyes, turning to the paperwork in front of him.

"We have a few things up our sleeves, too. I've been consulting with Glevum's PR reps, and we've come to an arrangement. I thought we should strike while the iron is hot, so to speak. We'll play this off as a drunken mistake, the excitement of Jordan's first match, and so on. I've arranged for a photo op tomorrow afternoon at a local sustainable, organic farm. Jordan and Theo will both attend, petting the animals, looking over the organic produce, and sharing drinks in the café."

"Wh—" Jordan's exclamation was cut off by Rory's pointed glance, and it was only my ability to lock down my emotions—most of the time, unless Jordan wound me up—that stopped me from visibly reacting. This was an awful idea.

"The press will eat it up." Amir repeated his earlier words, and this time, he seemed enthusiastic, nodding at Rory. Wonderful. They were both onside with this utterly ridiculous plan. Play nice with Jordan? At a farm, of all places?

"They'd better." Harvey stood. "I don't want to hear any more about this. You're dismissed, both of you."

Bumping my Aston Martin down the rutted track that led to the farm car park, I gritted my teeth. My mood was already low, thanks to the email I'd received this morning. A distant uncle had written to me on behalf of my estranged parents. Reading between the lines, it said that the family was disappointed in my conduct, and I shouldn't expect an invitation to any formal functions anytime soon. The wording was cleverly phrased, and I could easily picture my father at the formal desk in the manor house, dictating the words. I pushed away the spike of hurt, reminding myself that I'd done what was best for me and I didn't control the actions of my parents.

I parked the car, and as I climbed out, I saw Jordan exiting a dark grey Lexus. He was dressed casually in a red hoodie matching our team colour, ripped, soft-looking blue jeans, and his feet were clad in a pair of red-and-white Air Jordans. A backwards cap was shoved on top of his head.

My heartbeat stuttered. I hated the way this man got under my skin so easily.

"Where's your other car? In the garage?"

Jordan stared at me blankly for a moment as I stomped over to him, pointing my finger at his car. No, that wasn't correct. Theodore Lewin did not *stomp*. I walked. Heavily.

"My other car?"

"Well, I assume this is a rental. It's far too unassuming

for a poser like you." I gave him a disdainful once-over, and he grinned.

"It is, isn't it? But it's much better for the environment than *your* car. You should really look into getting a hybrid." He glanced over at my beautiful, gleaming machine before turning back to me. "Don't worry, when the money from my underwear endorsement comes in, I'll be sure to buy something extra flashy. Environmentally friendly, of course."

Before I could come up with an appropriately cutting response, Rory exited the passenger side of the car. He was followed by a guy with a huge camera slung around his neck, who climbed out of the back, along with…Amir?

"Amir?"

He gave me a pained smile. "I'm afraid I'm stuck on babysitting duty today."

"What about your other clients?" I hadn't been aware that our agents were going to be here. Although, when I thought about it, it was probably a good thing. It meant that there was more of a buffer between me and Jordan.

"My other clients don't exist today, according to Harvey Raines." Stepping closer, he lowered his voice. "This was your fuck-up, and you'd better be on your best behaviour in front of the photographer. I don't want this to happen again. It's been a nightmare trying to rejig my schedule so I could clear everything to be here today."

"I know. I'm sorry." I glared at Jordan. This was his fault. He caught my eye and glared right back, his eyes—which appeared to be a greyish green today—flashing dangerously.

"Ahem." Rory cleared his throat pointedly. "Theo, meet Rob. He's our photographer for today. He's going to follow you from a distance while you tour the farm and…"

Scanning a piece of paper he had clasped in his hand, he continued. "...sample the wares in the café and shop. Everyone good with that?"

Without waiting for a reply, he turned on his heel, striding towards the farm entrance.

I guessed it was showtime.

The first photo-op moment was in some sort of corrugated iron shed full of goats. Goats. I shuddered.

"What's your problem?" Jordan hissed as we entered. "Didn't you grow up in the countryside? This is basically your mother ship."

"I grew up in a manor house, you imbecile. Not a *farm*."

"My apologies, my lord." He dropped into a bow, and Rory immediately stepped over, cuffing him on the side of his head.

"Don't antagonise him, Jord."

"I wasn't." Jordan pouted, shooting Rory an injured look. I rolled my eyes, turning away from them both and pasting a smile on my face as the photographer was pointing his camera directly at me. From behind me, I heard Jordan ask Rory to take some photos of him with the animals for his social media. Of course. Any excuse for him to pose.

We entered a small enclosure at the behest of our tour guide, and I gingerly perched on the edge of a straw bale next to Amir. Jordan took a seat on the bale opposite me, his gaze fixed on the tiny white goat—kid? at his feet.

"Would you like to hold him?" The tour guide smiled down at Jordan, and his mouth curved into a wide, bright smile.

"Can I?"

The tour guide showed him how to hold the goat, but all I seemed to be able to pay attention to was the huge smile on Jordan's face. One of his real smiles, not his rehearsed ones. He tucked the goat's head under his chin with a happy sigh. Stroking over its fur, he murmured, "Ror, can I get a goat?"

"You absolutely cannot."

"Fun ruiner."

"Daddy! Daddy! Look! It's Jordan Emery and Theo Lewin!"

Everyone turned at the high, excited voice. A small blond boy of around six or seven was tugging a man by his sleeve, pointing at us and bouncing up and down.

"Look, Daddy! Jordan Emery has a goat!"

I glanced over at Jordan, who still had that smile on his face, but this time, it was directed at the child. "Wanna hold him?" His gaze slid to the tour guide. "Is that okay?"

The tour guide nodded, ushering the boy and his dad into the enclosure. The boy made a beeline straight for Jordan, hopping up onto the straw bale next to him, his legs swinging.

"Okay. Stay very still and hold out your arms." Carefully, Jordan transferred the goat to the little boy, supporting his arm where the goat's head rested. "He's cute, isn't he?"

Nodding, the boy stared down at the goat with wide eyes. "Look, Daddy. He likes me," he whispered. His dad smiled, holding up his phone to snap a picture of his son, and then turned to Jordan.

"Is it alright if I get a photo with you in it?"

"'Course."

My chest hurt.

Fucking stress. I needed to take a sleeping pill and get some rest, and I would as soon as this farce of a photo op was over.

Thankfully, we wrapped up the goat portion of our visit

quickly. As we were leaving the shed, the dad stopped me with a hand to my arm.

"Uh, Theo. Sorry. I know you probably don't want to be disturbed, but I just wanted to say that we're big fans of yours. You're doing a good job on the left."

"Yeah. I have your shirt! Number eleven!" the boy piped up.

A lump came into my throat, and I swallowed hard. Bloody hell, a stranger telling me I was doing a good job shouldn't affect me this way.

"He's great on the left, isn't he?" An arm was slung around my waist, and I immediately stiffened. The dad stared between Jordan and me, lowering his voice so he couldn't be heard by his son.

"You two are friends, then?"

"Yeah. The papers got it wrong. So wrong," my liar of a teammate said. "Me and Theo are besties. We just had a little disagreement. But he loves having me on the team, don't ya, bro?"

"Love it," I said through gritted teeth, still managing to keep the smile on my face. Jordan leaned his head on my shoulder, and I immediately jerked my arm upwards, knocking his cap off his head. "Oops."

"Accidents happen." Swiping his cap from the floor, he brushed off the bits of straw and then shoved it back on his head. His smile had turned into his professional, fake one, and I felt a sense of satisfaction that I'd managed to irritate him. "I think we need to move on to the next place now. Do you guys want an autograph before we go?"

As soon as we were alone, our minders and photographer sidetracked by a rare breed of sheep, I yanked Jordan around the back of a barn. "What the fuck was that? You just lied to a parent and his child."

"You don't wanna be besties?" His eyes sparked with amusement, and there was a challenge in them that I was powerless to resist.

Shoving him back against the barn door, I growled, "No. I do not, nor will I ever, want to be anything to you. You're nothing to me, I'm nothing to you, so let's keep it that way, okay?"

"But we could be the best of friends."

"That will never happen. I fucking loathe you, Jordan Emery." One more hard push, and suddenly, he was no longer there as the door gave way behind us, flying open with a loud creak, and I found myself falling forwards.

I landed on a hard body, and he reacted immediately, jerking up and then twisting, rolling us across the barn floor.

"Get...off...me...." Jordan panted, aiming blows at me as we rolled. I hit him back, gripping him with my legs and pinning him underneath me. He stilled, his eyes meeting mine. His cap had come off somewhere in the barn, and his hair was covered in straw, and there were smudges of dirt on his face.

"You're such a fucking brat," I whispered hoarsely, staring down at him. "Why can't you leave me alone?"

"I'm a brat? You're a fucking knobhead." His eyes never left mine. "Why can't you leave *me* alone? Why the fuck is it my fault?"

"It's your fault for existing."

"Fuck you." Anger flared in his gaze. Jerking upwards, he sent me flying to the side and climbed to his feet. "Leave me the fuck alone." He stalked out of the barn, only pausing to retrieve his cap from the floor.

When I caught up with the others, Rory was asking Jordan how he'd managed to get so dirty. As he took in my appearance, his brows pulled together, his mouth thinning.

Jordan followed his gaze, and he smirked. I wanted to smack that smirk off his face. "It was my fault. We were, uh, looking at the Jersey cows, and I was...I was leaning on a barn door that gave way. I grabbed onto Theo to stay upright, but I accidentally took him down with me."

I nodded, balling my fists at my sides, forcing myself to appear calm and unaffected. "He's right. It was an accident."

Rory clearly didn't believe us, but he didn't say anything else, no doubt because the photographer was pointing his lens in our direction. After I'd shaken the straw out of my hair and brushed myself off with the help of Amir, the photographer had us pose in front of the field of rare breed sheep. Seeming to sense that both Jordan and I were rapidly reaching the end of our tethers, Rory suggested skipping the café, instead ushering us into the farm shop to purchase some of the local goods.

"Organic, local cider. Bottled right here on the farm." Jordan held up a dark brown bottle. "This looks good. I might get some for my dad." Had he forgotten our animosity? Clearly so, because he continued speaking as if I was interested in the drivel coming from his mouth. "You getting anything for your parents?"

My estranged parents? "Fuck off," I muttered, pushing past him and exiting the shop.

I'd had enough of Jordan Emery.

All I wanted to do was to go home and forget this day had ever happened.

EIGHT

JORDAN

The football season was flying by, and I was loving every minute—except for those spent in Theodore Lewin's presence, but that was a given. Ever since our staged photo op at the farm, we'd done our best to avoid each other, but that wasn't practical when we played on the same team in almost the same position. I always felt his anger and resentment simmering under the surface, and I knew he was aware of mine, too. It wasn't ever going to go away.

There was one other small problem marring my season, and for a change, it wasn't a Theo-related problem. This one was all down to me. When I'd received the first payment from my endorsements, I'd put down a deposit on a house. It was a modern, detached place in a private development. It had come fully furnished, and it was close enough to get to Glevum's training grounds and the stadium in under twenty minutes. All good. The downside...I'd hosted a few parties in my new place...or more than a few...and they'd drawn the attention of the media. Now, I had a reputation as a party boy, in addition to the rumours that still swirled around me and Theo. Several girls had sold me out, which had never happened before—probably because no one would've been interested in a League Two player, as well as several anonymous sources who I just knew were my disgruntled neighbours, and so there were rumours flying around about sex and alcohol and things that weren't good when you were supposed to be a role model for kids.

It was so fucking hard to find a balance, though. Having a full house was great because it meant that I forgot how lonely I felt at times. Maybe "lonely" wasn't the right word. It was more of an emotional support thing, I guessed. Yeah, I had Rory and my dad, but Rory had a lot of other commitments, and my dad had his own life.

With my dad, having his own life wasn't even the issue. I'd never begrudge him that. Why would I? I was an adult, after all, and I wouldn't expect his world to revolve around me. I supposed it was mostly the fact that he wasn't the sort to show emotion. If he had emotions, he kept them locked down, unless it came to his beloved football. I'd seen him scream and shout and cry for his team. But in every other aspect of his life, he came across as quite emotionless. I knew that was the way he was raised, and it was how all his friends were, too, so it was nothing out of the ordinary. But it might've been nice to get a hug once in a while instead of a brief clap on the back. I knew without a doubt that he was proud of me, though, and he'd never given me any reason to doubt his support. I had more than a lot of people did, so I reminded myself to be grateful. Not only that, but my online fans were also great at getting behind me and supporting me with their comments and messages.

Other than the increased interest from the tabloids, things were good. Really fucking good. Glevum were currently ninth in the league, and if we managed to keep up our current streak, we might actually have a real shot at qualifying for the European tournaments. After today's match against Nottingham Forest, I had an interview with *Offside* magazine, which was one of the country's most respected football magazines with a huge online presence. That would raise my profile even more. I'd already been interviewed by them once over the phone, but this time, they were sending their digital editor to speak to me. The original, small feature they'd planned was being expanded to fill two issues, and there was already a lot of online buzz surrounding it.

I pushed all my thoughts of interviews and tabloids from my mind as I walked down the tunnel. It wasn't hard to slip into focus mode, concentrating fully on the upcoming match. According to the odds, it should be an easy win for us, but that was the thing about football—you could never take anything for granted. This was a crucial match. If we did manage to win, we'd move into the eighth position in the league, and we'd be one step closer to our goal.

Playing at home was unparalleled. Knowing you had the home fans behind you, on your own turf, where you were comfortable...there was nothing like it. And that was why a loss at home was even harder to take than an away loss. But I was going to do everything I could to make sure we got a win.

When the game started, I was fully focused on the ball, always ready to receive it and pass to Reuben or to take my own opportunity to take a shot at a goal. The first half passed in a blur, and by the time the whistle blew, we were winning, 1–0. Theo had been the one to score the goal, and I wasn't even pissed off about it. We needed this win too badly. It didn't matter who scored.

Except it did, and I fucked up. Badly. The series of events began two minutes into the second half, when Nottingham Forest managed to score. Harvey shouted instructions from the sidelines, telling us to push forwards, to move into an attacking formation. He subbed one of our defenders, and we threw everything we had into scoring another goal.

Nottingham Forest weren't going down without a fight, though. Their defence was all over Reuben, and when Grant booted the ball to me with just two minutes remaining on the clock, I could instantly see that there was no way I could pass to Reuben without the ball going to our opponents. Fuck. I glanced to my left, across the field, and that was when I saw Theo, wide open.

But if I passed to him, he'd score two goals, and he'd make my life unbearable.

I made a split-second decision, and instead of passing to him, I aimed the ball at the top-right corner of the goal.

It curved over the heads of the players, aiming exactly where I wanted it. Until one of Nottingham Forest's defenders leapt into the air, heading the ball away from the goal, and it was kicked out of play.

Fuck.

"What the fuck, Jordan?" Theo stormed over to me, shoving at my chest, practically spitting in my face. "I was wide open! There was no way I would've missed from my position, and now you've cost us the fucking match!"

"Fuck off!" Grabbing a handful of his shirt, I pushed him right back, lunging forwards as I did so, getting in his face. "I had a good chance, and I took it."

"You arrogant bastard! There was zero chance of you scoring!" He shoved at me again, and suddenly, I was being tugged backwards by Reuben while Grant was holding

Theo in place. The whistle blew, and the ref jogged over. The roaring in my ears drowned out his words, but I clearly saw when he reached into his pocket and withdrew a yellow card, which he held in the air, first in my direction, then Theo's.

Fucking fuck.

Theo was livid, I was livid, and the rest of the team were extremely pissed off with both of us. Moreso with me. I could see Harvey pacing on the sidelines, the vein protruding in his forehead, and I knew I was in for a tongue-lashing when this match ended.

In a few minutes, it was all over, and as we trudged off the pitch, the team and the crowd were united in their disapproval.

Nausea churned in my stomach. This was my fault and my fault alone. I'd let my hatred of Theo get the better of me, and it had cost us vital points. Yeah, there was a chance that the goalie would've saved Theo's shot, but he was right—he had been wide open, with no other players standing in his way.

I hung my head as Harvey ranted, completely irate. I took his anger and accepted it. When he was finally done, I slumped on the bench in the dressing room with my head in my hands. Hot tears stung at the back of my eyelids, but I refused to let them fall.

"Jordan."

Raising my head, I saw Rory crouching in front of me. "What are you doing here?" I rasped, scrubbing at my face.

"I came to see if you were okay. Officially, you made a bad decision, and the team paid for it. But unofficially, as your friend, everyone makes mistakes. We all fuck up." Climbing to his feet, he squeezed my shoulder. "Put it behind you and move on."

"I'll try." Glancing up at him, I attempted a smile. "Thanks."

"Chin up. Oh, and don't forget you have that interview with *Offside* magazine in an hour."

I groaned. I'd forgotten all about it. This was the worst timing possible.

"Okay. Yeah," I muttered.

"I'll leave you to it. I'll be waiting in the meeting room for you." He left me alone, and I began mechanically stripping down, grabbing my towel, and heading into the showers. I caught Theo's eye as I entered when he was exiting his shower with a towel wrapped around his waist, his raven hair wet and messy, droplets running down his defined torso. As soon as he saw me, his expression darkened, but for once, I didn't rise to the bait. Instead, I turned away, heading into the closest unoccupied shower without another word.

"Mr. Emery. Thanks for meeting us today." A tall, dark-haired guy in a suit rose to his feet when I entered the room. Next to him, a younger guy with chestnut hair glanced at me and then back at the dark-haired guy. He cleared his throat, chewing on his lip before he also climbed to his feet.

I barely paid him any attention because the first guy was introducing himself, and his name immediately set alarm bells ringing.

"Dean Lewin, *Offside* magazine's digital editor. This is my colleague, Adam Collins."

"Dean *Lewin*?" I clipped out, and Dean shook his head.

"Yes, Theo is my cousin, but that's irrelevant. I'm bound by the journalistic code, and regardless, Theo and I barely know each other." He shook his head again. "That's irrelevant, too. You have my word, and the word of *Offside* magazine, that we'll be completely impartial."

His gaze was sincere, but I was still on edge. I relaxed a little as he went through the pre-approved questions that Rory had already coached me on, answering them with ease. I knew that any questions about me and Theo were banned, so I was caught off guard by Dean's next question.

"Harvey Raines called you 'reckless' after your conduct on the pitch today. What do you have to say about that?"

My gaze shot to Rory, and he seemed as much at a loss for words as I was. Great.

"Reckless?" I said carefully.

Dean cleared his throat, glancing down at his iPad briefly. "Social media also refers to you with that moniker. There have been rumours of parties—"

"That's enough." Rory shot to his feet, his expression dark. "This interview is over."

Dean's eyes widened before he slumped in his chair, pinching his brow. "My apologies. Rest assured, neither of the previous two questions will appear in the interview. We're here to focus on Jordan's underwear brand deal."

The guy next to him, Adam, shot him a savage glare, which would've made me smile if I hadn't been so fucking out of sorts from the events of today.

We wrapped up the interview, and although I still had my suspicions around the fact that the journalist was Theo's fucking cousin, I believed him when he said he was impartial for some reason.

When I was finally back in my house, the silence reminding me that I was alone, I fell back onto the sofa with my eyes closed.

Today had been one of the worst days I'd experienced in a long time, and most of it had been my fault.

I needed to forget.

How could I forget? We had training tomorrow morning, so I couldn't drink myself into oblivion. I couldn't order junk food and sit on my sofa bingeing it.

And I definitely couldn't bury myself in a girl. Or I could…but with the way my luck had been going recently, she'd probably sell me out, just like the others had recently.

At least every girl that had sold me out had praised my dick. That was a plus, right?

With a sigh, I dragged myself off the sofa and headed into my bedroom. I stopped in front of the huge mirror that marked the entrance to my closet.

I tugged off my T-shirt and pasted a smile on my face as I angled my body to catch the evening sunlight streaming through the windows. My social media fans would appreciate me, even if no one else did.

NINE

THEO

Jordan Emery's house was exactly as I'd expected. Modern, bland, and soulless. Why was I here?

"Why are you here?"

"I've been asking myself the same question." Glancing up at Lars, I shook my head. "Grant 'strongly suggested' that I come after yesterday's incident. He seems to think that if Jordan and I interact outside of our place of work, we'll be able to put our differences aside. I told him that it would never work and reminded him what happened the last time we mixed me, Jordan, and alcohol. But he insisted."

Lars scrubbed a hand over his beard, his brows pulled together as he mulled over my words. "He may be correct. You are fighting too much. It's bad for team morale."

He was right about the team morale part...and I supposed he had a point about the fighting. After yesterday's away match against Manchester City, which we'd lost 3–0, Jordan had stormed over to me in a rage, ranting about the mistakes I'd supposedly made and how it had cost us the third goal. Yes, I had lost the ball, but we'd all made mistakes, and it wasn't fair of him to single me out. And this was Jordan, the man I loathed. It didn't take much to rile me up when he was involved, and I'd ended up grappling with him against the tunnel wall, both of us snarling insults at one another until we'd been pulled apart by our teammates.

I highly doubted that attending a party at the house of my enemy would fix anything, though. We were too broken for that.

"I'll try to...be polite." It was all I could offer.

"You're a good man, Theo." Lars clasped my shoulder. "We only have one more game left in the season, and then you can have a break. It will be good for you. Take a trip somewhere tropical and forget about your problems."

"That sounds good." Anywhere that was far away from Jordan sounded good.

One more game. Our dreams of qualifying for Europe were over, but there was always next season. If we won our final match, we'd finish in eighth position in the league, which was far higher than Glevum had ever placed before. So close to qualifying for Europe, but not close enough.

But it was something worth celebrating. *If* we could manage to do it. There were three teams vying for eighth position, and it would all come down to the final game. If we lost and two of the other teams won their games, it was possible that we'd finish in the bottom half of the table.

We couldn't allow that to happen.

"Theo, there you are." Grant appeared in the entryway that led into the kitchen area. His arm was slung around a pouting Jordan, whose expression darkened when he lifted his eyes to mine.

Grant tightened his grip on Jordan's shoulder and dragged him over to me. "Now. I want you two to shake hands and promise me that you'll be civil to each other. We've only got one game left this season, and we need to win it."

There was a long silence. Grant cleared his throat, and Lars nudged me. "Fine," Jordan muttered, holding out his hand.

I lifted mine and curved my fingers around his warm palm.

He immediately yanked his hand away, giving me a wide, fake smile. "Theodore. Welcome to my humble abode. Would you like a drink?"

I matched his fake smile with one of mine. "Thank you for having me. A drink would be lovely."

His smile dropped, and he jabbed a finger behind him. "Kitchen's through there. Help yourself."

"Jordan."

Because Grant was our captain, Jordan actually listened to his warning, and so I found myself in the kitchen with my hated rival. It was crowded and loud, which had the unfortunate side effect of Jordan stepping closer to me to be heard over the din.

The bastard smelled *delicious*. Cedar, tropical rainforests, and some other notes I couldn't decipher but combined to make an addictive, exotic scent. I'd caught a hint of it before, when he'd been hanging all over me when he was completely wasted, but I'd been drunk myself at the time. Now, with his body so close to mine, I had no choice but to breathe him in.

"Just to make it clear, I don't want you here, but if I don't play by Grant's rules, he's gonna be really pissed off with me."

I leaned in, my mouth far too close to his ear. "Just to make it clear, I don't want to be here. I'd rather be literally anywhere else than in your presence. Now, be a good boy and get me a drink."

"Fuck you." He pulled back from me, his eyes flashing with fire.

"Whatever you're thinking, don't." Reuben materialised next to us, his arm around the waist of a gorgeous brunette. "You're trouble, Jordan Emery."

Jordan deflated. "Nothing to see here. Just catching up with my bestie." He blew me a kiss, and I mouthed *fuck off*, which made him grin. Spinning away, he headed over to his gargantuan fridge and pulled out two bottles of beer. Twisting off the caps, he returned to us, handing one to me. Before I could decide whether to act polite and thank him, he turned his attention to the girl with Reuben.

"Evie. Did you come here on your own?"

Smirking, she peered up at him from beneath her lashes. "It's not like you to be subtle, Jordan. I came with Livvy and Gracie. Livvy was looking for you earlier."

Jordan smirked right back at her, and my jaw clenched. "Just what I wanted to hear. Excuse me, guys, but I have someone—I mean, some*thing* to do."

I glanced at my phone. I'd stay an hour. That was reasonable. Then I could get out of here and, as I did every time I was subjected to Jordan's presence, try to forget it had ever happened.

Heading out of the open bifold doors that ran along the back of the house, I stepped out onto the patio. The garden was small for the size of the house, but it was...nice. There was a large patio area, part of it covered, complete with wicker furniture and a small firepit. The bottom half of the garden was grass, with a football goal at the very end. Fairy lights illuminated the space with a soft, golden light. It was far less crowded out here, and the music from the party was muted. Taking a deep breath of the fresh night air, I found myself relaxing for the first time since I'd arrived.

"You're Theo Lewin, right? I haven't seen you at one of Jordan's parties before."

"Yeah." I turned to the girl who had spoken to me. She was gorgeous—just my type, with rich brown hair and light blue eyes. I smiled. Things were looking up. "Theo. And you are?"

She licked her soft-looking lips, extending a manicured hand to me. "Livvy."

Livvy. Was this the same girl Jordan had been looking for? Taking her hand, I pressed a kiss to the back of it. "It's a pleasure. Can I get you a drink?"

Holding up a bottle, she shook her head. "No, but you can stay and keep me company."

"Hmm." Taking a step closer, I leaned in, watching her pupils dilate. "I think I might."

"What the fuck!"

In the kitchen, just about to help myself to another drink, I suddenly found myself pinned up against the wall with an arm across my throat. Blinking, I recalibrated, focusing on my assailant.

Jordan. Fucking wonderful.

"What do you mean?" I raised a brow at him.

"You. This," he ground out, raising his hand and dragging the pad of his index finger across my lip, his gaze fixed on my mouth. My eyes widened at the completely unexpected move, my breath stuttering. "You have her lipstick all over you."

I cleared my throat. "There's no rules that say I can't partake in a completely consensual kiss, is there?"

"Partake in a kiss," he muttered. "Who the fuck says things like that?" Then he lifted his eyes to mine, pinning me with his grey-green-blue gaze. "Livvy was here for me. You knew that, and that's why you decided to hit on her."

"You really want to do this? Grant's right there." I gave a subtle nod to the left.

"Yes, I really do, fucker." He drew back, wrapping his fingers around my bicep, and then yanked me in the direction of a white door. Tugging it open, he shoved me through into a small utility room, flipping on a light and slamming the door behind us.

"What the fuck is your problem?" Folding his arms across his chest, he stared me down. "There are tons of girls here. Why did you do it? Are you purposely trying to piss me off so I look bad in front of the team? Because Grant specifically asked me to be on my best behaviour?" His eyes widened. "That's it, isn't it? You want me to snap because you know this will get back to Harvey and give him yet another reason to get rid of me."

What?

"Slow down with the conspiracy theories. For your information, she approached me. Why would I turn her down? She's gorgeous."

His jaw clenched. "Fine. Whatever. This party was ruined from the minute I saw your face." Spinning on his heel, he turned to leave.

"Wait." My arm shot out, and I grabbed his wrist, stopping him in his tracks. "Harvey's not going to get rid of you. You must know that."

"All I know is nothing is guaranteed in football." He

wrenched his arm out of my grip. "I would've thought you'd be happy at the thought of me leaving."

"Believe me, I will be fucking ecstatic when you leave. But I can't see it happening at the end of this season." Even though I wished it would. The truth was the club didn't have the funds for another decent winger. That was one of the reasons why it was so important for us to win our final game. The higher in the league we finished, the more money would come to the club.

"Maybe they'll sell you," Jordan mused.

"You wish."

"I do fucking wish. Every night."

"Did I ever tell you how much I hate you?" I stepped closer, caging him in against the wall.

His eyes darkened as he placed his hand on my chest. My heart was racing beneath his palm, and I could feel his beating just as hard where our bodies were pressed together. Sliding his hand up, he curled his fingers around my throat.

I forgot how to breathe.

Leaning in, he placed his mouth to my ear. "Did I ever tell you how much I hate you back?"

Keeping one hand planted on the wall, I mirrored his movements, placing my own hand around his throat. His pulse was wild beneath me, but he remained completely still. I misjudged the distance between us as I tilted my head, my lips brushing over his ear, and a tiny gasp fell from his throat. "You're the bane of my fucking existence, Jordan Emery."

He swallowed hard underneath my grip. "Yeah? You're—"

The door flew open, and we sprang apart, but not before Grant caught sight of our compromising position.

"For fuck's sake." He pinched his brow. "You two cannot be trusted to be alone in a room together. As the captain, I'm going to have to fine both of you for fighting."

As Jordan pushed me away and stormed out of the room, I sank against the wall, exhaling a shuddering breath.

It hadn't felt like we were fighting. Not in that moment. Not at all.

I didn't know what it was, and I didn't even want to think about what it might have been.

Jordan Emery was my antagonist, my rival, the thorn in my side that wouldn't go away.

And my teammate.

That was all he was and all he ever would be.

TEN

JORDAN

The whistle blew, and the second half began. I was on fire today—the whole team was, united in our need to win this match, to finish up the season in eighth place. We were playing Wolverhampton Wanderers at home, and the crowd were behind us every step of the way, keeping our morale high. Better yet, we were currently winning 2–1, and Reuben had scored both goals.

It was one of those rare matches where everything came together. We were completely in sync, and it was as if we could read each other's minds. We were unstoppable.

Wolves threw everything they had at us, but we kept pushing back. Then, in the eighty-third minute, something happened. Something that gave me déjà vu.

I had the ball, and there were too many players between me and Reuben. I couldn't see an opening. But Theo was wide open.

This time, I didn't hesitate. I didn't try and shoot myself. I booted the ball across the pitch, straight to Theo.

His foot connected with the ball, and he sent it soaring straight into the goal.

Fuck, yeah! I ran at him, along with half of the team, all of us piling on each other and celebrating. I didn't get too close to Theo, of course, because I still fucking loathed the guy, but I appreciated his skills on the pitch. And now we were two goals ahead, with only seven minutes remaining on the clock, plus however much time was added at the end.

We just had to hold on.

As it turned out, we didn't even have to do that. Theo's goal seemed to be the final nail in Wolves' coffin because they fell apart, and Reuben scored another blinder of a goal, top corner of the goal.

And then it was all over, and we'd officially finished in eighth place in the Premier League.

Fucking incredible.

Back in the dressing room, Harvey had nothing but praise for the team.

Or so I thought.

I shifted in my seat, clenching and unclenching my fists. Next to me, Theo was, of course, completely cool and calm —outwardly, at least.

Across the table, Harvey, Rory, and Amir stared at us in silence, identical serious expressions on their faces.

"Here's the thing," Harvey finally said. "I have a dilemma. Both of you are extremely talented players, but you've been causing me problems all season with your reckless behaviour." He levelled me with a look that managed to convey anger, disappointment, and sadness all at once. "You've been in the headlines more often than not, especially you, Emery. Then there are all the issues between the two of you that don't make the headlines. I heard about your little altercation last week, for example. Grant's very concerned about your failure to put aside your differences, and the things he's told me have only reinforced my own concerns."

Shit. This was not good. Not at all.

Harvey leaned back in his seat, folding his arms across his chest. "So here's my dilemma. Do I cut my losses and find replacements for one or both of you?"

Bile rose in my throat. "No. Please." I leaned forwards in my chair, planting my hands on the table. They were fucking shaking. "We—"

Harvey held up his hand. "I haven't finished. Today's match showed me that there is hope of you working together, given the right incentive. So here's what's going to happen. You're going to work on your shit during the off-season, and when we come back in August, you're going to work in perfect harmony, and you're going to be as friendly with each other as you are with the rest of your teammates. Do I make myself clear?"

I nodded violently. "Yeah. Clear. I'll do whatever it takes."

Theo, who had remained silent, cleared his throat. When he spoke, I detected a tiny tremor in his voice, the only way I could tell that he was as affected as I was. "Clear. I have a question, though. How, exactly, are we to be expected to 'work on our shit'?"

A smile appeared on Harvey's face, and it was one of those sadistic smiles he used whenever he wanted us to do something torturous in our training sessions. "I'll let your agents give you the details. They came up with the idea, after all."

Rory glanced at Amir, who gave a small nod, and then he directed his gaze first at Theo, then at me. His own expression remained serious, and the look in his eyes told me that I wasn't going to like what he was about to tell me.

"Have either of you heard of Black Diamond Resort?"

PART 2

ELEVEN

JORDAN

At first glance, the island looked like paradise, with soft white sands, palm trees, turquoise seas, and a fresh, tropical breeze in the air. But it was the furthest thing from paradise. To begin with, my travel companion was a Mr. Theodore Lewin, who happened to be the one person I couldn't stand to be in the presence of. The second, and maybe even worse thing, was that we'd both been sent to fucking rehab.

Rehab.

What the actual fuck?

Apparently, Rory had a friend he'd been at Cambridge uni with, and he'd called in a favour. His friend happened to own the land that this rehabilitation centre masquerading as a luxury resort was squatting on, and so here we were. It was a retreat for elite, rich assholes, and it was going to be my home for the next few weeks while I worked on my "issues."

From what Rory had told me, I knew that the island itself was somewhere in French Polynesia in the South Pacific, and it had been a long fucking journey to get here.

Thank fuck that whoever had made our travel arrangements had the good sense to seat me and Theo as far apart as possible.

Being apart from each other was the only upside. We'd flown first class by commercial plane to the USA—LAX—then had to switch planes to fly to Tahiti. That in itself had taken a total of *twenty-three fucking hours*. But that wasn't even the end of the journey. We'd barely even set foot in the airport when we'd been whisked off to a small private plane, which took us to our final destination.

Black Diamond Resort and Spa.

The island was split in two by a mountain range, with emerald-green hills, lush jungle, and high cliffs and sandy beaches on both sides. One side of the island had an actual luxury resort, and the side I was unlucky enough to be on was the rehab side—or the recovery centre, as it was known. Both sides of the island officially had the same name, which Rory said was to protect the privacy of the rich and famous when they were here to seek help.

A "Black Diamond Intake Liaison" named Lawrence Shaw had taken me by golf cart to the main building so I could check in. As for my unwanted travel companion? I'd heard him complaining about feeling sick during the last part of our journey, and then he'd actually thrown up. *Sucks to be him.* I didn't know or care where he'd been taken. As long as it was away from me, I was good with it.

When the cart came to a stop, Lawrence turned to me. "This is the main building, where you'll check in at the front desk. It houses the health centre with the gym and indoor pool, as well as the therapists' offices, group therapy rooms, and the restaurants."

Group therapy. I smirked, thinking about how Theo

would hate that. He always came across as a very private person.

Lawrence climbed out of the golf cart. "Leave your bags. They'll be taken to your bungalow. If you'd like to follow me, we'll get you checked in."

"When you say 'bungalow,' what exactly do you mean? Is all the accommodation here the same?"

He shook his head as we entered the spacious lobby, the air conditioning welcome after the humidity of the air outside. "Here at the recovery centre, we offer various forms of accommodation to cater to the varying needs of our guests. We have three resident buildings, which contain hotel-style rooms, and we also have hillside and waterside villa-style bungalows. You'll be staying in one of our hillside bungalows. They're usually reserved for those guests who need the least monitoring, and they offer the most privacy of all our accommodations."

Okay, this was starting to sound like it might be alright. If I had to sit through some therapy sessions in order to get my own private villa on a tropical island for a few weeks, then I was actually getting a pretty good deal, truth be told.

"Cheers, Lawrence. Sounds good."

The man had quite a haughty, posh air about him—he'd probably love Theo, come to think of it—but with my words, a corner of his mouth ticked up.

"You're welcome, Mr. Emery. My nephew is a huge fan of yours."

I flashed him a grin as he pressed the bell on the desk to call the receptionist. "Do you want me to sign something for him?"

"I'm afraid we are all bound by ironclad non-disclosure agreements. If I were to obtain your autograph, there would be questions regarding how I'd managed to get hold of it."

"Leave it with me. I'll send him a signed shirt when I get out of here. Just sneak me his address, and I'll make up an excuse."

Before Lawrence could reply, a petite brunette woman with a beaming white smile appeared behind the desk.

"Welcome to Black Diamond, Mr. Emery. My name's Katlyn, and I'll be checking you in today."

"Call me Jordan." I winked at her, and her cheeks flushed, her lashes fluttering at me. If only Theo was here to see the effect I had on women. Although...maybe not. I remembered the party and how Livvy had gone for him, even though I knew for a fact she was interested in me. There was no accounting for taste.

"Jordan." Her beaming smile widened. "Your bungalow is all ready for you. I know you've travelled a long way, and you must be exhausted, not to mention the eleven-hour time difference. It's late in the day, so I suggest we get you settled into your accommodation for now, and your intake session will take place in the morning at 10:00 a.m. You'll meet your therapists then, and they'll give you a rundown of what to expect during your stay." She tapped on her computer keyboard. "You'll find a room service menu inside your bungalow, so you can order refreshments, and you can enjoy your private pool and take in the beautiful views of our island."

"Did you say *private pool*?"

"I did indeed."

My own villa with its very own private pool. I hoped Theo got put in the hotel room block so I could rub it in his face.

Katlyn asked for my passport and had me sign a couple of forms, then handed me a black wristband with a shiny glass oval face, which acted like a key card and would allow me to access the facilities in addition to my bungalow. She went over a few housekeeping items before informing me that there was a blanket 10:00 p.m. curfew for all guests, without exception. Then, she asked for my phone.

What the fuck? My entire life was on my phone. My social media followers would be expecting to hear from me. How could I show off my villa and private pool without it?

She read my panicked expression, giving me a placating smile. "Please don't worry. Your phone will be kept in a secure lockbox for the duration of your stay, and none of the staff will have access to it. Your agent, Mr. Nash, left us with specific instructions and has provided you with an alternative phone for use during your stay. You'll find it waiting for you in your room."

Thanks, Rory. I'd better be able to access my social media, or we'd be having serious words.

When check-in was complete and my poor phone was placed in its temporary prison, Lawrence took me to my villa in the golf cart. The sun was just beginning to set, streaking the sky with pinks and oranges. Fuck, I needed my replacement phone ASAP. A selfie with this sunset would be fucking epic.

We wound our way through tropical vegetation, gradually ascending until we popped out into a clearing.

My jaw dropped. Before me was a villa, nestled into the hillside, all crisp white paint and rich brown wood. In front of the villa was a wooden decked area, partially covered, with sun loungers and an infinity pool. But that wasn't even the jaw-dropping part. That came from what lay beyond the pool.

The view.

I could see down the hillside to the white sand beach. The tops of buildings peeked out from the vegetation, but because of the layout of the resort, it felt like I had my own completely private piece of paradise. The turquoise sea sparkled in the setting sun, the rays painting it with golds and pinks and burnished orange tones. In the far distance, right on the horizon, I could make out the outline of another island. A white sailboat cruised slowly past my line of sight, the water rippling in its wake. The air was heavy with the scent of tropical flowers and salt water, and birds sang from the trees, hidden from view, until one burst from the leaves to swoop past me.

It was completely fucking stunning, like nowhere I'd ever been before.

"Ahem."

My head whipped around to see Lawrence eyeing me with what might have been amusement.

"Sorry. I, uh, was taking in the view."

"So I see. Now, if you'd like to follow me, I'll show you inside."

He told me to wave the oval face of my wristband over the scanner to let myself in, and if I had any problems, reception could reset the wristband for me. If it was out of hours, I could dial o from my bedside phone, twenty-four hours a day, and someone would be available to help me.

The interior of the villa had taken on the same colour scheme as the outside, with crisp whites and rich brown wood. The main door opened into a lounge/dining area that also contained a desk, and the space had doors that opened onto the pool deck. At the back of this area was a tiny kitchenette with a fridge stocked with beverages, a small cupboard with snacks, and drink-making facilities. The room service menu and ordering instructions were stacked next to the coffee maker. A door led to a spacious bathroom with a walk-in shower, a tub, double sinks, and a separate toilet, while another door led to my bedroom with two huge beds and a small ensuite bathroom —minus the shower and bath—and a walk-in closet.

After receiving instructions for adjusting the air conditioning, I opened the doors wide and stepped out onto the wooden deck.

This place really was beautiful. And I needed my phone, like now, so I could document it.

Lawrence cleared his throat again, startling me out of my thoughts. "I'll be back tomorrow at nine to pick you up for breakfast before your intake session. After tomorrow, you can make your own way to breakfast, or if you'd prefer to be chauffeured around, dial reception, and someone will come to collect you. Enjoy your stay."

"Cheers. See you tomorrow."

When I was alone, I headed back into my bedroom, spotting the white box with an envelope on top of the closest bedside table, with "Mr. Emery" written on the outside of the envelope in flowing cursive script.

I scanned the contents of the envelope. There was a letter welcoming me to the resort, with the rules and information that Katlyn at the front desk had briefly mentioned. A second sheet of paper had a weekly timetable of sessions and activities, with mandatory items marked in bold. It looked like I had one mandatory group therapy session each week, two private therapy sessions, and two joint therapy sessions—whatever those were. In addition to that, I had to do something called "Focus," which seemed to be a name for the activities on offer. The supplementary sheet said that the timetable was subject to change after I'd been assessed by the therapists or at any time during my stay, and if either myself or one of my therapists felt that I needed additional sessions, then a revised timetable would be created for me.

The list of activities at the resort sounded interesting. A few options caught my eye straight away—kayaking, paddleboarding, and snorkelling. I'd need to somehow find out which activities Theo was interested in, so I could sign up for whichever one he wasn't doing.

Tossing the papers onto the bedside table, I picked up the plain white box and lifted the lid. Inside was a shiny phone, complete with charging cable and earbuds. When I powered it on, I was greeted with a plain red background with the Glevum FC logo and five icons on the home screen. A phone, a text bubble, a camera, Spotify, and a folder with a padlock on it.

What the fuck? Where were all the other apps? I was guessing they were all hidden within the padlock folder. I tried clicking on it, and a message came up to tell me I needed to input a password. Fucking brilliant.

I opened the text app and found a message from Rory.

RECKLESS

RORY:

> I know what you're thinking, Jordan. Be grateful you even have a phone. The resort strongly discourages their use and most residents have a block on theirs. This phone has been set up so you can listen to music and take pictures (I know you're incapable of surviving without taking at least 10 selfies a day), and you can call me IN AN EMERGENCY ONLY. A real, actual emergency. You can text me if there's something you really need, and text your roommate as much as you want, but all other calls and texts are barred, as is internet usage. Please try to remember we're doing this for your own good. Play your part, get back to England, and help Glevum to get to Europe next season. YOU CAN DO IT

My fingers flew over the keys as I replied.

ME:

> No internet? How the fuck am I supposed to maintain my social media presence?

RORY:

> I see you found my gift. How's the recovery centre?

ME:

> It looks like paradise and I was feeling ok about it until you told me I HAVE NO FUCKING INTERNET

RORY:

> Send me your password and I'll update your accounts while you're away. Glevum has plenty of photos we can use for content

ME:

> Fine. I guess. But NO INTERNET?!! There are so many selfie opportunities here! Also WTF am I supposed to do for entertainment without it? My room doesn't even have a TV and the curfew is 10pm

RORY:

> Save your selfies for when you get home. As for entertainment, you're not there to be entertained, but I connected the phone to your Spotify account and downloaded all your most listened to playlists, so you have music. You could also try talking to your roommate. He's in the same boat as you

ME:

> I don't have a roommate

RORY:

> You do. Now, did you text me just to complain about your lack of internet? Because it's 4:30 in the morning here and I'd like to get at least a couple more hours of sleep before I have to start my very busy day of work

ME:

> Sorry forgot about the time difference. OK I'm going

RORY:

> Have fun. I mean it. Let yourself be open to things, and I think you'll surprise yourself in a good way. I'm proud of you for doing this

ME:

> Thanks. Get some sleep Grandad

RORY:

> Don't start

ME:

Love you too

When I exited out of my messages and explored the rest of the apps I was allowed access to, I found that my contact list had two numbers programmed into it.

One was my agent's.

The other number was listed as "Theo."

I glanced across the room to the other bed before returning to my messages, rereading the line that said, "text your roommate as much as you want."

No. They wouldn't put us together, would they? It was a *horrible* idea. In fact, if you listed every bad idea ever, forcing me and Theodore Lewin to share a bedroom would be close to the top. There was no way that wouldn't end in bloodshed.

But when I climbed off my bed and padded over to the other side of the room, I saw the white box placed on the other bedside table and the envelope with "Mr. Lewin" written on the outside.

Fuck.

TWELVE

JORDAN

After breakfast, followed by my intake session, where I had to fill in five million forms while being asked intrusive questions, I had some free time. I decided to head down to the beach because seeing it from my villa's vantage point and not being able to go there had been torture. As soon as I kicked off my sliders and stepped onto the softest, warmest white sand, the grains cradling my toes, a smile crossed my face.

This was amazing.

Leaving my sliders at the edge of the beach, I moved closer to the crystal-clear waters until my feet touched wet sand, leaving imprints in my wake. When my toes were finally kissed by the warm, foamy surf, I laughed out loud, high on life and a feeling of utter contentment that I didn't think I'd ever experienced before. Finding that here, of all places, was completely unexpected in the best way.

Whatever happened, I'd always have this memory.

All too soon, my time on the beach was up, and I had my first individual therapy session. I could still feel the sand between my toes as I entered Dr. Weaver's office. She was my initially assigned therapist for my individual sessions, and although I had no clue what to expect when I walked through her doorway, something about the room made me feel immediately at ease.

The office was bright and airy, with a wall of windows offering a view of the vegetation and a glimpse of the sea beyond. A black leather sofa was in the centre of the space, and the wall behind the desk was decorated with various diplomas and certifications.

Dr. Weaver smiled at me as I stepped inside, her expression warm and welcoming. Her brown hair was pulled into a tight bun, and wire-framed glasses were perched on the end of her nose. She was dressed professionally, but not in an intimidating way, her petite frame covered in black trousers and a light blue floaty blouse thing. She directed me to the sofa, and then she took a seat on a chair to my left, a pad and pen clasped in her hands.

"Thank you for choosing to meet with me today, Jordan. I thought we could begin with you telling me a little about yourself."

She made it sound like I had a choice in any of this when the truth was everything here was mandated. But if she wanted to hear the boring details of my life, I was more than prepared to tell her.

"Okay. I'm nineteen, and I'm a professional footballer in the English Premier League. I was transferred to my team in January, and before that, I played in League Two."

Dr. Weaver made a little note on her pad. "Tell me about your transfer and the adjustments you had to make."

"Uh..." Leaning back, I took a minute to really think about it. Everything had happened so fast, and I'd never actually taken the time to sit and think about the adjustments I'd made. "I guess...I mean, it was a big change. There are three professional leagues below the Premier League, and I was in the lowest one. I went from playing in front of a few thousand people to tens of thousands, and millions more on TV. I was up against some of the biggest footballing legends in the world, so I guess...there was a lot of pressure to perform. It was stressful, but I love it."

She hummed, scribbling something on her pad. "What about your relationship with your teammates? Did they welcome you?"

Surely she knew all about Theo—it was why I was here, after all, so I avoided mentioning him specifically. "They made me feel welcome. I get on well with most of them."

Thankfully, she didn't call me out, simply changing the subject. "I asked you to tell me a little about yourself, and you chose to focus on your recent career. Why don't you tell me a little about your childhood?"

I told her about my life growing up with my dad, our Saturday afternoons spent watching football, and then my time at the youth academy—avoiding mentions of Theo. When I ran out of words, she smiled, climbing to her feet and crossing to her desk. When she returned to her chair, she held out a brown leather notebook.

"I'd like you to try an exercise before our next session. In this notebook, I'd like you to list the important people in your life and what makes them important to you. Important can mean both positive and negative, so I'd like you to include anyone that has an influence in your life in either a positive or negative way."

Please don't say I have to write about Theo fucking Lewin. "What, like good and bad people?"

"We don't use 'good' or 'bad' to define people, but I would like you to include both positive and negative aspects. Write down everything you can think of, even if it's something that you think is small."

I took the notebook, glancing down at the smooth leather cover before I met her gaze again. "Will you be reading it?" I wasn't sure how I felt about that. Because if I had to include Theo, it wasn't going to be complimentary.

"No, not unless you want me to, but I hope that we will be able to discuss some of the contents in our future sessions."

"Okay. I'll try."

"That's all I ask."

Outside in the fresh air again, I slid my sunglasses on and headed in the direction of the path that led up to my villa. I'd done it. I'd survived my first therapy session, and I hadn't even had to talk about why I was here. Somehow, I couldn't imagine Theo's first session going so smoothly.

When I reached the villa, the second bed was undisturbed, and the box and the envelope were still in the same position. It was weird. Don't get me wrong, I was glad to postpone any interaction with Theo, but where the fuck was he?

THIRTEEN

THEO

The minute I'd opened my bag on the plane, I knew I was completely and utterly fucked.

I'd forgotten my sleeping pills. I distinctly remembered counting out the amount I needed to get me through my time away, and then I'd been distracted by a phone call from my agent. By the time the call ended, the taxi was waiting outside to take me to the airport, and in the ensuing rush, I'd forgotten to put the pills in my bag.

I'd been awake the entire flight, and when we arrived in Tahiti, I'd started feeling nauseous, and then the vomiting began. My throat was raw, I hadn't slept, and I was fucking miserable. I had no clue where I was, other than in a sterile room with monitors and an IV drip attached to me.

A short, grey-haired man holding a tablet and wearing a lab coat entered the room. "Morning, Mr. Lewin. How are you feeling today?"

"Terrible," I rasped. That much should have been obvious.

He left the room and returned a minute later, holding a

paper cup brimming with water. "For your throat. Small sips."

My bed had a remote control to raise and lower it, so I raised myself into a seated position, taking the cup and sipping from it. I'd stopped throwing up, but I was still nauseous, so I only allowed myself to drink a small amount.

When I'd placed the cup down on the table next to my bed, the grey-haired man pulled up a chair, eyeing me over the top of his tablet. "My name is Dr. Ross, and I'm one of the psychiatrists and medical doctors here at Black Diamond Recovery Centre. We weren't aware of any medical issues prior to your arrival, so I need to ask you a few questions, if you're feeling up to answering them. We have the medical information that your soccer club sent through to us, and as far as I can tell, you're a perfectly healthy nineteen-year-old. Do you have any idea of what may be causing your symptoms?"

Yes.

Fuck. I bit down on my cracked lower lip. I was going to have to tell him, wasn't I? If it was the pills, then he might be able to help me. Closing my eyes, I exhaled shakily. "I—I've been taking sleeping pills. I...forgot to bring them with me."

"I see." He scrolled on his tablet for a minute, scanning the screen before he met my gaze again. His eyes were knowing, but there was no judgement in them. "Are these the prescribed pills mentioned in your medical information?"

"Uh...yes and no." My voice was barely above a whisper. "I've been prescribed them, but I needed more..." I trailed off, swiping my trembling hand across my face.

Picking up the cup, I sipped my water. The cup shook in my grip. "It was only supposed to be temporary." I swallowed hard, forcing the rest of the words out. "I never meant for it to get so out of hand. I don't...I know I have a problem."

"Mr. Lewin. Or would you prefer me to call you Theo?" At my nod, he continued. "Theo. Let me ask you a question, and I want you to answer honestly. Yes or no. Do you want to rely on pills to help you sleep?"

Of course I didn't *want* to. "N—no."

"Okay. One more question with a yes or no answer. Would you like me to help you to stop relying on them?"

"*Yes.*"

He gave me a warm smile. "Then I will help you."

Three days later, my nausea finally subsided. I hadn't had much sleep, and Dr. Ross had informed me that I would probably experience something known as "rebound insomnia" for a week or so, which was like a double dose of insomnia each night. According to him, the usual way he'd get someone to detox from sleeping pills was to gradually decrease the dosage, but because I'd gone cold turkey, my symptoms were more intense.

On the plus side, because I'd only been taking the pills for around nine months, my symptoms shouldn't be as severe or last for as long as someone who had been taking them for years. My peak physical fitness was another factor that would allow me to recover quickly, and so I'd finally been allowed to move out of the medical wing and into my prearranged accommodation. I had to have a daily medical check, and if any of my symptoms worsened, I could be readmitted or receive medical treatment, but other than that, I could proceed as normal.

Dr. Ross was confident that I'd recover quickly. He told me that the main symptoms I'd be likely to experience for the next week or two were the insomnia, anxiety and mood swings, possible nightmares, and a craving for the pills. It was possible that I'd experience other things like confusion, muscle pain, and headaches, but because of the aforementioned reasons and the type of sleeping pills I'd been taking, it was unlikely.

The cravings were the worst. They were constant and something Dr. Ross would be working on with me through therapy. I knew I'd be able to handle them here because I had no other choice, but I didn't know what would happen when I got back home. I only hoped I'd be strong enough to resist. After three days of in-depth conversations with Dr. Ross, I'd come to realise that I had an addiction. I'd never thought of it in those terms before—I'd always told myself that it was okay to take the pills because so many players relied on them to help them sleep before games, and I thought I could stop at any time. But I'd become too reliant on them, to the point where I couldn't function without taking them. Accidentally leaving them behind and going through withdrawal had been the wake-up call I needed.

One day at a time.

That was all I had to do. Take it one day at a time, beginning with today.

I opened the door to my villa and stepped inside.

FOURTEEN

JORDAN

"What the fuck!"

My head shot up at the angry exclamation from a very familiar voice. A wide grin spread across my face, and my heart rate kicked into overdrive. Shaking the water from my hair, I ascended the steps of the infinity pool. By the time I reached the wooden deck, Theo had burst through the doorway, his face twisted in rage and his blue eyes flashing with fire.

When he caught sight of me, he came to a sudden stop, his gaze drifting down my dripping body before returning to my face. His mouth opened, but I spoke first.

"Where the fuck have you been?"

He slammed his mouth closed, folding his arms across his chest and glaring at me. I rolled my eyes.

"You look like shit. What's going on, Lewin? Where have you been hiding?"

"I haven't been hiding," he bit out. "I've been in the medical wing."

Shit. "Are you...uh...okay?" The words tripped

awkwardly off my tongue. I wasn't used to this, not with him.

"I'm fine. Why are we sharing a fucking bedroom?"

He clearly wasn't fine. His skin had a grey pallor, and there were dark circles under his bloodshot eyes. But whatever. He clearly didn't want to talk about it, and that was fine by me.

"Your guess is as good as mine. Believe me, I'm as unhappy about it as you are."

His gaze trailed down my body again, and for some reason, my dick decided to wake up. I knew it was muscle memory or whatever from the way women eyed me with blatant interest—not that Theo was looking at me with interest, more like jealousy over the way I looked—and I realised that I hadn't actually fucked anyone for over a week or even had a wank since the day before yesterday. What the fuck was that all about?

I'd rectify that tonight. In the meantime, I needed a shower. Grabbing my towel from the sun lounger, I wrapped it around my waist and then sidled around Theo, making my way into the bathroom and closing the door firmly behind me.

By the time I'd showered and dressed in a clean pair of shorts, Theo had disappeared. I noticed that the white box next to his bed had been emptied, so I knew that wherever he'd gone, I could reach him. I'd completed my day's therapy session—this morning had been a group session where they tried to teach us to meditate, unsuccessfully in my case—and spent two hours in the gym, and now I had the rest of the day free.

I was bored. Yeah, I was in paradise, but I was alone, and Theo was the only person I knew here. Even though we hated each other, antagonising him until he exploded could be a way to pass the time until dinner.

ME:
Where are you?

THEO:
Go away, Jordan

ME:
Rude. What are you doing?

THEO:
Leave me alone

ME:
I'll keep texting until you reply

Theo

THEODORE

THEODORE LEWIN

LORD LEWIN

THEO:
Fuck OFF, Emery

ME:
Nope

THEO:
You are the most irritating person I've ever met. Where I am and what I'm doing is none of your concern

ME:
I'm bored

THEO:
I don't care

> **ME:**
> I'm your teammate. You should care

> **THEO:**
> I don't. I've been through three days of hell, and all I want to do now is survive the rest of my time here as far away from you as possible. Leave me alone. I won't be replying to you anymore

> **ME:**
> Fuck you then

Fine. He wanted to be left alone? I'd go and find someone else to entertain me.

With that thought in mind, I fastened my wristband, grabbed my sunglasses, earbuds, and the notebook the therapist had given me, and then headed down to the main building.

"Jordan!"

As I entered the lobby, I saw Katlyn waving at me from behind the front desk. I headed over to her, enjoying the way her gaze raked over my shirtless body. First, Theo was looking at me with undisguised jealousy; now, she was looking at me with undisguised lust. As it should be.

"I was going to have this delivered to your room, but since you're here..." Her fingers flew across the keyboard, and a minute later, the printer whirred to life, spitting out a single sheet of paper. "This is your revised timetable. I have another for your roommate; would you mind taking it for him?"

I already had a revised timetable? Scanning the sheet of paper, I saw that a few of the timings had changed, but it looked to be similar to the original timetable I'd been given. Then I glanced at Theo's timetable and groaned out loud.

Other than a recurring appointment at nine thirty each morning, labelled as "Dr. Ross," all of his other sessions lined up with mine. Dr. Ross was his individual therapist, and I still had Dr. Weaver, but our group therapy sessions and activity sessions were at the same time with the same therapists. Even worse...the slots that had simply been labelled as "joint therapy" on my original timetable now informed me that I was expected to attend these sessions *with Theo*.

Fucking brilliant.

"Thanks, Katlyn." Leaning across the desk, flexing my muscles, I shot her a bright grin. "I'll make sure my roommate gets this. Speaking of, do you happen to know where he's been the past few days?" Lowering my voice, I let my smile drop. "He doesn't seem like himself, and I'm a little worried about him."

She bit down on her lip, her gaze darting around her before she gave a tiny shake of her head. "I'm not at liberty to say."

Well, fuck. Time to pull out the big guns. I eyed her from beneath my lashes as I put on my most pleading expression. "I'd never get you into trouble. I'm just concerned for my friend." *Friend.* It made me nauseous to even think of using that word in connection with Theo. "He told me he'd been in the medical wing. I want to make sure I'm doing everything I can to help him. He's the type of person who refuses to ask for help, even when he needs it."

I could see her cracking. "All I know is that he was taken to the medical wing when he arrived, and he's been put under the care of Dr. Ross, who's one of our psychiatrists and medical doctors. Dr. Ross usually works with guests who have, um, substance abuse problems."

Substance abuse? What the fuck? No, that couldn't apply to Theo. We had random drug tests throughout the season, so there was no way that would've gone unnoticed. That had to be a coincidence.

"Why was he in the medical wing?"

"I don't know. I'm sorry." She gave me a small smile. "You're a good friend, wanting to look out for him."

A tiny niggle of guilt prodded at the back of my mind. What if there was really something wrong with him?

No, there couldn't be.

I pushed the guilt away. "Thanks, Katlyn. I'll make sure he gets the timetable." Folding the pieces of paper, I shoved them into my pocket.

Well, that had wasted ten minutes of my time. Now what? Connecting my earbuds to my phone, I decided to head down to the beach. I hadn't explored much of the island yet, but I'd walked the entire length of this strip of sand three times already.

As soon as I stepped onto the deserted beach, the sea breeze ruffling my hair and the sun warm on my face, I smiled. This was perfection.

After taking a quick selfie with the sea in the background, ready to post when I was back in the real world, I glanced around me. My smile fell from my face.

Because of the way the sea worked—I was no aquatic expert, but I knew it was something to do with tides and the weather—shit got washed up on the shore every now and then. Plastic. The bane of my life. Or the second bane of my life, if I included Theo in the list. As I walked down the beach, I scooped up four broken bottles, an old flip-flop, three straws, a toothbrush, a length of frayed blue fishing rope, and a toy doll missing its head. All made of plastic.

Taking a seat on a flat rock at the far end of the beach, I made a little pile of the debris I'd collected so I could deal with it later and pulled out my notebook.

Who was important in my life? Who had an influence in either a positive or a negative way? I decided to make a list of names to begin with, and then I could come up with reasons later.

PEOPLE IN MY LIFE
Rog Emery (my dad)
Rory Nash (my agent)
Harvey Raines (my manager)
Grant Evans (my team captain)

I stopped and thought for a minute. There were people from my old team, school, and youth academy that I spoke to, but as far as having an influence on my life went...they didn't affect me either way. Same with ex-girlfriends—I'd never had any serious relationships, so there hadn't ever been a girl who had been important enough to me to make the list. I'd never known my mum—she'd left right after I was born and had passed away when I was four or five, and my dad had been an only child whose parents had both passed away before I was born, so I had no other relatives I knew of.

I guessed I could include some of my new teammates. A few of them already felt like friends, not just teammates.

I added three more names to the list.

Reuben Mendy (my teammate)
Lars Nielsen (my teammate)
Ainsley Shaw (my teammate)

The blank space below Ainsley's name stared at me accusingly. I growled under my breath, almost stabbing my pen through the page as I added one final name.

Theo Lewin (my teammate/hated rival/pretentious wanker)

FIFTEEN

THEO

Of course, the place I'd chosen to come to for some peace and quiet was also the place my unwanted roommate had chosen. It appeared that he was scribbling in a notebook, and he had earbuds in, so with any luck, he wouldn't notice me. I began to circle around the back of the rocks and then stopped.

"What's that?"

Jordan's head shot up. When he caught sight of me, he slapped his notebook shut, yanking his earbuds out of his ears. "Oh, now you've decided you want to talk to me?"

This had been a mistake. "No. I simply asked a question."

"I didn't hear you. Music." He pointed at his ears and then pushed his sunglasses on top of his head. Today, his eye colour matched the sea. "What did you say?"

"I asked what that was." I nodded towards the pile of rubbish at his feet.

"Oh, that?" He grinned, and I had to look away. "It's debris that got washed up on the beach. I collected it as I was walking."

Despite the fact that I should have stepped away, I moved closer, crouching down to examine the pile. "Why?"

"Why was it washed up, or why did I collect it?" For once, there was no hostility in his tone, just curiosity.

"The second one." Picking up a headless doll, I examined it before throwing it back down with a shudder. Creepy. "What exactly do you plan to do with all of this?"

"I'm going to dispose of it responsibly. All this shit is really bad for the environment, you know. And the island's ecosystem."

I stared at him, temporarily lost for words. "You care about the environment?"

"No need to sound so surprised," he muttered, his lips forming a bratty little pout. I rolled my eyes.

"I didn't know you cared about anything other than yourself. Oh, that's it, isn't it? You're doing this to score points, to make yourself look good."

His eyes darkened, real anger entering them. Throwing his notebook down, he leapt to his feet and shoved at my chest, hard. I hadn't been expecting it, and I fell backwards, taking him with me.

"You arrogant fucking knobhead," he snarled as we rolled, sand flying around us, getting *everywhere*. "Just because I like to show the body I work fucking hard to get doesn't mean I'm a brainless himbo. I care about things, not only myself. You're just too fucking stuck-up to see past the end of your own nose."

"What the fuck does that mean?" I kicked at his shin while he got in a blow to my kidneys that left me gasping.

He stilled above me, gripping my wrists painfully to hold me in place. "It means that you judge me by your own fucking upper-class standards, which means I'll always be found lacking in your eyes. You did it from the first day we met, and you're still fucking doing it now."

"Maybe if you showed this side of yourself once in a while instead of just posing for endless selfies and fucking underwear brands, then people might realise that you're not as shallow as you come across."

"Fuck. You." He shoved at me again and then launched himself to his feet. Grimacing, he rubbed at his shin where I'd kicked him. "Asshole."

Swiping his notebook from the rock, he shoved it into the pocket of his board shorts and then scooped the rubbish into his arms. "For your information, I do share some of this stuff online, but you've obviously got a selective memory. Even if I didn't, it wouldn't matter. I don't need to shout about the things I care about. It's none of your business or anyone else's." He shook his head violently, sending sand cascading everywhere. I barely noticed, my gaze caught on his tanned torso, which, even now, he appeared to be flexing. When he spun around and stormed away, my eyes followed the shift and ripple of his muscles until he was a distant speck.

Collapsing back on the sand, I closed my eyes. I loathed Jordan, but from the moment I'd seen him sitting on that rock, I'd forgotten about my troubles. For that short time when I'd given him my full focus, there was nothing else in my mind. No worries, no stress about the sleeping pills.

All that remained was him. And as much as I hated the fact that he was the one to command my attention, it had been a welcome respite.

Not welcome enough to repeat, though. I needed and wanted to stay away from Jordan Emery. He was nothing but trouble.

After I'd brushed off the worst of the sand and eaten a solitary dinner at the restaurant, stretching it out as long as possible, I knew that I couldn't avoid returning to the villa any longer. I was at optimum physical fitness, but I had spent three days in bed with very little sleep, and my symptoms seemed to be coming back again. My palms were sweating, and my heart was racing from anxiety I couldn't pinpoint the source of, and I had the beginnings of a headache. I craved the relief of the pills, but I knew I would have to push through and bear it. So I allowed myself to be chauffeured back up the hill by golf cart.

A sliver of light shone from beneath the closed bedroom door. In the hope that Jordan would be asleep by the time I went to bed, I decided to take a long, hot shower to get the sand out of the places it really shouldn't be and then read for a while. Perhaps it would tire me out enough to sleep for at least a few hours. Of course, I had the rebound insomnia to contend with, but I was so very tired.

I rubbed at my gritty eyes with shaking hands.

The cravings for the pills were getting worse.

It was going to be a long, long night.

SIXTEEN

JORDAN

Stretching out in my huge bed, I yawned widely. I was going to sleep well tonight. But before I turned off my lamp and closed my eyes, I had some important business to take care of. Dick-related business.

I removed my earbuds, placing them on the side table next to my phone. Rory had been kind enough to download some football podcasts to my Spotify, so I'd passed the time listening to a couple while I was lying here, waiting for Theo to get out of the shower. The shower noise had stopped a while ago, and there was still no sign of him, so I guessed that probably meant he was sleeping in the lounge area. Stubborn bastard. I would rather share a room with just about anyone other than him, but I sure as fuck wouldn't attempt to sleep on that sofa. It was made for style, not comfort, and it was a two-seater, so it was far too short for either of us to stretch out on.

Whatever. It was his choice. Meanwhile, I was going to have a nice, satisfying wank and then pass out until morning.

I shoved my boxer briefs down, kicking them off, and

then wrapped my hand around my cock. I wasn't fully hard yet, but it wouldn't take much to get me there. Closing my eyes, I lay back, giving my balls a light tug as I stroked my shaft, feeling it hardening in my grip.

Oh, yeah.

"What the fuck?"

My eyes flew open to see Theo standing in the doorway, wrapped in a fluffy white bathrobe with his mouth wide open and his gaze fixed on the place where my hand was lazily stroking my erection. The lower part of my body was hidden by the covers, but it was obvious what I was doing.

"Evening, bestie." I blew him a kiss.

His cheeks flushed as he raised his gaze to mine, his blue eyes glittering with anger or something. "What the fuck," he repeated in a hoarse voice.

I continued to stroke my cock, which was now rock-hard and throbbing. If he was expecting me to stop, he'd be severely disappointed because I wasn't shy about what I was doing. Why would I be? I had a great body, a fucking great dick, and I had every right to satisfy myself before I went to sleep. If Theo had a problem with it, he could leave.

"What are you doing?"

Was it my imagination, or had he moved closer? I could've sworn he was standing in the doorway, and now he was right at the end of my bed.

"You really don't know? Do you want a visual?" I smirked at him, my words slightly breathless as I rolled my foreskin back, dragging my thumb across the exposed head of my cock. It felt so fucking good. Way better than it usually did.

"N—no. *No.*"

Of course not. He was a posh git and was probably a complete prude. Maybe I should really give him a shock.

Before I could second-guess myself, I threw back the covers, and there I was, exposed in all my naked glory. Fucking hell, I bet I looked amazing from where he was standing. If it had been anyone else, I might've been tempted to ask them to take a picture. But not Theo.

He froze in place, so still that I couldn't even see him breathing. The only movement came from his clenched fists, which looked like they were trembling slightly.

"Feels so fucking good," I moaned, closing my eyes and concentrating on the way my hand was moving over my dick.

"Jordan," he whispered hoarsely. "Stop it."

"No." Spreading my legs a little, I reached down to my balls, gently tugging at them again. So. Good. "I've got a better idea. Why don't you get into your bed and do the same thing I'm doing? It might help to loosen you up. Or are you too prudish to touch your dick when you're in the same room as another person?"

"*No.*"

I heard movement, and when I opened my eyes again, he was in his bed underneath the covers, the bathrobe discarded on the floor.

And he was still fucking watching me.

"What are you so scared of?" I met his gaze. "It's nothing to be ashamed of."

"I'm not ashamed," he bit out. His jaw was clenched so hard that I could hear his teeth grinding together, and his hands were still shaking.

Fuck. I'd probably taken things too far.

My hand stilled on my dick, my enthusiasm suddenly waning. "Sorry," I muttered. "Goodnight."

Flipping off the lamp, I plunged us into darkness.

It suddenly seemed so quiet, other than the soft hum of

the air conditioning. I could hear Theo's rapid breaths and the slide of the bedcovers against his body as he shifted position.

My dick jerked.

He was naked under there, wasn't he?

I curled my fingers around my shaft again, giving it one long, slow stroke. Fuuuck.

"Why are you doing it?"

"Because it feels good, and it'll help me sleep." My whisper was just as quiet as his.

"Will it help me sleep?" He exhaled sharply. "Forget I said that."

I remembered the dark circles under his eyes. "Uh...it might. Worth a try, at least."

"Okay."

Fucking hell, was he actually going to do it? I'd been trying to get under his skin earlier. At no point had I actually expected him to go ahead. But maybe it really would loosen him up. Fuck knows he needed it.

Because of the silence, it was easy to hear the sounds he made, even though they were muffled by the covers. The slide of his hand over his erection. His breathing getting heavier and heavier, and his bitten-off groans. My cock was throbbing and leaking as my own hand moved faster, chasing my release. I had to beat him to the finish line. I couldn't allow him to win this.

"Fuck," I groaned as my balls drew up and my climax hit me, cum shooting over my abs, painting my skin. *"Fuck."*

Theo gave up on staying quiet, his low moan filling the room as he came, his bed giving a soft creak as his hips arched up and came back down again.

Then the only sounds in the room were our combined rapid breaths, eventually slowing. I fumbled for the box of tissues on my bedside table, knocking the lamp and my phone before I found it. When I'd cleaned up, I tugged the covers over my body and settled on my side.

Before my brain could process what had just happened, sleep took me under.

SEVENTEEN

THEO

"You don't need therapy for anger management." Flora, the woman tasked with our joint therapy sessions, gave me a beaming smile, her bangles jangling as she waved her hands in the air. Her blonde hair, shot through with pastel pink, whipped around her face in the sea breeze. We were seated on yoga mats in a flat, grassy area close to the beach, and I was doing my best to ignore the person sprawled out to my left.

Last night...what the fuck had Jordan been thinking? What had *I* been thinking, more to the point? I never should have let him goad me into it.

He had been right, though. It had helped me to sleep, for a few blissful hours at least, until I'd woken up again, sweating and with a racing heart. After tossing and turning for another couple of hours, I'd given up and got out of bed, taking a cool shower and then sitting out on the deck with a mint tea, watching the sky lighten on the horizon.

"Your case is a little different," Flora continued. "While I think you will both greatly benefit from continuing with your individual therapy sessions, we're going to try another approach for your joint sessions. I'm all for thinking outside the box, so here's what we're going to do. You're teammates who need to learn to work together, and that's going to be our goal. Each day, I want you to do two things together. Firstly, I want you to sign up for one of the activities on offer. To avoid arguments, you'll each take a turn to choose the activity. Secondly, I'd like you both to do something together of your own choosing. It can be something as simple as sharing a meal, or taking a walk along the beach, or even working out. As long as you do it together, every day. At the end of the week, the three of us will meet again, and I want you to tell me some things you've learned about each other."

"Every day?" Jordan's horrified tone matched my thoughts.

"Every day. And I want you to make an effort to really talk to each other and to listen." She paused, her gaze scanning mine, then Jordan's. "I believe this approach will work for you, but you both need to commit to putting the effort in. It's up to you. I can't do this for you. You need to choose to work at it."

Jordan sighed. Out of the corner of my eye, I could see him rubbing his hand over his jaw, which was lightly dusted with stubble, instead of his usual clean-shaven look. "I guess...I mean, that's why we're here, right? I don't wanna be transferred to another team. I—I can try." When I glanced over at him, I saw that his mouth was downturned, his expression defeated.

"Theo?" Flora gave me an encouraging smile.

I couldn't say no, not when Jordan had already agreed. It would reflect badly on me. I nodded, and she clapped her hands together.

"Perfect! There's no time like the present. Go and sign

up for one of today's Focus activities. I'll see you back here at the end of the week at the same time. Good luck, boys."

"I'm choosing the first activity," Jordan announced as I fell into step next to him. The sooner we got this over with, the better.

"No, I'm choosing. I have seniority over you."

He stopped dead, staring at me. "How exactly did you come to that conclusion?"

"I'm older than you, and I've been at Glevum longer than you."

"Not by much, and you were only there for half a season before I showed up."

"I'm choosing." Picking up the pace, I strode towards the main building, leaving Jordan pouting in the middle of the path. I didn't have time for his antics. All I wanted was to get this nightmare over with.

"The waterfall's this way."

"For fuck's sake, Theo. We're following the yellow markers, not the orange ones. It's this way, I guarantee."

"Fuck *off*," I shouted, swatting away yet another mosquito from my arm. "Fucking bloodsucking bastards!"

A laugh burst from Jordan's throat. "Wow, you really don't like mozzies, huh?"

"Stop making such idiotic comments." I wiped at my forehead. It was so humid today, and ominous, heavy grey clouds were gathering overhead. I was already jittery and on edge from the lack of sleep combined with my withdrawal symptoms, and the weather wasn't helping. I was stuck in a mosquito-infused jungle hell with my rival, and now, thanks to his insistence on hiking in the wrong direction, we were hopelessly lost.

"I'm so hot." Jordan shrugged off his pack, pulling out his canteen and gulping down half of its contents. When he was done, he swiped his hand across his mouth and then peeled off his T-shirt, leaving him in nothing but a pair of extremely short blue swim shorts that looked like they could pass for underwear.

My own mouth was suddenly dry, and I spun away from him, reaching for my own canteen. When I'd sufficiently lubricated my throat, I decided to remove my own T-shirt because it was sticking to my skin in an extremely uncomfortable way. It was only when I'd shoved it inside my small pack that I realised my swim shorts were almost as short as Jordan's.

Jordan turned to me, his gaze dropping to my abs. He tugged his bottom lip between his teeth as he stared at me. Then he moved forwards, and I moved back, but he took a step closer. Then another, and another, until he was right in front of me and I was backed up against a tree.

"How do you get such good definition here?" His finger traced lightly over the lower part of my left oblique, and goosebumps pebbled all over my skin. "Mine don't look like this."

"Uh. Yours are defined." I should've been pushing him away, but I was frozen in place.

"They are, yeah, but not like this." He trailed his finger down the muscle again, and fucking hell, my dick jumped. This was bad, bad, bad.

"Side planks," I ground out, pushing him away from me and picking up my pack. "Come on. It's going to rain."

"No, it isn't." Jordan's voice held a bit of a rasp, and when I dared to shoot him a glance, I noticed the flush on his high cheekbones and the redness of his full lower lip, where he'd been biting down on it. "It's not going to rain today. It's—"

A streak of white lightning split the sky, and a loud crack of thunder echoed around us.

Then the rain came, a torrential downpour that we had no hope of escaping, and so we ran.

Within minutes, both of us were soaked to the bone, slipping and sliding as the ground beneath us turned into a mudslide. We were even more hopelessly lost, and I'd lost sight of any trail markers of any colour.

The rain stopped just as suddenly as it had started, and Jordan skidded to a halt, throwing his pack to the ground. "Fucking great! Everything's soaked, and I'm lost in the jungle with *you*!"

I threw my own pack down. I was so sick and tired of his attitude. Enough was fucking enough.

"I don't want to be here with you, either." I pushed at his chest, my hand slipping on his wet skin.

"You're the worst person in the whole world." He launched himself at me, but I sidestepped him, and he went crashing down to the muddy ground with a wet splat and a punched-out cry.

He didn't move.

Fuck. What if he was injured?

"Jordan. Jordan?" Taking a cautious step closer, I tried again. "Jordan?"

There was no movement.

What had I done?

I crouched down next to him, placing my palm on his soaked skin.

Quick as lightning, he flipped over, yanking me down

with him, and rolled us, pressing my face down into the mud with the heel of his hand.

Spitting mud from my mouth, I scooped up a handful, wiping it across his face.

"You wanker! Stop trying to get one over me!" He flung a dollop of mud straight at my eyes, but I twisted us over, making it fall uselessly to the ground. I was so fucking pissed off that I could barely think straight. Getting on top of his body, slippery from the mud and the rain, I pinned his wrists above his head, meeting his irate gaze.

"Just submit, Jordan! Fucking hell, you stubborn twat!" I shouted in his face, and he froze for a second before bucking his body upwards, trying to throw me off.

"No! I'll never submit to you!"

"Yeah?" I dipped my head, my voice low and dangerous. "You think so? We'll see, you insufferable fucking brat."

His eyes widened, his mouth forming an O. I smirked down at him. Finally, I had the upper hand.

At least, I thought I did.

"Fucking. Make. Me." He yanked one of his wrists free, shoving me to the side and rolling with me, his fingers digging into my arm, right where I'd been feasted on by the bloodthirsty mosquito.

"The storm's over, boys. Do carry on with today's Focus activity."

Jordan and I both jumped at the commanding voice coming from behind us. I quickly rolled off Jordan, climbing to my knees. Wiping the worst of the mud from my face, I turned to the brown-haired man who'd interrupted our fight. His piercing grey eyes scanned us both as we drew apart.

He looked to be around a similar age to Jordan's agent, and he was accompanied by a guy around my age, maybe a little older, with windswept brown hair and deep brown eyes. The younger guy looked familiar, but I couldn't put my finger on it.

"Who the fuck are you? The activities police?" Pulling himself upright, Jordan shot the older guy a cocky grin.

The younger guy burst out laughing. "Yeah, Cal. Are you the activity police? Island security, maybe?" He turned back to Jordan with a grin that was just as cocky as my teammate's. "I wouldn't be surprised, Jordan. The man wears many hats around here. I'm Jett Roman, by the way, and this grumpy old dude is Callum Ryan. And I already know who you both are! I'm a huge fan."

Jett Roman. Now I remembered who he was. An American child star who, from what I could remember, was in the tabloids a lot. He'd found a kindred spirit in Jordan, then.

Callum side-eyed Jett, clearly unamused. "You both need to continue with your Focus."

Predictably, Jordan ignored him, focusing on Jett. His eyes sparkled as he shot Jett one of his bright, mischievous smiles, and I gritted my teeth. "This is absolutely insane! I can't believe it. We just saw your movie—that really sad one where you're a rock star and you die at the end? What's it called?" He snapped his fingers. "Oh, yeah! *Destined for the Stars.* Theo cried like a little baby!" An obnoxious laugh fell from his throat.

Fucking liar. We didn't even have a TV in our villa, and if we had, we certainly wouldn't have been watching movies together. No. Instead, we'd both— *Fuck.* Last night had been a mistake of epic proportions.

"Jordan." I gave him a warning look.

"Theodore." He put on an extremely irritating, mocking voice. His lips curved into a smile as he lifted his hand, motioning at his cheek. "You've got a bit of dirt, just there."

I ignored him.

"You didn't get it. Here, let me." He scooted closer.

"Don't touch me, you wanker."

Before I could duck out of the way, he smeared a handful of dripping mud over my head, sending it cascading down my face. Both Jett and Jordan laughed, but Jordan's was abruptly cut off when I lunged for him, taking him down again. This bastard was going to pay for that. I straddled him, shaking the mud from my face and hair, sending it splattering all over his face.

"Fine! You win!" Jordan spat mud from his mouth. His words were music to my ears, but I hadn't finished teaching him a lesson yet.

Except, it seemed that Callum had other ideas. He tugged me away from Jordan's prone body. "Enough, you two! Are you not teammates? What is going on?"

Jordan smirked, clearly happy that I was in trouble as well as him. Whoever this Callum guy was, he had an air of authority about him, and that probably meant that he was one of the people in charge around here.

"Why are you both here? Why are you so angry? Why are you fighting in the jungle during a dangerous storm? I don't need those answers. I just want you to think about them and maybe ask yourself later. See if you can let the people here help you." He shot Jett a warning look. "That goes for you, too, Mr. Roman."

Jett rolled his eyes. "I don't *need* help, *Mr. Ryan*."

"Exactly, mate! Neither do we," Jordan added. He really needed to learn when to keep his mouth shut.

Callum acted as if neither of them had spoken. "Now, as I said earlier, continue on your way, boys. The waterfall is straight down this path. Follow the arrow, and don't veer off again."

Jordan rolled his eyes as he clambered to his feet, picking up his pack. I did the same, turning in the direction Callum had indicated. "Fucking activities police, I'm positive," my asshole teammate muttered before raising his voice. "Catch you later, Jett!"

"Made a new best friend, did you?"

"Nah, you're still my bestie. Best bros for life." He nudged me with his elbow, and I glared at him. "Can you believe we just got to meet Jett Roman? Shit, I should've got a selfie with him."

I ignored him. I was tired. My entire body ached after our race through the jungle and subsequent fight. All I wanted to do was get to the waterfall, wash this mud from my body, and then go back to the villa.

Thankfully, Callum had been right. We turned a corner, and the waterfall was there, cascading down a rocky face into a pool surrounded by greenery.

Jordan threw his pack to the ground and dived for the pool without even checking to see if it was safe.

Something inside me snapped. I threw my own pack down, uncaring where it landed, and entered the pool, swimming over to him in three long strokes. Pushing down, my feet found the bottom of the pool, and I launched myself into a standing position. "You fucking idiot! You could've got yourself killed!"

"That would make your life easier, wouldn't it?" His eyes flashed with fire. "You'd probably throw a party."

"I don't want you to fucking *die*!" I gripped him around the back of his neck, jerking him forwards into me. "Where's your sense of self-preservation?"

"I—I don't...I—"

I. Was. So. Fucking. Tired of his shit.

"Jordan."

"Y—yeah?" We were pressed together, and I could feel him tremble. Our faces were so close, and his breath was warm on my chilled lips. His eyes were wide and dark, a question in them that I didn't have the answer for.

I angled my head forwards, and my heart stuttered when soft lips brushed against mine. "For once in your life, do what you're told, and shut the fuck up."

"Okay," he breathed.

I kissed the word from his mouth.

EIGHTEEN

JORDAN

My heart was pounding so hard, a drumbeat in my ears that almost drowned out the roar of the waterfall. I was sure it could be heard all across the island. Theo's hand was in my hair, holding my head in place as his mouth moved against mine. He tasted of rain and mud and salt, and even though I could've done without the mud part, I made no attempt to break the kiss.

Fuck. My dick was really into this, lengthening inside my shorts, tenting the fabric and brushing against Theo's hard cock.

Theo. Hard cock.

Whoa, hold the fuck up.

Theo Lewin. Who was a man, for a start, and I was one hundred percent straight. And he was the one person I hated, and oh, yeah, did I mention that he was a fucking man, and even worse, he was *Theo fucking Lewin*?

My head reeled as the pieces slotted into place, and then I broke out of his hold, pushing at his chest so violently he went flying back into the water with a huge splash, a tsunami crashing over both of our bodies.

"What the fuck was that?" I wiped at my mouth and then spat into the water, needing to get rid of the taste of him from my tongue. "What the fuck, Lewin?"

Clearly at a loss for words, his mouth opened and closed a few times, but then he recovered, his eyes glittering dangerously. "Yeah, what the fuck. Don't pretend you didn't want that."

"I absolutely did not. *You* wanted it. You're the one who kissed me."

"It was the only way to get you to shut up. It was that or punch your smug fucking face. I'm at the end of my tether, Jordan. My symptoms are—" Cutting himself off with an angry exhale, his nostrils flaring, he pursed his lips, sinking down into the water so only his head and the tops of his shoulders remained above the surface.

My curiosity was piqued again. Wading across the pool, tracked by his wary gaze, I stopped in front of him and sank down to his level. "What symptoms?"

He shook his head, sending mud sliding from his hair to streak down the side of his throat. "It doesn't matter."

Cupping my hand, I lifted it carefully, letting the water trickle down the side of his head, following the streaks of dirt and washing it away. He stared at me with heavy-lidded eyes, his lips slightly parted, watching me with that same wary look as I repeated the process, this time with two hands, cleansing his raven hair of the remaining mud. "Tell me. Please."

His eyes closed, his shoulders slumping as the breath whooshed from his lungs on a heavy sigh. "I can't."

I pushed aside the tangled knot of barbed wire that made up my feelings regarding him and moved even closer, placing a hand on his shoulder, my thumb brushing over his collarbone. "Tell me, *please*. I won't be Jordan. I'll be...I'll be someone who cares. Pretend I'm not me."

He swallowed hard, his Adam's apple bobbing. "I...I have a problem with sleeping pills." *Fuuuck.* Of all the things he could've told me, I'd never have even guessed it was anything like this. "At—at first, I was only taking them before games, like some of the other players do. Then I...I got used to the effect. I liked it. I've had trouble sleeping since—for a long time, and it... I liked being able to fall asleep at night. I started taking them more often, and then they weren't enough. Some days, I had to have two or three. Most days, lately. When you joined the team, it got even worse, and then I couldn't stop."

A shocked cry tore from my throat, my eyes widening and filling with unexpected moisture. *Me?* Fucking hell, I was to blame for—

"Don't, Jordan."

I raised my blurry gaze to Theo's. His hand came up, catching a stray tear with his thumb.

"It's not your fault, okay? It's mine. You had nothing to do with it."

"But I made it worse."

"You didn't. You made my life hell—you *make* my life hell—but this is all on me."

"Okay," I whispered, biting down on my lip. I didn't believe him, and he must've known what I was thinking because he rolled his eyes and then sighed.

"As much as I'd love to blame you, this was all me, I promise. As for the symptoms... To cut a long story short, I forgot to bring my pills with me. I was sick on the plane, which turned out to be the first of my withdrawal symptoms. I've also had anxiety and mood swings and headaches. The insomnia and the cravings have been the worst, though."

"You know, I wouldn't have guessed about the mood thing. Although...now I think about it, it has been easier to rile you up since we've been here," I mused. "I've got the bruises to show for it."

Beneath the water, his hand found mine, and he lifted it, placing it on his arm where I'd grabbed it earlier when we were fighting. "I have the bruises to show for it, and they're right where that mosquito bit me."

"If you're looking for sympathy for that, you won't be getting it. You deserved everything I gave you." Tugging my hand out of his grip, I dunked my body underwater, head and all. A question kept trying to come out of my mouth, and I needed to drown it before it could be asked.

When I resurfaced, Theo's brows were raised.

"What?" I glared at him.

"Ask it."

Was he a fucking mind reader? The only reason I responded to him was because I felt guilty for the sleeping pills thing. "Was kissing me one of the withdrawal side effects?"

He stared at me incredulously for a second, and then his lips curved into a smile, and suddenly, we were both laughing. Yeah, okay, that was a ridiculously stupid question.

"I kissed you for one reason only—to shut you up, you fucking brat," he murmured, still smiling at me. "And it worked."

"Still feel like making me shut up?" What the fuck was I saying?

"Do you want me to shut you up?"

"N—no. I—I don't." I was so confused.

His expression shuttered, and I couldn't get a read on him. "I don't, either. I don't know what I was thinking."

"Neither of us were thinking. It's probably the weather or the mosquitos or something." Backing away from him, water sloshing around me, I shook my head. We needed to take our minds off this confusing, weird set of events that had transpired today. "Race you to the waterfall."

Before he could respond, I dived under the water. There was no way I was going to let him win.

By the time we made it back to the recovery centre, my stomach was protesting at the lack of food. Luckily, our clothes were more or less dry, so for the second of our two daily forced activities, I suggested grabbing some food in the restaurant. We ate in silence for the most part, and when we did speak, we kept to safe topics. The weather. How annoying mosquitos were. What the best exercises were for getting more defined abs.

It was...surprisingly okay. Things still weren't comfortable between us, and we still loathed each other, but for us to even be able to eat in the same room without tearing each other's heads off would have been unheard of before today. Maybe Flora did have a point.

When we got back to the villa, it was fully dark. Opening the doors onto the deck, I switched on the infinity pool and deck lights, leaving the lights inside the villa off. Kicking off my trainers and peeling off my T-shirt, I stood in the doorway for a moment, thinking, before I turned around.

"I'm gonna have a quick swim. Might be nice before

bed. The extra exercise and fresh air's good for making you feel sleepy."

Theo gave me a short nod. "Have fun."

What was I thinking? He wasn't interested in spending any more time with me, and I'd had enough of him today, anyway. Stepping out onto the deck, I peeled off my swim shorts and then lowered myself into the illuminated pool, naked. The warm water rippled around me as I swam to the far side, hooking my arms over the infinity edge and staring out into the darkness.

There was a splash behind me. I smiled.

"Flora wants us to share some things we've learned about each other." Theo's voice was hushed in the night. "Shall I tell her that I found out you're a bit of an exhibitionist? First last night, and now this?"

I turned around, watching as he swam towards me. My gaze dipped lower, into the rippling water. "I could tell her the same thing about you."

When our eyes met again, his were blazing with blue fire, burning me alive. He planted his hands on the lip of the pool on either side of me, leaning in. "Why do you love the attention so much, Jordan?"

"Are you really a prude, Theo?" I countered, angling my hips forwards. Just to see if my suspicions were correct. "Or is that aloof, stuck-up persona a front?"

He didn't answer me, but I could feel the proof against my thigh. Strangely, I wasn't scared. More...intrigued. Theo Lewin was hard because of *me*. What that meant, I didn't know, and it was too big of a thought to wrap my head around. But what I did know was that it was very fucking flattering. Theo, if I looked at him objectively, was hot. Really, really fucking hot, if I tried to view him through the lens of a straight woman or, I dunno, someone that was attracted to men.

There was that coal-black hair and matching brows and lashes. Those light blue eyes that flashed with fire whenever I riled him up...and maybe when he was turned on. That fucking fit body, chiselled to perfection, and—and his big dick.

Fuck. Was it bigger than mine? That couldn't be possible; he'd lord it over me forever.

"It seems as if you love the attention." His head lowered, his nose brushing over the skin beneath my ear. I shivered involuntarily, my cock hard and aching. This had to be one of those sex-starved situations, right?

"It seems as if you love that I love the attention."

"What?" He pulled back, arching a brow at me, and I curled my fingers around the back of his neck, stopping him from moving any further away.

"I don't know. I—I..." I forgot how to form words.

What in the actual fucking fuck was happening?

"It's fascinating." Lifting his hand, he traced a finger across my lips, his gaze dark and hot. Pressing closer, he moved under the water, his erection sliding against my thigh. "How can I loathe you so much, and yet you have this effect on me? Why do you insist on fucking with me like this, Jordan?"

NINETEEN

THEO

Jordan was lost for words, and I relished it. Seeing his beautiful eyes widening, his mouth struggling to form coherent sentences while I had him pinned against the edge of the pool, was so satisfying.

His tongue slid across his lips. "I—I don't know what's happening."

That made two of us, but the way he was so fucking pliant and at my mercy was addictive, in a completely different way to the sleeping pills.

"Are you interested in men?"

He immediately shook his head. "No. Nooo. Never have been. Are you?"

That was a question with a complicated answer. Jordan Emery was the kind of person that lit up a room the minute he walked into it. People couldn't help but notice him. Lately, *I'd* noticed him. And he was undeniably beautiful. So beautiful, in a way that made my heart race, as much as I wished it didn't.

It had been easy to keep my distance when we were at each other's throats. Easy to ignore all those things when all

I had to do was hate him. Easy when I could keep him in a box—that shallow, cocky boy that had stolen my place and had been my hated rival for years. But here, well out of both of our comfort zones, forced together and with nothing and no one else to provide a distraction, it was getting harder and harder to deny the effect he had on me.

But going down that road would lead to nothing but trouble. Serious trouble.

"I'm not interested," I lied, forcing myself to move back, creating a sliver of space between us.

"Wait." His eyes widened as soon as the word fell from his throat. Dragging a hand through his hair, he lowered his lashes, hiding his gaze from me. "Are...uh...yeah. Never mind. It's getting late, isn't it? I'm, uh, gonna shower. Then go to bed. Goodnight, Theo."

"Goodnight." I watched him leave, the perfect globes of his ass flexing as he ascended the steps, and when he turned towards the bathroom, I caught a glimpse of the heavy weight of his erection, the outdoor lights giving me a hint of what he was packing.

Submerging myself in the pool, I held my breath for as long as I could, allowing my own erection to subside. Then I swam laps until my muscles screamed for mercy, and as I dragged my exhausted, aching body out of the pool and into the shower, I just hoped it was enough to finally silence my mind and allow me to sleep.

"Theodore. Stop that racket this instant!"

I lifted my tear-stained face from my pillow, blinking at my father, who stood silhouetted in the doorway, the light from the corridor spilling into the darkness of my bedroom.

"I h—had a bad—a bad d—dream," I stuttered out between sobs. *"Th—the monster was c—coming to get me, and—and—and I couldn't move!"*

"Nonsense. There is no such thing as monsters. I'm going to have a word with Angela in the morning. Has she been allowing you to read those books again?"

"They—they're only fairy tales," I sniffed. My nanny read to me in the afternoons, and I loved story time. It was an escape into magical worlds, with heroes and villains, and if I could, I would have spent all day listening to her fantastical tales.

"Regardless of their definition, your ridiculous screaming is keeping your mother awake. She needs her sleep, Theodore. I have an important meeting tomorrow, and I must be well-rested, too. I don't want to hear any more noise from you. This is the third time I've warned you this week, and you're walking a very thin line. If you don't stop this nonsense, I'll be forced to take action."

No. Not the attic bedroom. My father had been threatening me with it for weeks, ever since my nightmares had begun. I didn't want to go up there, in that cold, draughty room, where spiders made a home and the creaks and groans of the weathered wood sounded like all my nightmares were coming true.

I couldn't be moved up there.

"S—sorry. I promise I won't make any more noise."

"See that you don't." Without another word, he closed the door, leaving me to be swallowed by the darkness.

As soon as he was gone, the stifling terror returned. Curling myself into a ball, making myself as small as possible, I pulled my bedcovers over my shaking body and covered my mouth with my hand so no one would hear my cries.

My pillow soon became wet with tears, but my sobs were silent. I refused to let myself fall asleep again because if I did, the nightmares might come again, and no one would come to comfort me. Only to threaten me with retribution.

"Theo! Theo!"

Gasping, I shot up in bed, my eyes flying open. Illuminated by the light coming from the now-open door, Jordan stared down at me, concern written all over his face.

"Are you, uh, okay?" He bit down on his lower lip. "Uh, sorry to wake you, but you were, um, making noises, and, and, kind of thrashing around."

Fuck. I wiped my hand over my face, and it came away wet with tears.

How was I going to explain any of this?

Breathing in and out deeply, I attempted to regain my composure. "I'm sorry I disturbed your sleep. I'll go and sleep in the lounge so you can get some rest."

"Fuck that," he snapped. "I don't give a shit that you woke me up. Are you okay?"

To my horror, my eyes filled with fresh tears, and I shook my head. Jordan stared at me for a moment, open-mouthed, and then he did the last thing I'd expected from him.

He took a seat on the edge of my bed and wrapped his arm around my shoulder. "Uh, is this okay? I don't really know what I'm doing." He huffed out a laugh. "I know that if I have a nightmare, I want to be comforted, so I guess, I mean, it's probably the same for you, right? I know I'm probably the last person you want to be here. No, not probably, definitely. But yeah, I'm the only one here, so, yeah…uh…"

"Thanks," I rasped out, leaning into him and letting him take my weight. He fell backwards against the headboard with a cry of surprise.

With another soft laugh, he straightened up, still keeping his arm firmly around me. "You were heavier than I was expecting. Must be all that muscle mass. Have you been overdoing it at the gym? Trying to get abs like mine?"

When I glanced at his face, he was smirking at me, and just like that, the lump in my throat dissolved, and I could breathe again.

"I seem to remember you complimenting my obliques earlier. In fact, I believe you admitted that they were more defined than yours."

"Nah, you must be mistaken. That doesn't sound like something I'd say. Anyway, we're talking about how amazing my abs are, not your obliques. Look at them! They're a work of art." He stroked his free hand down his stomach, grinning widely.

"Always trying to make it about yourself." I rolled my eyes, but I couldn't stop myself from smiling.

"Theo?"

"Yeah?"

"Seriously, though. Is there, uh, anything you need? Want me to get you some water? Or put the light on? Or—or...uh, anything else?"

I sighed. "No. I probably won't sleep again tonight, but there's nothing that'll help."

"Oh." His face fell. "Okay. Do you want to talk about it?"

"No." The word came out much more harshly than I'd intended, and he recoiled, pulling his arm away from me.

"Okay. I'll leave you to it." Diving for his own bed, he yanked the covers up over his body.

Rubbing my hand across my gritty eyes, I groaned. "Sorry. I'm not used to talking about it with anyone. I...I went through a period as a child where I had nightmares most nights. My parents...they...they weren't pleased. I began keeping myself awake at night so I wouldn't disturb them, and I don't know...my sleep patterns ended up being fucked up. I've had trouble sleeping for years. I don't have nightmares very often these days, though, but Dr. Ross did mention that might be one of the side effects of my withdrawal."

Jordan had stayed completely silent while I spoke my confession into the night, but as soon as I finished, words burst from him as he flipped onto his side to face me, rage darkening his eyes.

"That is complete fucking bollocks! What the fuck were your parents on? Bloody hell, Theo, you were a kid, and that was something that was happening when you were asleep. It was completely out of your control. What the actual fucking fuck?"

His outrage on my behalf soothed me like a balm, smoothing over some of the cracks in my heart.

"It's in the past now. Other than the withdrawal symptoms, I suppose. I can't promise that I won't wake you again with more nightmares, but I can sleep in the lounge."

"Fuck off. I don't care about that. I can nap in the day if I get too tired." He studied me intently. "The more important question is, how can we make sure that you get some nightmare-free sleep?"

Something inside me melted. "I don't think there's a way."

"Nope. That can't be true. There has to be a way." He had that stubborn look on his face, his eyes narrowed in determination and his lips curved into a pretty pout—a pretty annoying pout, I meant. That look always made my blood boil, except this time, it was on my behalf.

"Believe me, I've tried everything. The only guaranteed way is to stay awake."

Suddenly, his pout disappeared, and in its place was a sly smile. "What about what we did last night? That worked, didn't it?"

Yes. "That was a mere coincidence."

"A mere coincidence," he repeated mockingly. "Or it could be that you're scared to do it again and prove me right."

"I'm not scared."

"Prove it."

"Okay. I will."

The atmosphere in the room changed as quickly as a snap of my fingers, and my nightmare was forgotten. Jordan kicked off his bedcovers, never needing an excuse to show off his chiselled body, his hand moving south. I didn't dare to look down at what he was doing, but I also couldn't look away.

"Are you gonna hide under the covers this time, Theo? Or are you going to prove that you're not scared?"

Gritting my teeth and twisting my head to fix my gaze on the ceiling, I yanked my own bedcovers down and tugged off my boxer briefs, throwing them to the floor next to his. "I'm *not* scared."

I wasn't scared. I was terrified. Not of showing my body but because it left me nowhere to hide. The proof that I was into this was right there for us both to see.

"Fuck, yeah. Feels good, doesn't it?" Jordan had no such reservations, and for a second, I wished that I could be as open and as free as he was.

"Yeah," I admitted in a whisper, taking hold of my

erection. I was already hard. I had been from the minute Jordan had mentioned doing this again.

When I slid my fingers down my shaft, a soft groan escaped my lips. Getting into a slow, steady rhythm, I did my best to block out the knowledge that my teammate was here in the room with me, concentrating only on the movement of my hand and how good it felt.

The other side of the room was quiet. Too quiet. I darted a quick glance over at Jordan's bed and then did a double take. He wasn't even touching his cock. Instead, he was watching me with his brows pulled together.

I suddenly felt very, very exposed.

"What?" My voice lashed out into the room, my hand stilling on my cock.

"Nothing. I was, uh, thinking."

"About?"

His cheeks flushed. "Who has the biggest dick."

"For fuck's sake, Emery."

"You asked."

"Yes, but I didn't think you were thinking of that." Almost against my will, my gaze slid down over the ridges of his body to his dick, big, hard, and glistening with precum. I immediately ripped my gaze away from his erection, my heart pounding. Fuck. Now he'd mentioned it, I was a little curious about whose was bigger, too. And I was incredibly turned on.

I swallowed. "Mine's bigger."

"Mine is," he shot back immediately.

"Do you have a ruler handy?" That was the only way we'd settle this.

His eyes narrowed. "No, but I know how we can solve this. Get out of bed."

"Excuse me?"

"Out of bed. We'll measure." Before I had time to process his words, he was standing right in front of my bed, and his erection was in line with my eye level, pointing at me. Bloody hell. I shot upright, clasping my chest.

"What the fuck are you doing?"

His fingers wrapped around my bicep, and he yanked me to my feet, bringing our bodies level with one another. When my cock brushed against his hip, his eyes widened, and he suddenly seemed lost for words. I fucking loved it when that happened, and it gave me a surge of confidence.

"How do you want to measure, Jordan?"

"Uh." He licked his plush lips, and my gaze tracked the movement of his tongue.

Lowering my voice, I placed my hand on his chest, right over his racing heart. "Shall I measure?"

"Y—yeah."

I slid my hand down his torso while he stood as still as a statue. He was so fucking fit, and I couldn't deny that his body had a measurable effect on my dick. Why it had to be him, of all people, that made me appreciate a man's body in a whole new way, I didn't know. Fate had a twisted sense of humour.

When the back of my hand knocked against the tip of his erection, precum smearing over my skin, we both gasped. My confidence faltered, but I'd come this far, and I wasn't a quitter. I angled my hips so we were lined up with each other and met Jordan's heated gaze. "Ready?"

He jerked his head in acquiescence, and I wrapped my hand around both of our cocks, as far as it would go. I was only trying to line them up, but for some reason, my hand moved of its own accord in an experimental stroke up our rigid lengths. My breath caught in my throat at the feel of his foreskin sliding against mine, our cocks hard and leaking in my hand.

"Fuck." His groan seemed to echo around the room. "Why does that feel so good?"

"I don't know." I had absolutely no idea what I was doing, but he was right. It felt *so* good, too good to stop. I repeated the movement, releasing a shuddering breath. I'd never touched another cock before, but now I had, I...I found myself wanting more. His cock felt like mine but different, too, and when I touched him, it had an immediate effect on my dick.

This was like nothing I'd ever experienced before.

I'd forgotten why we were doing this, and as I gained confidence in my movements, falling into a steady rhythm, all I could concentrate on was Jordan. His body, warm and solid against mine. His cock, throbbing and leaking in my grip, turning me on beyond belief. His panted breaths, hot on my skin, as his head dropped forwards to rest against mine, both of our gazes fixed on our cocks sliding together.

"This is so much better than porn. So much better than —" His hips jerked, and I had a front-row view of his hot, hard dick coming in my hand, his erection jerking in my grip as his release covered my fingers and his torso.

"Fuuuuck. *Jordan.*" My orgasm overtook me, my cum combining with his and soaking my hand. Out of breath, with my heart racing and my head spinning, I fell forwards, sending him staggering back. We crashed onto his bed, my body collapsing onto his, both of us sweat-soaked and spent. I had no idea how or why that had just happened. How were we supposed to navigate this new and utterly unexpected dynamic between us?

"It's after midnight."

I raised my head when Jordan's voice rumbled against

me, meeting his gaze. As if his brain had a direct line to mine, we both scrambled away from one another, and I knew that if I could see my own face, it would mirror the shock and confusion in his expression as the reality of what we'd done hit us both. I threw myself onto my bed, wrapping the covers around me, and he did the same, burrowing beneath his bedsheets so only his head and neck were exposed. He reached out to his bedside table to grab a handful of tissues before he hid back under his sheets, and I did the same, cleaning away the evidence of what had just happened.

Rather than lie in an awkward silence and overthink everything, I spoke up. "What about it?"

It took a moment for him to gather his thoughts, but eventually, he cleared his throat. "It's after midnight, which means it's a new day. Do you think what we just did counts as one of our two daily activities?"

I stared at him before an unexpected laugh burst from my throat. "I'd like to see you tell Flora about this."

"Maybe I will." There was an evil gleam in his eye. "I might tell her how we measured our dicks, and mine was bigger."

"It was not." In actuality, I would have said that we were around the same size—not enough to quibble over, at least. "But yeah, you go ahead and tell her."

"I might."

I rolled my eyes. "Goodnight, Jordan."

"Night." He turned away from me, facing the wall. I closed my eyes. Even if I didn't get any more sleep tonight, I couldn't deny that I was relaxed and sated.

My nightmare was a distant memory.

I had much bigger things to worry about now.

TWENTY

JORDAN

On my way to my appointment with Dr. Weaver, I texted Rory. This definitely qualified as an emergency. It was now day three since the thing that I was avoiding thinking about had happened with Theo, and we'd both been tiptoeing around each other. The daily activities we'd picked had been group activities, so we didn't have to be alone together, and our other forced interactions had consisted of a mostly silent breakfast yesterday and a completely silent dinner the day before—both in the restaurant.

Both nights, Theo had woken me with his nightmares, and both times, he refused to let me comfort him, turning his back to me and ignoring me. I was used to being able to rile him up, to go up against him and force a reaction from him, but this new wall of ice between us was a whole different ball game.

ME:
RORY I HAVE AN EMERGENCY

Luckily, it was the evening in the UK, and he responded almost instantly.

> **RORY:**
> What's wrong?
>
> **ME:**
> I can't ask Google and I need help
>
> **RORY:**
> OK tell me. This had better qualify as an emergency
>
> **ME:**
> If I was having some nightmares what could I do to make them better? Also if something happened with someone and it made things weird what could I do?
>
> **RORY:**
> Your second question is very vague and quite alarming. What have you done?
>
> **ME:**
> Nothing bad!

Extremely inadvisable and completely unexpected, but not *bad*. It was...something that shouldn't have happened, but it had, and now I needed things to go back to normal again.

> **RORY:**
> Hmm. I'm not sure I believe you. Regarding your first question, here's what the internet suggests...
>
> Regular sleep schedule
>
> Talk about the dream with someone, to reassure yourself the nightmare isn't real

> Stress relief activities e.g. meditation and relaxation techniques
>
> Establish a relaxing bedtime routine
>
> Most of the other suggestions pertain to children, and there are medical treatments which I'm assuming you don't require? You don't usually suffer from nightmares do you?

ME:

> Thanks Ror you're the best. No I don't need medical treatment. I'll try those things

Or Theo would, even if I had to force him. I couldn't deal with another night of him waking up all distressed, of seeing those dark circles under his bloodshot eyes that seemed to become more prominent each morning.

I'd feel the same about anyone. I'd do this for anyone, not just him.

ME:

> What about the other thing?

RORY:

> Can you give me any more details? You're being very vague

ME:

> There's a guest on the island and I might have done something with them that was inadvisable. Now things between us are weird

RORY:

> You're going to give me grey hairs, I swear. What thing? It better not be illegal. Who was the guest?

> ME:
>
> You know I can't say because we have those NDAs but no it was nothing illegal so your hair's safe

> RORY:
>
> Without anything else to go on, all I can suggest is that you talk to them. I'm assuming that this is something to do with a woman, knowing you. I feel the need to remind you that you're not there on holiday, you're there to learn how to get on with your teammate. How is Theo anyway?

Doing his best to avoid me.

> ME:
>
> He's fine. Thanks for the help. How's everything at home? Did my Offside issue come out? I guarantee it'll be their biggest seller this year

> RORY:
>
> Your ego knows no bounds. But no it hasn't come out yet. When it does I'll buy you a copy

> ME:
>
> Thanks for the help. Got to go to my therapy session now. Wish me luck

> RORY:
>
> You don't need luck. Take care of yourself J

> ME:
>
> You too

Pocketing my phone, I scanned my wristband to enter the main building and made my way to Dr. Weaver's office.

As soon as she asked me if I wanted to share any of the names from the list in my notebook and why they were important to me, I found Theo's name coming out of my mouth. What the fuck was that all about?

"He thinks I'm a brainless, cocky asshole. Sorry for swearing. He's made a lot of comments about me being shallow and a poser and, y'know, insinuating that the only thing I'm interested in is myself, which isn't true at all."

Dr. Weaver scribbled something on her notepad and then studied me from behind her wire-framed glasses. "Why do you believe that he has those thoughts about you?"

Instead of letting more words escape unchecked, I thought about it. "I post a lot of selfies, and I put a lot of effort into making myself look good, I guess. I also landed an endorsement for an underwear brand when I first signed with the team, and I suppose that didn't help. Then there're the tabloid stories." I gritted my teeth as I thought about the headlines. "They like to paint me as a shallow party boy with a grudge against Theo."

"What do you believe?" Her tone was gentle, and there was no judgement in her eyes.

"I...I think that I am those things. But I think there's more to me." Biting down on my bottom lip, I clenched my fists, my nails digging into my palms. "There *has* to be more to me. That *can't* be all that I am." To my horror, my voice cracked, and I blinked rapidly, desperately trying to hang on to the fraying threads of my composure.

Dr. Weaver thankfully remained silent while I gathered myself. When I eventually sucked in a deep, shuddering breath, giving her a small nod, her lips curved upwards.

"There's so much more to you, Jordan. The picture you've painted is...a simplistic scene. Every single human is made up of many complex layers, and there are always far greater depths beneath the surface." Tapping her pen on her pad, she hummed. "I'd like to use an iceberg analogy because it's easy to picture. Let's imagine, for a moment, that you are an iceberg. Someone may look at you and see the parts of you that are visible on the surface. What do you think those might be, if it were someone who didn't know you?"

"I guess...if they knew of me...then probably the things I already mentioned, and me being a footballer?"

She gave me an encouraging smile. "Now, have you ever seen a diagram or photograph of an iceberg? The view from the surface is only a tiny fraction of its mass. It goes far beneath the waterline, into the deep, layer upon layer of ice, all packed tightly together, strong and solid in the depths of the ocean."

I exhaled harshly, her meaning hitting me all at once.

Tears filled my eyes once again.

After my session with Dr. Weaver, I was feeling too raw to face Theo, even in a group setting. We'd signed up for a tai chi session, but I needed some time alone. Instead of going to the session, I headed to the gym for a workout before I took a long shower, followed by a very late lunch. I didn't want to go back to the villa in case I ran into Theo, so I decided to sneak around the side of the main building. Maybe there was a part of it I hadn't discovered yet. Something new that would take my mind off my problems and allow me to escape my reality.

"This area is out of bounds."

I spun around at the haughty tone, a grin tugging at my lips as I took in Lawrence, the Black Diamond employee who had taken care of me when I first arrived on this island. "Sorry, Law. Can I call you that?"

His mouth wrinkled in distaste, and he immediately shook his head. "Absolutely not."

"Sorry. Look, I need to take my mind off things, and so I thought I'd go exploring."

He sighed. "What 'things' might you be referring to?"

Slumping back against the wall, I shrugged. "Things that happened here recently that I shouldn't have done with a certain person."

The only change in Lawrence's expression was his eyebrows lifting almost imperceptibly. "Hmm. You know, there's a saying among some of the staff here. What happens on the island stays on the island."

"Is that really a saying?"

Instead of answering me, he began walking. With a lack of anything else to do, I followed him until he came to a halt in front of a shed-like structure, all rickety wooden boards creaking in the wind.

"Help yourself." Pulling open the door, he gestured towards the interior. "And remember. What happens on the island stays on the island."

He melted away into the shadows, and I was left alone.

When my eyes adjusted to the darkness, I saw that the shed was filled with miscellaneous beach and sports equipment. Lilos, pool noodles, beach balls, tennis racquets, a volleyball...

But one thing immediately grabbed my attention.

A perfectly inflated football lying in the corner of the shed.

I jogged over to it, and as soon as I scooped it up, a smile spread across my face.

I'd missed football so fucking much. With all the drama surrounding the circumstances that had landed me on this island, I hadn't even realised just how much I'd missed it until now. But I did. Fuck. It was a part of me. A part of my soul. And now I was holding this leather ball in my hands, all I wanted was to be back at Barnwood Park, the Glevum FC stadium, playing with my team and helping to bring us to victory.

The homesickness was sudden and so intense I sank to the floor, cradling the ball in my arms, my breath catching in my throat.

I needed to get back. As beautiful as this island was, it wasn't home.

"I miss you," I whispered out loud. Fucking hell, people would probably give anything to be here. But I missed England, with its unpredictable weather—too hot, too cold, too rainy, or too dry—whatever it was, people loved to complain. I missed Marmite on toast, tea and crumpets while my dad swore at the football commentary on the radio, the people in my neighbourhood who got very fucking particular about how and when to queue... But most of all, I missed football. It was my life, and I was good at it, and I wanted to be a team player, to help my team do the best they ever had in the league.

And if that meant working with Theo, I knew right then that I was prepared to do whatever it took. I'd do anything.

With that thought in mind, I climbed to my feet, still holding the ball, and headed for the beach.

TWENTY-ONE

THEO

Jordan had been missing all day.

I shouldn't have noticed or cared, but there was a niggle of worry inside me that wouldn't go away. I hadn't actively looked for him, but I'd been up to the villa twice, as well as making a circuit of the main building, and I hadn't caught a glimpse of him anywhere. I doubted he would've gone off hiking in the jungle on his own, not after our experience getting lost on the trails, and so I decided to walk down to the beach.

I didn't *want* to find him... I just... No. I couldn't even explain it to myself. We'd both put distance between us after that night...the night I couldn't stop thinking about. Now everything inside me was so twisted—even more so than before, and with the cravings for the pills constantly at the back of my mind, as well as the nightmares and anxiety, my brain felt as if it was going to explode.

The sun was setting as I stepped onto the sand, bathing everything in a golden glow. Down at the water's edge, silhouetted against the burnished rays reflecting on the surface of the sea, a barefoot figure in a backwards cap and a pair of loose shorts was playing with a football, alternating between keepy-uppies and juggling the ball between his feet, the muscles in his powerful legs flexing as he enacted a series of complicated twisting manoeuvres.

Then he spun and saw me, and he stopped dead, his chest heaving. He was too far away for me to see the expression in his eyes. I kicked off my trainers, leaving them well away from the tide line next to his, and moved towards him. As I drew closer, I couldn't stop my gaze from dragging down over the contours of his lean, strong body, all the way down to his feet. My heart was pounding, and my mouth was dry, and as much as I wanted to blame that on my withdrawal side effects, it had nothing to do with the withdrawal and everything to do with the man standing in front of me.

When I reached him, he studied me warily for a moment before he huffed out a soft, resigned breath, the corners of his lips curving up.

He kicked the ball over to me, and I smiled.

We played until the sun sank beneath the horizon, passing to each other, dribbling the ball along the beach, doing headers, working in perfect harmony without ever exchanging a word.

When it grew too dark to see what we were doing, Jordan picked up the ball, tucking it under his arm, and spoke for the first time since I'd arrived on the beach.

"I missed this. Football. I didn't realise how much until I found the ball earlier."

"Me too." This was the first time that I really felt as if we were teammates. Spending time with him, passing the ball back and forth, had eased something inside of me, and I felt so much lighter. More positive. Maybe things really would work out. Jordan and I were beginning to manage to spend time together without hostility...or much less of it than before, my withdrawal symptoms were lessening, and although I knew the cravings for the pills would take longer to go away, my therapy sessions with Dr. Ross were helping me to get through it.

"Theo?" Wiping his feet off on the grass at the edge of the beach, Jordan tugged his trainers back on.

"Yeah?" I followed suit, dusting off the worst of the sand before lacing up my shoes. When I straightened up, he was staring at his feet, his bottom lip tugged between his teeth, his dark lashes sweeping downwards and hiding his expression from me.

"Someone said something to me. What happens on the island stays on the island."

"And?" We began walking up the path, our way lit by tiki torches.

"And...uh. It means that the thing that happened doesn't count because it happened here."

I didn't have to ask him to clarify the "thing" he was referring to because we both knew exactly what it was. "So what are you saying?"

His cheeks flushed, and he exhaled shakily. "I'm saying, can we forget it happened, and please can you stop ignoring me? It felt like we were making a bit of progress, and then things got weird."

Forget it happened. I wasn't sure that I could, but I wanted to. I had to make myself want to.

"Okay. If that's what you want."

He came to a sudden halt, his wide eyes flying to mine. "Isn't that what you want?"

My gaze traced the angles and lines of his beautiful face, and I swallowed hard, forcing myself to nod. "It's what

I want. I...we'll forget what happened, and we'll keep working on our...issues. I'll try harder."

I was such a liar.

He gave me a hesitant smile. "Okay. Yeah. Good. I'll try, too." His voice grew quiet. "I don't want to transfer to another team."

A horrible thought hit me out of nowhere, shocking me like a bolt of lightning to my body.

Even though all the things I hated about him were still there, I didn't want him to transfer, either.

Showered and full from the room service dinner we'd eaten, I lay back on my bed with a low groan of satisfaction, my muscles expanding and contracting as I stretched out my joints. I hoped that I'd sleep better tonight. Dr. Ross had said the nightmares could last for a few more days, maybe even a week, and the rebound insomnia was still in full swing. But he was certain that once the withdrawal symptoms were out of my system, we could help my body to relearn effective sleep patterns.

Across from me, Jordan was studying his phone with a frown on his face. I tried so hard not to notice the way he looked, clad in nothing but a tight black pair of boxer briefs with all that smooth, tanned skin on display, but now I'd started, I couldn't seem to stop.

He suddenly looked up, and our gazes caught, his eyes a gorgeous light grey green today, the darker ring around the edge of his irises making them pop as he stared at me.

"Do..." He licked his lips and then began again. "Your nightmares. There are some things we could try that might help, if you want."

"What things?"

Glancing down at his phone screen, he cleared his throat. "We need to establish a relaxing bedtime routine and do some stress-relieving activities."

"Where are you getting that from? Does your phone have access to Google or something?"

He shook his head. "Uh, no. I asked Rory to google for me. Don't worry, I told him it was for me." His gaze flew to mine again, and his expression was defiant. "And before you say it, I didn't do it because I was pissed off with you keeping me awake or anything. I wanted to help."

My entire body filled with warmth as I stared at him in shock. I was honestly lost for words.

"One of the things Rory sent me suggested meditation, but I don't think that'll work for us. I thought about what I like to do to relax, and I thought maybe I could—" He bit down on his lip again, screwing up his face as if he was about to say something unpleasant. "I could give you a massage, if you want. I haven't given one to anyone before, but I've had a lot of them, not just sports massage, and I think I can do an okay job."

Jordan's hands all over me when I was starting to notice him against my will was a terrible idea. I should have instantly shut him down, but instead, I hesitated. "Uh... We don't have any massage oils, do we?"

"We have that organic aloe vera after-sun gel I brought with me. Or...lemme check what's in the bathroom. There might be something in there." He disappeared into the bathroom, and when he returned, he had a wide grin on his face, and he was brandishing a bottle triumphantly. "Look! Body oil, and it even says it's infused with extracts for calming and relaxing and shit."

I scrubbed my hand over my face. There was no excuse not to do this, then.

It looked like I was about to find out just how much of an effect Jordan had on me.

Fuck.

TWENTY-TWO

JORDAN

I stared down at the smooth, broad expanse of Theo's back. Now that I was faced with the reality of my idea, I was suddenly a little nervous. Also...I really wanted to take a photo. Not a selfie, but a photo of my teammate, lying in front of me.

Fuck it. I snapped a quick photo. It wasn't like anyone else was going to see it. I'd never post anything like this to my social media.

Propping my phone up on Theo's side table, I hit my "Relaxxx" playlist, and "The Beach" by The Neighbourhood began playing at a low volume. I'd already done what I could with the lighting by turning off the overhead lights and just keeping on my bedside lamp, and that was as relaxing as it was going to get. Some of the massages I'd had in the past had incense or candles or whatever, but I didn't have any of that here.

"Do you wanna get naked, or are you feeling prudish?"

Theo's body stiffened. "For the last time, I'm not prudish. But I'm not getting naked."

It was probably for the best because now I thought

about it, that was a weird question for me to ask my probably straight teammate. Straight…except for thinking that kissing me was a good way to shut me up. And that other thing that happened that I wasn't going to think about, although that was an accident. Maybe. Probably. No, definitely.

My cock jerked, and I glared down at it. There would be no shenanigans until I could have some alone time with my hand. Now, it was time to concentrate on what I was here to do.

Opening the bottle carefully, I drizzled some of the oil onto my palm and then rubbed my hands together, warming it.

When I placed my hands on the backs of Theo's shoulders, he exhaled sharply but stayed still, and I took that as my cue to begin. I was straddling his thighs, his leg hair brushing against mine, and if this had been any other situation, I might've questioned myself. But I was here for one reason only—to relax him enough that he actually got a decent sleep, and so I began. Sweeping my hands down his body in slow, kneading strokes, I covered his back in the oil, massaging it into his warm, soft skin.

As I moved my hands lower, he shifted beneath me, a soft sigh escaping him, and for some reason, my heart beat a little bit faster. When I reached the top of his tight underwear, I stopped for a second, debating whether to go any lower before I decided to reposition myself so I could massage his thighs and calves.

When I started on his thighs, I realised just how close to his ass I was. Fuck, it was…it was nice. Aesthetically. Athletically. A perfect, muscular curve. If he'd wanted to, he could give me a serious run for my money with underwear modelling.

"Do you ever wear a jockstrap?"

Why the fuck had I said that aloud?

"No. Why?" Theo's voice was slow and lazy, and despite my momentary panic, I felt a sense of satisfaction that I was obviously relaxing him.

I ignored the way that it was having the opposite effect on my dick.

"No reason." I resumed massaging his thighs, moving down to his calves and willing my dick to behave. Thinking of Harvey shouting at me did the trick, and I was mostly composed when I said, "Wanna turn over?"

Theo's tone was suddenly sharp. "No. This is fine. More than fine."

"Okay." I moved back up his body again, kneading the backs of his shoulders, working the pads of my fingers into his muscles until he was boneless beneath me. A soft sigh fell from his lips, and for some reason, it gave me a tickly, warm feeling inside. A feeling I'd only associated with girls that I'd been attracted to—and very, very rarely at that.

That thought was shocking enough to have me scrambling off him and diving onto my stomach on my bed, squeezing my eyes shut.

"Want me to do you now?" The low voice coming from my teammate's bed sent my eyes flying open again.

No. "If you want." My dick was lengthening again, and I pressed down into the sheets with a frustrated groan that I muffled with my pillow.

"Do you want to get naked, or are you feeling prudish?" My question repeated back to me in Theo's haughty, mocking tone should have pissed me off, but...it didn't. Fuck. This was bad.

Whatever. If he tried to play this game with me, he had to know he wouldn't win. Keeping my body averted so he couldn't see the dickuation I had going on, I tugged off my underwear and settled back on my stomach. Turning my head to face him, I attempted to get us back to our usual dynamic by smirking at him. "All naked and ready for you, bestie. You can massage my glutes. I like that."

His eyes darkened. "You don't get to tell me what to do, brat."

"Enough with the fucking brat thing, already."

He climbed off his bed and fuck me, he was *hard*. I couldn't help but notice it with the way his cock was blatantly straining at his boxer briefs, tenting the fabric. Catching my glance, his expression darkened even further, even as his cheeks flushed.

"It happens to a lot of people when they get massages. It's a physiological response, nothing to do with you," he ground out.

Ohhhh...yeah. That could be my excuse, too, if he noticed that I had a semi— No, who was I kidding? This was going to be the most awkward massage session I'd ever had.

I shot him a wink. "Don't worry about it. I know I have magic hands."

He bared his teeth at me but said nothing, swiping the massage oil from his side table, and then he stalked over to me. "If you really want me to do this, you need to lie there and shut up. I don't want to hear another fucking word from your mouth."

Fuuuck. My eyes widened, and I swallowed hard. My dick was *throbbing*.

"You can't tell me what to do," I managed to croak out, and he laughed humourlessly as he straddled my thighs. Lowering his head to my ear, he breathed across my skin, and my entire body jerked.

I noticed two things at once. His hot breath as his lips touched my ear, and secondly, *his erection, which was touching my ass.* I froze beneath him, my heart hammering, and he stilled above me, clearly noticing the same thing I had. I did my best to melt into the mattress to create some space between us. Instead of getting off me, he carefully angled his hips away from me as his mouth dipped to my ear. "Shut up, Jordan."

Then his hands were on my body, and I had to bite down on my lip to stop myself from making any incriminating noises. What was it about Theo's large, capable hands that made this massage so different from all the others?

When he reached the top of my ass, I heard him suck in a harsh breath. "Too scared to massage my glutes?" My words were supposed to be taunting, but the rasp in my voice gave me away.

"I'm not fucking scared." He dragged his hands down onto my ass cheeks, kneading my flesh with his fingers, and I fucking *moaned.*

I clamped my mouth shut straight away, horrified, but the damage was done.

His movements instantly stopped. "Turn over."

"Fucking hell," I mumbled into the pillow. My face was on fire. This was a special kind of torture, and I didn't like it at all. "No."

"Turn over. Please?"

"I *can't*. You know why."

He traced a finger across the curve of my ass, and my body trembled. I bit down on my lip so hard I almost broke the skin. "Remember what I said. It's a physiological response to the massage. Please, Jordan. I want to see you." Lifting himself to his knees, he held himself still, and with a defeated sigh, I turned onto my back.

I stared up at him defiantly, daring him to say anything. He looked down at me in silence, his gaze still fixed on mine, not even flicking to our erections, even though they were almost impossible to ignore. His eyes were wide and so dark, and when he released a shuddering breath, I couldn't stand it anymore.

I reached up, curled my fingers around the back of his neck, and pulled him down to me.

There was a millisecond when he hesitated, but then our lips met, and both of us were completely lost.

His mouth opened for me, his soft, soft lips sliding against mine. How could this feel so fucking right and perfect when it was so different to anything I'd experienced before? Here I was, lying on my bed, with my very male teammate pinning me down and kissing me like my mouth contained the air he needed to breathe, and instead of bucking him off, I was pulling him closer. Even worse, I'd been the one to initiate the kiss.

His stubble scraped against mine as he deepened the kiss, his hands sliding into my hair to hold my head in place. His body was all warm skin and defined muscles, and there was only a thin layer of fabric separating his erection from mine.

Fuck.

"Jordan." He buried his face in my throat, panting. "What are we doing?"

My head was spinning. What were words? I managed to get my brain to work enough to form a breathless sentence. "Uh...I guess you're trying to shut me up again."

His head lifted, and his lips curved. "I think it was you trying to shut me up this time."

My fingers threaded through his hair, my nails lightly dragging across his scalp. "You weren't saying anything."

Staring down at me, his pupils so blown that there was barely any blue remaining, he blinked, his coal-black lashes sweeping down. "Does that mean you actually wanted to kiss me?"

"*No.* Why would I do that? I'm straight, and I'm not into you. You're my—my— We're—"

Lowering his head, he rolled his hips, and I gasped as his clothed erection slid against my bare, dripping cock. "So straight," he murmured, smirking against my mouth. Arrogant asshole.

"That's physiological. *You're* not so straight." I kissed him again so he couldn't accuse me of anything else.

"It's beginning to appear that way," he mused before he captured my mouth again. And again. And again, until my lips were swollen, and the skin of my jaw tingled from the rasp of his stubble against mine.

Tearing my mouth away from his, I rolled us on the bed so I was the one on top. "I want to feel what it's like to be on top of you." I sat up, staring down at him, taking a minute to allow myself to appreciate the view of my teammate. His jet-black hair, all tousled and falling into his eyes, his soft mouth, his angular features, and that powerful body that was easily as ripped as mine, although I'd probably never admit it to him. Then there was the large bulge in his underwear and his strong thighs, which I was currently straddling, the muscles solid beneath me. *Did* I appreciate the view in more than an aesthetic way? From the way I couldn't catch my breath when I looked at him, my heart pounding out of my chest, and my very, very hard dick, it appeared that yes, yes, I did.

Fucking hell.

Speaking of my dick, I was so on edge, I felt like I could come at any second. I wrapped my fingers around my erection, squeezing. When the urge to orgasm subsided, I returned my gaze to Theo, who was staring at my cock in a way that I could only describe as hungry. My heart stuttered, and my cock jerked in my grip. We needed to even things up. "Why am I the only one naked?"

His eyes flashed with fire. "If you want me to be naked, get me naked."

"Fine." If he thought I wouldn't do it, he was wrong. Not allowing myself any time to overthink it, I pulled down his boxer briefs, doing my best to avoid his cock. But there was no avoiding it, not when he groaned as it sprung free, solid and throbbing, the head glistening with the proof of his arousal.

"Oh fuck," I whispered. It was one thing to have a dick-measuring contest that might have possibly accidentally turned into something more, but this...there was no other way I could play it off. There was nothing I could say to excuse the fact that I, Jordan Emery, professional footballer and underwear model, was naked in bed with Glevum's star winger, both of us clearly aroused. Nothing.

"Jordan?" There was concern in Theo's voice. "Are you okay? We don't have to do... Fuck. I don't even know what we're doing here."

"That makes two of us." I dragged my gaze away from his dick, focusing on his mouth. "Let's kiss again."

At least when we kissed, I didn't have to think.

He slid his fingers into my hair as he tugged me down to him. His hands felt big, and fuck, I liked it. I really, really liked it.

I lost myself in the heat of his mouth again, grinding my dick against his. I was so fucking close—

"What the fuck!"

Theo's shocked gasp, followed by his body jerking up, made me jump a mile. I flew backwards, scrambling away from him. "What? What is it?"

He climbed to his knees, grimacing. "The massage oil. We must've knocked it over."

I followed his gaze. Shit. The oil was pooling on the bedsheets, a large stain that was spreading rapidly.

Theo quickly picked up the bottle, popping the cap back down, but it was too late to salvage my bed. My shoulders slumped as I let out a defeated groan.

"Fucking brilliant. Cockblocked by a bottle of body oil, and my bed's completely ruined."

A laugh burst from Theo's throat. "You're so dramatic."

I pouted, and he just laughed harder, clambering off the bed and then tugging me upright. "Stop pouting, brat."

"I'm not a brat." I lunged forwards, nipping at his lower lip. He moaned, and so I did it again, then licked across it. It somehow turned into me being pressed up against the wall with Theo's arms wrapped around me and my hands curved around the back of his head, our tongues sliding together as we traded hot, deep kisses.

His mouth moved to my throat, his teeth scraping deliciously over my skin. "You taste so fucking good."

"Mmm. So do you." Fuck, he was turning me on beyond belief. I was going to die if I didn't get to come soon. Death by Theo. What a way to go. "Need to come."

"Can I suck you?"

The words were murmured softly into my shoulder as his kisses moved lower.

I didn't care about the weirdness of this situation anymore. Who cared if he wanted to suck my dick and I wanted him to? There was no one else here, just us. And all

I wanted right now was to finally, finally come. "Yeah. Fuck. *Please*. I'm going to die if I don't come soon."

"Dramatic." He flicked my left nipple, and I yelped, then realised I liked it.

"Do that again."

With a smirk, he repeated his action and then closed his mouth over my nipple, sucking and lightly nipping at it. When he moved his mouth to the right one, I groaned.

"I've never been so hard in my life. Please suck me off."

"Patience. I've never done this before. Give me a minute."

The note of uncertainty in his voice gave me pause, and I squeezed my dick again, willing it to calm down. "Sorry. Yeah. Fuck. I can't think straight. Literally."

"I know. Me neither." He kissed lower, down over my abs, and I threaded my fingers through his hair, stroking him as he dropped to his knees in front of me. "Tell me if I'm doing anything you don't like, okay?"

"I'll like it all." My cock was soaked with precum and painfully erect, the head exposed and so sensitive. As Theo opened his mouth and took me in, I exhaled a long, shuddering breath. That fucking mouth and that fucking tongue that had been used to lash me with hurtful words was now licking and sucking me with such care. And it felt good. So. Good. I'd been the recipient of so many blowjobs, but nothing compared to this. It was evident that it was his first time, but he was so into it and trying so hard to make me feel good that I was turned on beyond belief.

"Fuck," I whispered. "Theo."

His gaze met mine, heavy-lidded as he stared up at me from beneath his lashes, and my stomach jolted when it hit me. There was a connection between us that I'd never had with any of my other sexual partners. A connection that had been there from the moment we met, even though it had always been warped and acerbic. That had to be why everything was so different.

Because it was *him*. He was the one making me feel this way. And he was on his knees for me because he wanted to be.

He licked over the head of my cock, and I shuddered as my balls drew up.

"I'm gonna come." My fingers tightened in his hair, tugging him off my erection. He didn't waste a second, wrapping his fingers around my length and stroking me through my orgasm. My entire body shook, my knees going weak as my cock pulsed in his grip for what felt like forever.

When I came down from my high, panting and completely spent, I realised that I was slumped over him, letting him take my weight.

"Sorry." I straightened up, my legs still weak and shaky. "Fuck, Theo. I think you almost sucked my entire life out of my dick. It was nearly death by blowjob."

He rolled his eyes, but his lips were curved into a smug smile. I couldn't even be mad at him. Although...now, I had something to prove. I eyed his thick erection with trepidation. But he'd done it to me, and therefore, I could do it to him.

"Get on your bed so I can suck your brains out."

"What an offer." His tone was dry, but I noticed that he moved immediately, sprawling out on his back on his crisp, white, oil-free bedsheets.

"You're not gonna get a better one tonight." Tugging my own ruined bedsheets off my bed, I wiped myself off and then climbed onto his bed and knelt between his legs. Okay...so... I just needed to put my mouth on him and suck his dick. Simple. And make sure I didn't bite him. Oh, and use my tongue, too. It felt fucking amazing when he did that thing with his tongue on the head of my cock.

Curving my fingers around the base of his erection so I could guide it into my mouth, I lowered my head.

His dick was warm—no, hot, and so hard but also soft. I tentatively licked at the precum coating the head, and I was rewarded with a low groan. It tasted...okay, actually, and I dragged my tongue across his head again, needing another taste.

"Jordan," he said hoarsely, his hands fisting the sheets. "Fuck. *Jordan.*"

I guessed that meant I was doing a good job so far. But there was always room for improvement. My mind scanned through all the things I liked, and I smiled to myself. Time to up the stakes so I could prove that I was naturally gifted at all things, not just football. I cupped his balls, which made him gasp, and as I took him further into my mouth, I felt just behind them, pressing on his perineum. He bucked his hips up, making me yank my head back, coughing as tears sprang to my eyes.

"Sorry, sorry. Wasn't expecting it. Feels so good." He looked down at me, sliding his thumb across my lips. "Your mouth. Fucking perfect."

My smile was helpless, even as I blinked back the tears. "Yeah? You like it?"

"Mmm. Keep going."

"Yes, my lord."

He flicked my ear. I bit his thigh in retaliation, and he growled down at me. With a grin, I pressed a kiss to the small mark I'd left and then kissed back up to his cock, trailing my lips up his shaft as I stroked over his perineum again. When I reached the tip, I took it back into my mouth, already feeling more confident in my movements.

I got into a rhythm, mouthing and licking up and down his shaft and over his cockhead, all the while using my hand to tease his balls and perineum, and it felt like it was only a couple of minutes before he yanked at my hair, pulling me off him. I watched, unable to tear my gaze away as his cock pulsed and jerked, sending his cum all over his stomach.

"That's so fucking hot." Pressing a kiss to the inside of his thigh, I stroked my palm up his trembling leg. Then I froze. What was I doing? The sex things were all finished, and now we could pretend it had never happened. So why was I kissing and touching him still?

A heavy silence descended between us. I moved into a seated position, pulling my knees up and leaning my back against the wall at the side of the bed. There were rustling sounds as Theo cleaned himself up and then lay back down.

"Are you going to sit there all night?"

My gaze swung to his. He raised a brow, giving my bare mattress a pointed glance before returning to me.

"No. I guess I'll sleep on the sofa."

When I went to get off the bed, he gripped my wrist, stopping me. "These beds are huge. There's plenty of room for us both." He hesitated. "It's more than likely that I'll wake you up with my nightmares, but it'll be more comfortable than the sofa."

"Yeah. I guess that's okay." I gave him a casual shrug, even though my heart was racing.

"You need to wear underwear."

Obviously. I wasn't going to sleep naked with him. We'd already crossed so many lines tonight, and now we needed space to regroup. Space...while sharing a bed.

I sighed as I retrieved a jockstrap from the closet. At this rate, I'd be the one with insomnia while he had a full night's sleep. Now that everything was over, my brain was blaring alarms that all went along the lines of *what the fuck did you just do with your teammate?*

When I'd turned out the light and slipped under the covers, the darkness blanketing me, I closed my eyes and tried to switch off my brain.

Sleep never came.

TWENTY-THREE

THEO

Something had woken me. I blinked, rubbing at my face. When my eyes adjusted, I noticed two things—firstly, my phone was telling me that it was 3:40 a.m., which meant that I'd managed to sleep for more than three hours in a row for the first time since I'd been here, and secondly, and most importantly, it hadn't been a nightmare that had woken me.

The reason for my rude awakening became clear when the bed shifted, then shifted again, and a frustrated huff came from my right.

Jordan. What had I been thinking, inviting him into my bed?

Reaching across him, I flipped on the lamp, and he gave a shout of surprise, burrowing his head under his pillow. I glanced over at him, my stomach flipping as I took in the sight of my teammate's fit body sprawled out on my bed, naked other than his jockstrap, which, from the view I had, he might as well have not been wearing. All it did was accentuate the rounded, muscular curves of his ass.

"Why're you burning my eyes?" he mumbled from beneath the pillow. I ripped the pillow away from him, and he blinked up at me, all tousled hair, sleepy grey eyes, and pouting lips.

I wanted to kiss him. I shouldn't want to kiss him. I didn't even think he wanted me to kiss him—there had been a disconcerted expression on his face when he'd been sitting on my bed last night, hugging his knees, looking so vulnerable and confused that all I'd wanted to do was to take him in my arms and promise him that everything was going to be okay. That was a feeling I'd never experienced with him before, and it wasn't something I was going to act on, either.

"You woke me up in the early hours of the morning with all your tossing and turning." I narrowed my eyes at him. "Stay still, or I'll kick you out of my bed, and you can go and sleep on the sofa."

He glared back at me, now fully awake. "Is this how you treat all your bed partners?"

"Is this how you do?" I countered. "You were moving around and making enough noise to pull me out of my sleep—a sleep that was actually nightmare-free, for once."

His face fell. Rolling onto his back, he rubbed his hand over his jaw. "Ah. Sorry. I'm not...I couldn't sleep. I'll take the sofa."

Instead of following the sensible course of action, I placed a hand on his forearm. "Want to talk about it?"

"Not really." He laughed without humour.

"What if I turn the light off?" Lowering my voice, I flipped off the lamp. "Want to talk about it now?"

He sighed. With the lamp off, his face was only dimly lit by the sliver of light coming from the doorway, but I could easily see the way his mouth twisted, his eyes falling shut as he tugged on a handful of his hair. "I don't want to...but...fuck. Dr. Weaver. I keep hearing her in my head, telling me that it's better to talk about it. If I tell you, you have to promise not to laugh at me or take the piss."

"I won't."

"I'm serious, Lewin. Keep your judgemental thoughts to yourself, and if you laugh or take the piss, I can and will punch you in the mouth."

"For fuck's sake. Just tell me."

Another defeated sigh came from him. "Fine. I can't stop thinking about what we did last night. And not in a good way, either. It's...it's fucking with my head, and I don't know what to do or even what to think."

That made two of us. But one thing I knew for sure after the events of last night was that I was undeniably attracted to my teammate. Did he feel the same way, or had he just been caught up in the moment?

My hand was still on his arm, and I rubbed at his skin lightly with my thumb. I'd never had to comfort someone before outside of a football-related situation, and that was more about teammates consoling each other after a loss. I'd barely even experienced anyone comforting me, so I was having to rely on my instincts—which, fortunately, was something I was extremely good at.

"What about that saying you told me? What happens on the island stays on the island?"

His head turned to mine. "Hey, give me my pillow back. I don't like being lower than you."

Making sure that he saw my eye roll, I retrieved his pillow from the end of the bed, where I'd thrown it. Taking my place again and pulling the covers over both of us, I shifted onto my side to face him. He huffed at me covering up his body but didn't protest. If we were talking about last night, it was better for my sanity if his delectable body wasn't on display.

The silence between us stretched until he eventually cracked. "What about the saying?"

"My point is, if we both enjoyed it—and I'm more or less certain that we did—then what does it matter? We're on a private island, thousands of miles from home, with no paparazzi, and staff and guests with ironclad NDAs."

"Aren't you worrying about it? Even a bit? I'm *straight*, Theo. I don't...I *can't* be interested in men. It would have huge consequences for my career, my sponsorship opportunities—every single thing I've worked for would be affected. Not to mention my friends...my *dad*. It would affect everything. Everything that has meaning in my life."

Nausea rose in my stomach. His concerns completely echoed my own. "I *am* worrying about it, and I have the same concerns as you. But—" I paused, shifting closer to him, my head on the edge of my pillow. "—there's one difference. I'm fairly certain that I'm not completely straight."

His eyes widened. Clearly, he hadn't expected me to admit it. "W—why do you say that?"

I looked my annoying, obnoxious roommate straight in the eyes. "Because somehow, I've found myself attracted to a man."

Cheeks flushing, he bit down on his lower lip. "W—who?"

He was so fucking cute when he got all flustered. "You might know him. He plays football for Glevum FC Number 22. He stole my position on the right wing. What else? Hmm...he loves to show off his body whenever and wherever he can. He's cocky and arrogant and extremely argumentative."

Jordan peeked at me from beneath his lashes, the

corners of his lips turning up into a smile that I could only describe as shy. "He sounds great."

My stomach flipped. I wanted to smile back at him, to kiss him, but I kept my face blank. "He's actually a bit of a wanker, and he likes to fight me all the time. He's the last person on this earth that I should be interested in."

I watched as Jordan rolled onto his side to face me. His gaze lowered, and there was a tremor in his hands that I only noticed because the tip of his finger was brushing against mine. He took a small, shaky breath. "I think...I think he might not be completely straight, either."

"It's okay," I whispered, sliding my hand over his.

There was a pause, and then he gave a tiny nod. "I know. I—I know the attraction's okay. It's...surprising and very fucking confusing, and it came out of nowhere, but it's not even that part that I'm worried about, really. It's the consequences of it."

He looked and sounded so tortured that a lump came into my throat, my heart lurching. Reacting on instinct, I pulled him into me, wrapping him in my arms. "It's okay, baby. It's just you and me here. No one else will ever know. When we go home, everything will go back to normal. We're teammates, and when we're around our team again, all of this will go away."

His head lifted, his eyes wide as he stared at me. "You called me 'baby.'"

I could feel my cheeks heating. What had possessed me to say that word? "Uh, yeah. It slipped out. Why don't we pretend it didn't happen?"

A proper smile curved over his plush lips, taking my breath away. "Nope. It happened, and guess what? I think I liked it."

I raised a brow. "Did you?"

"Yeah. It's nicer than you calling me wanker or—" His expression darkened. "—brat."

"You love it when I call you a brat."

"I do not."

"You do."

Leaning forwards, he tugged my bottom lip between his teeth, biting down lightly and making me hiss. "Yeah? Well, you love it when I call you 'my lord.'"

"Shut up, Jordan."

"Make me."

I did, by yanking his head to mine and kissing him until both of us were breathless. When we came up for air, Jordan now beneath me, pliant and at my mercy, I opened my mouth to continue our conversation, but he beat me to it.

"What happens on the island stays on the island? And after this, we go back to our normal lives?"

I nodded. "Normal…but without us riling each other up."

"But it's so much fun to rile you up." He smirked at me, and I had to wipe the smirk off his face, which resulted in another round of kissing, and this time, neither of us held back. When Jordan kissed down my throat, his hand going to my erection, trapped in my underwear, I wasted no time in ensuring we were both naked in under five seconds. Gripping the delicious curves of his ass, I ground my hips against his, our erections sliding together, all hot, wet friction.

"Fuck, Theo. This feels so good." His words were panted against my throat as our movements sped up.

"Mmm. Are you going to come for me, baby?"

He whimpered, his fingers digging into my skin as his climax hit, his cum smearing across our stomachs and my dick, and the feel of it on my skin was all it took to send me over the edge after him.

Afterwards, when we'd cleaned up and Jordan had finally fallen asleep, I lay on my back, staring unseeing at the ceiling. If I were to be completely honest with myself, what we'd just done and had been doing were some of the best sexual experiences of my life, and despite my reassurances to Jordan, I was worried about what it might mean for my future.

I breathed in and out deeply, until my racing heartbeat slowed. What happened on the island stayed on the island. By the time we left, I'd make sure that Jordan Emery was out of my system. For good.

TWENTY-FOUR

THEO

"You're over the worst of the physical symptoms now." Dr. Ross placed his stylus and tablet down on his desk, giving me a warm smile. "Your vitals are all perfectly normal, and from everything you've told me, I'd say that any remaining withdrawal symptoms should fade in the next day or two. Now, before we move on, we need to discuss your cravings."

I nodded. He'd been asking me the same questions daily, in the same order, and I'd come to take comfort in this little routine. I knew what to expect and when, and I found that it eased something in my mind.

"You've told me that they've been manageable while you've been here. With your end date drawing closer, I want to start discussing your situation at home. Here at Black Diamond, you've been in...let's call it a bubble. A new environment where you can stay busy and distracted. Managing to control your cravings is easier here. But when you're at home, back in your usual routine, it's likely that you'll find the cravings more difficult to ignore."

Wonderful. I shifted on the leather chaise longue, Dr.

Ross' preferred seat for me after the first week, when we'd been based in the medical wing.

He continued speaking after giving me another of his reassuring smiles. "We're going to start focusing on some techniques you can use when you get home. I've also put together a shortlist of therapists in your vicinity that I think will be a good fit for you—and of course, you're welcome to continue your sessions with me over video, if you prefer. My goal is to support you, and whatever you need, I'll do my best to provide it. I'm not going to abandon you when you leave, Theo."

I swallowed hard around the lump in my throat. This man, who owed me nothing, was offering to be there for me, to support me through my most vulnerable moments. Yes, he was more than likely being paid an obscene amount of money, but even so, it was clear that he genuinely cared.

"Thank you. I...I know there's a long way to go, and I appreciate all that you've done for me. I want to conquer this."

His smile widened. "And I have no doubt that you will. Now, have you heard of CBT? Cognitive behavioural therapy?"

When I nodded, he tapped his stylus on his tablet. "That's where we'll begin. It's my belief that it will help you to address the underlying cause of your sleep issues, and in turn, will make the cravings much more manageable."

The underlying causes.

My parents.

My...inability to switch off my thoughts at night.

I met his gaze. "I'm willing to do whatever it takes."

"Snorkelling was fun. If we could do that every day for our Focus activity, I'd be happy." Jordan gave me a bright smile as we sat across from one another in the restaurant, dishes of poulet fafa in front of us. He speared a piece of chicken on his fork, his full lips closing around it as he gave a blissful sigh. I discreetly adjusted my cock under the table. Fuck. This man had such an effect on me, and he didn't even know it.

"Yeah."

Swallowing his mouthful, he glanced over at me. "Not feeling talkative today?"

I shook my head with a small sigh. "I... This morning was a lot."

The smile slipped from his face. I knew he'd had his own therapy session this morning, and yesterday, we'd had a joint session with Flora, which had gone just like our other sessions with her. She asked us to tell her something about the other person and give her a rundown of the activities we'd done together. After that, she reminded us that we needed to continue to work together during our two daily activities. Although she hadn't directly said it, it seemed as though she was satisfied with the progress we'd made together, and when I thought back to that first session we'd had with her, it was clear that we'd come a long way.

As Jordan leaned across the table, I felt his leg slide against mine in a deliberate movement. This was so unlike us that I stared at him in shock. Ever since the night we'd confessed our attraction, we'd been cautious around one another. There had been no more bed sharing. What we *had* shared had been a lot of heated looks and a few stolen kisses. It had only been three days, but those days had felt as if they were never-ending. We were both holding back, restraining ourselves, and neither of us dared to push for more. I knew that what had happened between us had scared me, and I had no doubt it had scared Jordan, too. When we took the consequences of our actions into account, who wouldn't be scared?

What happened on the island, stayed on the island... and that worked in theory, but in the cold light of day, we both knew that it wasn't that simple. Getting involved with my teammate was unacceptable. It was impossible.

But I *craved* him, and the more time we spent together, the more I wanted him.

"Want to talk about it?" His voice was soft. "You know I won't judge you. Not for this."

"Maybe later."

"Okay." Accepting my words with an easy shrug, he flashed me another grin. "Want to sneak out after curfew one night this week? I overheard a couple of the staff mentioning the bioluminescent plankton."

"The what?"

"Bioluminescent plankton." His eyes shone as he described how the ocean would apparently glow blue when the tiny organisms were disturbed by movement. It sounded fantastical and unbelievable, but Jordan was so animated and enthusiastic I couldn't even attempt to burst his bubble. When he finally finished speaking, he batted his lashes at me, his eyes wide, and fuck him for being so gorgeous that I'd agree to anything, even breaking the strict curfew we were under.

I hooked my ankle around his, satisfied when his cheeks flushed. "Do you know exactly when and where we can see it?"

Shaking his head, he speared another piece of chicken on his fork. "Nope, but I'll find out."

"I don't know about this. You'd better not get us into trouble."

His mouth fell open in the fakest expression of outrage I'd ever seen. "As if I would."

"Of course not."

"You like getting into trouble with me, though, don't you?"

I raised a brow. That smirk he was directing at me was about to get him into trouble. *Brat*, I mouthed, and I was rewarded with a glare. So predictable.

"Say that to me outside, and you won't like the consequences," he hissed.

My gaze flicked to our almost empty dishes, and I made a decision.

"Outside, now."

For once, he followed me without question. When we were outside, blanketed by the night, the air heavy with the scent of the sea and the tropical plant life around us, I pulled him off the path, into the shadows, and backed him up against a palm tree.

Pressing my body into his, I dipped my mouth to his ear. "You're nothing but trouble, baby."

He shivered against me, his arms winding around my shoulders. Nipping at my jaw, he tugged me closer. "You fucking love trouble."

"Hmmm." I trailed my lips down the side of his neck. "You'd better make it worth my while."

"I always do." He gripped my throat, forcing my head up. We shared the same oxygen, so close that his lips touched mine every time we exhaled. "Let's not waste time pretending that you don't want this as much as I do."

We weren't talking about sneaking out after curfew anymore.

I closed the final millimetres of distance between us and took his mouth in a hard, possessive kiss. "I fucking want this." *I want you.*

He moaned, his cock rapidly hardening against mine. "Fuck. Theo."

"We shouldn't be doing this." I kissed him again.

"I know. It's just gonna fuck things up for us, isn't it?"

My hand slid over the planes of his stomach and down inside his shorts. "It already has."

"Fuuuuuck." His head slammed back against the tree, making the branches above us shake. I latched onto his throat, sucking a mark into his smooth skin. *My* mark.

"You like that?"

"You know I fucking do," he rasped, tugging at the waistband of my shorts. When his fingers wrapped around my cock, it was my turn to moan. I couldn't think when he was this close to me. All my perfectly rational reasons for staying away from him disappeared beneath his touch.

Burying my face in his throat, breathing in his delicious scent, I brought him right to the edge with my hand until he was a gasping, panting mess, his own hand movements uncoordinated and jerky as the pleasure took over. I was barely able to focus myself, surrounded by him, but I needed him to come first. I wanted to feel the proof of just how much I affected my mouthy, bratty teammate.

"Theo," he whimpered, and I bit down on his throat just as I twisted my hand over the head of his cock. His body stiffened, and then he came, pulsing in my grip, his release coating my palm and my fingers.

My moan vibrated against his skin, my erection throbbing in his grip. I'd never been this desperate for anyone, had never found such pleasure in bringing pleasure to another person. When he sucked in a shuddering breath, his hand resuming its movements, I found myself spiralling towards the edge, tipping over when he rasped out my name in the sexiest tone I'd ever heard in my life.

"Staying away from you isn't working." His sigh was loud in the sudden silence.

"Were you trying to stay away?" I winced at the feel of my cum soaking the inside of my shorts as we made our way back to the path that led to our villa. Of course Jordan had managed to wipe his hand all over them, making the situation even worse.

"Walk faster. I need a shower and to get out of these shorts." Breaking into a light jog, he pulled ahead of me, so I increased my pace to match his. When I drew level with him, he glanced over at me. "You know I was. You were, too. I couldn't hold back from kissing you, but I thought...I thought it might be better if we didn't take it any further." He shook his head, huffing out a laugh. "I only managed to last three days. I'm not sure I like this effect you have on me, Lewin."

"I didn't do any better," I reminded him. "And it's the same for me. You of all people being the one to affect me this way—it's extremely inconvenient and quite irritating."

With a laugh, he elbowed me in the side, making me stumble, and when I shot him a glare, he sped up, racing up the path to the villa.

As we reached the villa, he lifted his arm to scan his wristband, and when the door unlocked, he stood aside to let me go first.

That small gesture made me warm all over. And even warmer when he said, "You can use the shower first."

"You don't want to join me?" As soon as the words fell from my lips, I regretted them. We shouldn't be pushing this thing between us any further, especially when he'd just admitted that he'd been trying to stay away from me.

Jordan shook his head with a small smile. "I do...but I'm trying to, y'know, be sensible or whatever."

"I don't think I like you being sensible," I admitted, and his smile widened. Darting forwards, he pressed a hard, quick kiss to my lips before moving out of my reach.

"I don't like it either. But when you're all..." He waved his hand up and down my body. "Fucking hot and distracting and all wet in the shower... Fuck. Just go. Before I end up mauling you or something."

The conflicted look in his eyes was the only thing that gave me the strength to turn my back on him and enter the bathroom, closing the door behind me.

But when I was in the shower, all I could think about was him, and as I wrapped my hand around my cock and brought myself to the second orgasm of the evening, he was all that I saw.

TWENTY-FIVE

JORDAN

I came out of the shower to find Theo sitting on my bed, tracing his fingers over the leather cover of the notebook that Dr. Weaver had given to me. When he saw me, he snatched his hand away, a guilty expression appearing on his face.

"I didn't look inside. I promise."

I believed him. He was too moral to snoop around my private things. But I could tell that he wanted to ask about it, and for some reason, I wanted to share. I mean, most of the shit inside was about him, after all.

Taking a seat on the bed next to him, leaning back against the wall, our shoulders brushing, I held out my hand. "Pass it here."

When he handed the notebook to me, I flipped it open, bypassing the page where I'd made my original list of people who were important to me, and found the page I wanted.

Theo Lewin

(my teammate/hated rival/pretentious wanker/nemesis)

"You get a whole section to yourself." I showed him the page, and his brows flew up.

"What's this?"

"My therapist wanted me to write about the people who...uh, affect my life the most. In either a positive or negative way. So here you are. Look." I tapped on the first paragraph below his name and description.

His eyes lowered to the page where I was pointing, and he slowly read aloud, "Influences me in a positive and negative way. Positive—makes me want to try harder and improve my skills so he doesn't have a chance to lord it over me. Negative—he's arrogant, haughty, aloof, cold. He thinks he's better than me and has done ever since we first met. Not only for his football skills but in general. The upper-class bastard constantly gets under my skin, and I wish he'd be transferred to another team, preferably in a different league so I didn't ever have to interact with him again."

Hurt flashed in his gaze. "Is this what you really think of me?"

It was fucking insane that we were sitting here having this conversation at all, let alone that my first instinct was to reassure him. But here we were, and so I turned to him with a small shake of my head and then pressed a kiss to his cheek. "It was. Before we started spending time together. Now...you know things have changed. We've both said and thought hurtful things about each other in the past, haven't we? I mean, you really hurt me when you said all that shit to me that night when we left the club. I was drunk, but I remember it all."

He rubbed his hand across his face. "I'm sorry."

"I didn't bring that up to make you feel bad. I'm...some of the things you said just brought my own insecurities to the surface, I guess. It's something I've been working on with Dr. Weaver. Anyway, my point is, we thought those things about each other, and a lot of them aren't really true, are they?"

Exhaling unsteadily, he clenched and unclenched his fist. "What would you say now?"

I'd begun this by allowing him to read the first entry, and I guessed it was only fair that he saw what I thought about him now. Even though it was going to be really fucking embarrassing for me. I had to, though. I couldn't stand that hurt expression on his face anymore. "You can read the latest page I wrote." I flipped to the latest entry in my notebook.

Theo Lewin
(my teammate)

Influences me in a positive and negative way.
Negative: he's arrogant, but I can be too, so I can't be mad at him for that. I worry that he still thinks that I'm shallow and there's nothing more to me than football and showing off my body, even though we're getting on better now. He's annoyingly hot, and now I've noticed I can't stop noticing. I need an off switch for this. He made me question my sexuality for the first time in my life. I can't blame him for that but it's fucked up.
Positive: He's got a vulnerable side that I don't think many people know about, and it makes me want to take care of him. He's an AMAZING footballer. He's hotter than the sun. His smirks make my dick

hard and I like it when he calls me baby. He makes me feel safe. When he says something nice to me, something validating, it feels good.

Dr. Weaver says that my need for validation and acknowledgement stems from me always having to work for what I want while receiving little acknowledgement for it (or something along those lines). Not like I can complain about my childhood, but my dad wasn't one for praising me. That's just the way he is, he's never known any different. BTW Rory—if you're snooping here, this DOES NOT mean I have a praise kink. Apparently when I post selfies to my social media and get positive comments and likes, it gives me a little high. It trips something in my brain, and then I crave more. But I've been getting the same high from riling up Theo, and that's fucked up, isn't it? Who enjoys pissing someone off that much, unless they're a sadist or something. Again, Rory, if you're snooping, I am NOT a sadist. Things have changed between us and now I enjoy riling him up in a fun way. I like it even more when it involves my dick. Or my mouth/his mouth. I like it when he lets me take care of him like I did with his nightmares and the massage, even though he ruined my bed with the oil. I like feeling him on top of me. Weird, because I was all about a girl's curves before, but something about his body gets me going like nothing else. Is this just temporary insanity from being on the island? Will I still feel like this when I go home?

I think I like him.

I'm fucked.

My cheeks were flaming, and I buried my face in my hands so I didn't have to see Theo's expression as he read the words I'd written yesterday, sitting on my favourite flat rock on the beach. They'd come pouring out of me, and I'd meant everything I said. But to have my private thoughts and feelings spelled out for him in ink...I'd never felt so vulnerable in my life.

He was silent for a long time, and I was feeling more and more agitated as the time stretched. When he eventually cleared his throat, his voice was raspy. "Jordan. Look at me."

Dragging my hands away from my face was so difficult when all I wanted to do was hide. But when I dared to meet his gaze, his expression was so soft, and his eyes were suspiciously shiny.

He closed the notebook, carefully placing it down on my side table, and then turned to me, his hand coming up to cup my jaw, his thumb rubbing over my stubble. With his other hand, he stroked over my eyelashes with the tip of his finger. "Your eyes are so beautiful. They change colour all the time, did you know that?"

"Well...uh, yeah, I mean, they're grey eyes. That's what they do. But yours are, uh, amazing. I love the—"

His fingers tightened on my jaw, and I immediately stopped speaking. "I haven't finished yet. There's a reason so many people like and comment on your selfies. It's because *you* are beautiful. I can say that with certainty, as a man that's never looked at another man before and thought, *I want him*. Not until you. You know you're gorgeous, and yes, that does manifest in your annoying tendency to pose all the fucking time, but that's not a bad thing." He slid his free hand into my hair. "How's this for some validation? I don't think you're shallow. Not at all."

My eyes widened. "Y-you don't?"

"No. I think you—" He broke off with a harsh exhale. "Fuck, this is difficult to say to your face."

"What if we both close our eyes?" I felt like my brain and my heart and my stomach were going to explode if he kept looking at me the way he was and saying these things to me.

"Okay." A small smile curved over his lips. "Keep them closed until I'm finished."

"I will." My lids lowered, and my other senses were immediately heightened. I was even more aware of the places he was touching me, the heat from his body, his breath tickling my skin.

"I think you might be the person who knows me the best. It's absolutely mind-blowing because it's you and me, and our history hasn't exactly been conducive to us growing closer. Dr. Ross told me that in situations like this, when we're thrown together in an unfamiliar environment, people become closer far more quickly than they would in the outside world. A day here can be equivalent to a week outside, and maybe that's why we're here right now and I'm telling you this. You've seen some of my most vulnerable parts, and you're the only person in the world who knows about my sleeping issues, other than Dr. Ross." His lips skimmed over mine. "I don't think you're shallow. You're kind, and caring, and utterly gorgeous. You try to make a difference in little ways that most people probably aren't even aware of, like picking up that beach litter. You don't do that for kudos; you do it because you believe it's the right thing to do. You took the time to research how to help me with my nightmares, and I have *never* had anyone who cared enough to do something like that for me before."

The resignation and sadness in his voice *killed* me.

"People care about you, Theo. I bet if you opened up to them, you'd see that. You're so liked and respected by your teammates, and I've never heard anyone say a bad word about you...unless it involved me."

I brushed a soft kiss over his lips, and he sighed. "Maybe you're right. I just...I never really felt like I fit in anywhere. There was never anyone I was close to. Then I got my place on the team and thought, finally, maybe I'll fit in here. Then you came along, and the rug was pulled from under my feet."

"Fucking hell, Theo. Come here. No, lie down." My eyes opened to find his were wet, and it made my heart fucking hurt. I pushed him down onto the bed and wrapped my arms around him. "You do fit in. The guys love you. We're working on our issues, aren't we? We're gonna be proper besties when we get back, not just me telling you you're my bestie because I love to watch the way you get angry when I say it."

My words earned me a tremulous smile. "You're such a wanker." His voice was soft. "I had... This morning's session with Dr. Ross was heavy. I think—I think I want to talk about some of it with you."

"'Course. You know I won't share anything with anyone else. You can trust me." I kissed the side of his head. It felt so right to be here with him, in our own little world, opening up to each other in a way I'd never experienced before.

"Yeah. I can." He closed his eyes. "I'll give you the highlights. I didn't exactly grow up in a loving home. Yes, from the outside, it looked good—two parents, a beautiful manor house in the countryside, no money worries. But my parents...to them, I was a commodity. Or so it felt. If I didn't toe the line, didn't follow the exact path they'd planned out for me... Well. The threat of being disowned was a constant in my life."

"Fuck, baby." Now I was the one using that word. "I'm sorry for all the times I called you 'my lord' and all those other things I accused you of."

He smiled. "I don't mind it, coming from you. But you weren't wrong. I did have a sense of entitlement, especially when I was younger. It was soon knocked out of me when I joined the youth academy. It was pure luck I was able to do so, and my parents had no inkling that it would ever be more than a teenage hobby. But when I was there, I found that my upbringing set me apart from the other boys in the academy. I didn't know how to act any differently, and so I... I shut down. I put on a front, acted as if I were untouchable. You were the only one who ever managed to get past my defences, and you did it so effortlessly. What is it about you?"

"I guess I'm just that good."

He smacked my arm. "Sometimes I think your sole purpose in life is to irritate me until I snap."

"Sometimes it is." I shrugged and then kissed the spot just below his ear. "Tell me more. I want to know everything."

"Okay. As I just said, my upbringing set me apart from the other boys at the academy. But I soon found that football set me apart from the boys at my school. My school was probably just as you imagine—a boys' school filled with the sons of politicians and lords and other influential figures, costing thousands of pounds a year to attend. No one could seem to understand my passion for football and my disinterest in a career in law, or politics, or any number of other ambitions that I had no interest in. All I wanted was to play football, and there was no one in my life that understood that."

"Theo. I wish I'd known...I might have—"

"There's no use in thinking about what might have been. All we can do is acknowledge the past and move forwards. My parents certainly didn't understand. Do you know, they've never been to any of my games? Not one. They refused to support that part of my life. I'm now estranged from them, for the most part." He laughed bitterly. "So that's my life in a nutshell. My sleeping issues stem from my childhood nightmares, which I already told you about, and ever since, I've had trouble switching off my thoughts when I go to bed. I always spent my nights tossing and turning, and when I joined Glevum and sleeping pills were casually dropped into conversations, it seemed like a miracle solution. I started out taking them the night before a match, as some of the other players do, but I soon grew to rely on them. Getting a full night's sleep without my thoughts troubling me...it was...well, it became an addiction. Dr. Ross is helping me to learn techniques to deal with everything, and the aim is that I'll eventually be able to fall into a regular sleep pattern, but for now, all I can do is try to get through one day at a time. One night at a time."

I wrapped my arms more tightly around him. I wanted to take all that pain from him, to make it better, but all I could do was trust that Dr. Ross knew what he was talking about, and eventually, Theo would be able to sleep properly again. And I'd do whatever I could to help that happen if he'd let me.

I didn't know how to articulate the things I wanted to say, but I had to try. "You don't have to go through this alone anymore. I'll be here. Even when we get back, and we're, y'know, back to being teammates. I want to be your friend,

Theo, and I'll be here to support you. You can talk to me about anything. Anytime. Okay?"

He stared at me for a moment, and then his whole face just crumpled. "Fuck. You have no idea." Burying his head in my throat, he breathed in and out, short, fast breaths, and I rubbed my hand up and down his back, doing my best to soothe him. When his breathing slowed, he spoke again. "I've always been lonely. It sounds ridiculous, I know. I'm doing my dream job, getting paid more in a week than some people make in a year, and yet—"

"It doesn't sound ridiculous. To tell the truth, I'm lonely, too. I mean, I have Rory and my dad and the guys on the team, but. I dunno...it's different. What we're doing now...I can't imagine experiencing all this with anyone else. Let alone doing this." I placed a kiss to his lips. "Or this." I kissed him again.

"Or this," he agreed, taking control of this kiss and rolling me onto my back, his body pressing me down into the bed. "I think you mentioned that you like feeling me on top of you, didn't you? And there was something about thinking I was hotter than the sun?"

I glared up at him when he smirked at me. "I wish I'd never let you read that."

"I'm glad you did." His expression became serious. "And just so you know. I think I like you, too, Jordan."

TWENTY-SIX

JORDAN

The paddles of my kayak cut through the turquoise waters with barely a ripple. Next to me in his own kayak, Theo's brow was furrowed in concentration as he focused on dipping his paddle into the sea at the perfect angle, pulling slightly ahead of my kayak. I glanced up at the cliffs. There was the tree shaped like a dancing figure, just as the staff member I'd bribed with my natural charm had described, which meant that the cove should be just around the next corner. Sure enough, as we rounded the cliff edge, there it was—a small crescent of soft white sand surrounded by cliffs, the waves lapping gently at the shore.

"There." I inclined my head towards the cove, and Theo gave me a short nod, steering his kayak towards it. We pulled the kayaks up onto the beach, removing our life jackets, and then flopped back on the sand.

"So you really want me to break the curfew rules to come back here after dark?" Theo glanced around us. It had taken me a good few days to talk him into my plan, which he'd been hesitant about when I told him that it involved "borrowing" the kayaks from the lockup, i.e. stealing them.

Except it wasn't stealing if you were putting them back, right?

"We only have two more days left here. We have to do this. It's a once-in-a-lifetime opportunity." I sighed heavily, pouting my lips and lowering my eyes. "I guess I can come back on my own if you don't want to."

He leaned over, tugging my earlobe between his teeth. "I know what you're doing, brat. Stop trying to manipulate me."

I turned my head, darting forwards to bite at his lower lip. "Is it working, though?"

"Yes." His eyes narrowed. "You'd better make it worth my while."

"Oh, I will." Slowly and deliberately, I slid my tongue across my lips. "I'll make it *so* worth your while." I had a plan. Ever since our heart-to-heart, we'd stopped holding back, and I'd given Theo so many blowjobs that I probably needed to ice my jaw. But we hadn't gone further than blowjobs and handjobs and that thing where we rubbed our dicks together, which was possibly my number one sex thing ever. I knew we both wanted to go further, but it was a big fucking step. Penetrative sex. Who would be the one doing the penetrating? Would it hurt? Would we end up fighting instead of fucking?

So many questions, but although I was nervous and unsure, I wanted it. So badly. And if all went to plan, I might just get it.

"Come here," he murmured. "Kiss me properly, you little cocktease."

And just because I lived to annoy him, I whispered, "No," against his mouth and then jumped to my feet and made a run for the sea. He chased after me as I knew he would, and I finally let him catch me when we were both shoulder-deep in the warm, crystal-clear water. Fish swam around our legs, and the sand was soft beneath my toes. I turned to face him. "If you want me to kiss you, you'll have to come down here."

Then I took a deep breath and dropped beneath the surface.

Theo didn't waste a second, following me down and grabbing me around the waist to pull me into him. Underwater, our movements were a lot more difficult, but I wrapped my legs around him, clasping the sides of his face as we sank to the ocean floor, and then our lips met.

When we resurfaced, both of us gulping in lungfuls of fresh sea air, he looked at me with a wide, happy grin on his face. He tugged me close, kissing me again. "Never change, Jordan."

"Oh, so you're telling me you like it when I do the opposite of what you want?"

"Stop putting words into my mouth."

"I'll put my tongue in there instead."

And I did.

Sneaking out of our villa had been relatively easy. Okay, it had involved two precariously balanced sun loungers, followed by scaling a tree from our pool deck, with a branch or two digging uncomfortably into sensitive body parts, but we'd made it all the way down to the kayak storage area without encountering anyone. The kayaks themselves were on racks in a storage shed behind a locked door, but the lock was a simple combination padlock that fortunately, I knew how to pick. My knowledge of lock picking involved one weekend when I was home alone at sixteen, following several YouTube tutorials and a desire to get inside my dad's shed where he hid his vodka, but Theo didn't need to know about that. As far as he was concerned, it was all down to my natural talent.

The padlock clicked open, and we made quick work of removing the two closest kayaks from the rack and grabbing some paddles and life jackets. The moon was full and bright overhead, lighting our way as we made our way around the cliff to our cove. Our paddles splashed softly in the water, taking us closer to our destination.

When we rounded the corner of the cliff, I gasped, swallowing hard around the sudden lump in my throat as I took in the incredible sight before me. Nothing could have prepared me for this.

Where the surf was breaking, there was a swathe of shining blue lights, glimmering along the shoreline of the cove. They lit up the water, a dancing, shimmering glow of bioluminescence that looked like a starry sky, an entire galaxy beneath the waves.

"Oh, wow," I whispered.

Theo's jaw dropped, his eyes wide as he stared at the awe-inspiring sight that only the two of us were here to witness, in the still of the warm, tropical night with the moon shining on the sea and millions of tiny stars dotting the sky. "Jordan. This is…this is…"

"I know."

We paddled to the edge of the cove. Both of us remained silent, hushed by this once-in-a-lifetime moment that we were experiencing together. It was unforgettable. It was fucking magical. And I was so glad that he was here with me.

I placed the waterproof bag I'd brought with me on the beach, and after removing my life jacket, I opened it up.

Almost everything in here had involved me promising increasingly outrageous things for Lawrence's nephew. A season pass to a sports channel so he could watch our matches. A signed shirt. A signed picture from the whole team. Grant Evans' autograph. Whatever it took, I'd agreed to do it.

In return, Lawrence had come up with the goods. I laid out a large, thick blanket, soft on the top and backed with a material that stopped the dampness from the sand filtering through. Next, I pulled out a bottle of champagne, scooping out a dip in the sand to ensure it wouldn't tip over. A couple of beach towels followed the champagne, and then finally, my hands closed over the remaining items in the bag.

Biodegradable wipes, condoms, and lube.

I wasn't sure who had been the most uncomfortable with my request—me or Lawrence. But despite his distaste, his affection for his nephew had won out, and if everything went well, it would all be worth hearing his haughty tones asking what on earth I wanted condoms and lube for, as if it wasn't blatantly obvious.

"Theo." I glanced up at him. He was standing on the shore, clad in a pair of blue swim shorts that matched his eyes, staring at the blue shimmer of the bioluminescent plankton with his phone in his hand. "Theo," I said again, and this time, he turned to me. I crooked a finger at him, and he came, crowding me back on the blanket, his body draping over mine. His phone dropped to the sand, forgotten.

He trailed his nose up the side of my throat. "You got me here. What do you want to do with me?"

I dragged my nails down his back, mouthing at his jaw. "I want us to fuck."

"Fuck." He groaned low in his throat. "I want that, too."

"Yeah? Open the champagne."

Without another word, he shifted onto his knees, opening the bottle quickly and easily. When the champagne came bubbling out of the top, he tipped the bottle, drizzling a trail of champagne down my pecs and abs.

"Delicious," he murmured, his hot tongue chasing the cool champagne as it trickled down my body, giving me goosebumps.

"My turn." I gripped his shoulders and twisted us, pressing him down into the blanket. I poured a generous trickle over his torso, following the line of liquid down the centre of his abs, licking down his v line until I got to his shorts. "Fuck, Theo," I rasped, raising my head as I closed my fingers around the waistband of his shorts. "You're so fucking lickable."

"So are you." He lifted his hips, allowing me to slide his shorts off. "Your turn."

I found myself on my back, my own shorts removed in record time, and then more champagne was being poured over me, with Theo's tongue lapping up every drop and driving me completely fucking insane. Over his shoulders, I could see those incredible illuminated waves breaking against the shore, and I couldn't imagine *anything* better than this moment.

Until Theo abandoned the champagne and took my cock into his mouth.

"Fuuuck. Don't make me come yet. Wanna fuck."

He lifted his gaze to mine, his eyes wide and dark. Releasing my cock, he licked across his lips in the sexiest move I'd ever seen. "How do you want to do it?"

I bit down on my lip, suddenly unsure. "I've done anal before, but obviously not the other way round, y'know."

"Same." He smiled at me then, slow and dangerous.

"I'm enjoying the thought of shoving my cock inside my brat and making him moan for me."

Fuuuck. "For the last fucking time, I'm not a brat," I growled, barely able to get the words out, but he pounced on me, kissing the breath from my lungs.

"Maybe not, but tonight, you're mine, and I want to see you come on my cock."

I shivered at his low threat. "Uh, yeah. Okay. Yeah. We can do that. As long as I get to return the favour."

His gaze softened as he gazed down at me. "I'll let you do whatever you want to me," he promised, softly and sincerely. "Do you want to turn over? I think it'll be easier."

My heart pounded as I shifted onto my stomach, my erection rubbing against the blanket. I was turned on beyond belief, but I was also apprehensive about what was going to happen.

Very apprehensive.

"Here." Theo slid one of the beach towels beneath me, raising my ass. "I'll be careful, I promise. Tell me if anything feels uncomfortable, and I'll stop."

I heard the click of the lube cap, and then a careful finger circled around my hole. I'd never been so simultaneously scared and turned on in my life.

It's only a fucking finger, Jordan.

I breathed out. "Wait. Let's turn the other way so I can see the sea." It would help me to distract myself from what was about to happen. Yeah, people did this every day, but this was uncharted territory for me, and Theo had a big dick. No bigger than mine, of course, but imagine shoving a fucking rounders bat up your ass. Okay...that was an exaggeration, but the point was it was big.

When I was back in the same position, this time facing the amazing view in front of me, I relaxed a bit. I wanted this. Wanted Theo. And this place...it was like something out of a fantasy world.

"Relax, baby." Theo pressed a line of soft kisses down my spine. "I'm not going to hurt you."

This time, when his finger circled my hole, I didn't tense up. I watched the waves, focusing on the sound of them breaking on the shore, reminding myself that I was so lucky to be here and lucky to be experiencing this with Theo.

He pressed inside me, so slowly and gently, and it didn't even hurt.

"Keep going." I pushed back, hoping he'd understand what I meant without me having to spell it out for him.

He understood exactly what I meant, easing another finger inside. I concentrated on the waves, taking slow, steady breaths, and it was...it was different, but it was okay.

I thought it was okay, until he crooked his fingers and made me see fucking stars. More stars, joining those in the sky and the ocean. I knew about my prostate, in vague terms, but I'd never...I'd never...

"Theo. Why the fuck... What... How..." I panted as he added another finger, lighting me up in ways I'd never imagined. Fucking hell, I was writhing on the blanket, grinding my hard, leaking dick into the towel beneath me, and I couldn't even fucking *think*.

Dimly, I was aware of a ripping sound, and then he withdrew his fingers, and something much bigger was pressing against my hole.

I groaned as he entered me. Dual sensations of pleasure and pain warred within me, and I had no idea which way was up and which way was down. He was so fucking *big*, and I was so fucking full. I could never have imagined this, and I was going to return this favour as soon as I recovered so he could experience it, too. It was only fair.

"Fucking hell, Jordan. Your sexy ass swallowing my dick is the hottest sight I've ever seen." Theo's voice was strangled, his body tense and stiff as he did his best to hold himself completely still.

"Take a photo. For me." I wanted to see myself split open on his thick cock. Wanted a reminder of this moment. I heard a soft click, and then his body curled over mine.

"You're so fucking sexy. I want you so much. I want to see you stretched open, to see you fall apart on my cock. I want to see you to come for me. I want to see your cum all over this blanket."

I groaned. My teammate was a dirty, dirty boy. "Fuck me, baby. Make me come."

He thrust into me, but I could tell he was holding himself back. I appreciated him taking care, because I still hadn't adjusted to his length inside of me, but at the same time, I wanted him to lose control.

"Don't hold back. I won't when it's my turn," I promised him, and that was all it took. He withdrew almost all the way and then thrust back inside, hard. I rocked forwards with a moan. It burned, but it was so good.

"That's it. More."

He took it as the invitation it was.

His hips snapped forwards, and he fucked me. Hard. Somehow, his angle was perfectly calculated to hit that spot inside of me that had me seeing stars, and as his movements grew faster and more uncoordinated, I reached down to grab my dick, stroking it hard and fast, coming on his thick cock seconds before he found his own release, filling the condom as he slumped over my back, panting and moaning in my ear.

"Did I hurt you?" he whispered when he'd withdrawn from me, tying off the condom and stashing it in the spare pocket of the bag.

Grabbing a couple of the wipes, I quickly cleaned myself up and then shifted onto my side, facing him. He was lying on his back, naked and gorgeous, and all I wanted to do was wrap myself up in him and stay here all night under the stars, with the blue glow dancing in the waves. "I'll definitely be sore tomorrow, but no, you didn't hurt me."

"Good." He pulled me down to him, and we kissed softly before I settled my head on his shoulder, draping my arm over his chest.

We slept until dawn.

TWENTY-SEVEN

THEO

The time had come. It was our last night on the island. We had most of the day tomorrow until we needed to leave to catch our flight, but this was our final night in the villa.

Jordan and I had spent all day together, excluding our respective therapy sessions. We'd visited the beach, lazed around the villa, taken a walk on one of the short trails, during which we'd somehow ended up hand in hand. Everything between us had been so easy, but it had been overshadowed by the knowledge that tomorrow, we'd be going back to reality, and our time together would be over.

But before I let Jordan go, before we went back to our normal lives, we had tonight. We needed to make it count.

I descended the pool steps, fully nude, my cock hard and heavy. Jordan lounged at the far side, watching me through heavy-lidded eyes with his elbows propped up on the lip of the pool, water cascading over the edge. My dick hardened even further at the sight. I'd come to terms with my attraction for him, and I let my gaze trail over him appreciatively. He was the most beautiful person I'd ever seen.

When I reached him, his lips curved into a sultry smile. "You look fucking hot. Come here. I want to take a selfie. Just for us."

I let him wrap his arm around my shoulders, smiling as he pointed his phone camera at us, and then just before he could take another photo, I twisted my body to the side and kissed his jaw.

"Whoa!" Slipping on the pool tiles, he flailed for a second before he regained his balance. "Let me just..." He ducked under my arm, swimming to the side and placing his phone down before returning to me.

The night sky was black velvet, streaked with stars, and the soft underwater lighting of the pool bathed everything in a blue glow. It reminded me of our night in our cove, when I'd discovered what it felt like to be inside Jordan. It was a night I'd never, ever forget.

It was going to be so different when we got home.

That was a thought I wasn't going to entertain, not when I had Jordan here right now, and we had tonight. Our last night together.

When Jordan planted his hands on either side of me, mouthing at my neck, I groaned. I knew what he wanted, and I was going to give it to him.

Backed up against the edge of the pool, the water splashing around my chest, I met his lips in a hot, hungry kiss. His cock was so hard against mine, and his mouth was insistent, desperate, his hands all over me, just as mine were all over him.

"I want you so fucking much." He bit at my lip, his hands gripping my ass as he lifted me. My legs wrapped around his waist as we kissed and kissed and kissed, my back pressed up against the infinity edge of the pool, my erection trapped between us. "I can't wait to be inside you."

I stared down at my sexy teammate, his hair wet from the pool, droplets of water trailing down his body. My heart lurched, and my dick pulsed, and I *wanted*.

He ran his hand up my back as I lowered my head to his. "Get me ready, Jordan."

It took us a long time to make it across the pool, out of the water, and onto the lounger because neither of us wanted to stop kissing or to let go of each other. When I was finally on the lounger and he had two fingers buried inside me, I was so close to the edge I wasn't sure I'd last more than a few minutes longer. He'd been so gentle and careful, but his fingers felt so good. When he inserted another finger, I moaned, fumbling to my left for the condom packet so I could cover his cock. I needed to know how it felt having him inside me.

When I rolled the condom over his thick length, he shuddered against me, his breath stuttering. "Fuck, Theo. I know I'm not gonna last. Not this time."

"Me neither." I let him drag me back into the pool, our bodies entwined and our mouths and tongues sliding together. He pushed me back up against the far edge, and this time, he reached down between us, gripping my hips, and lined me up with his dick.

He lowered me so slowly, but it still burned.

I didn't care. I'd take anything for him.

When he was fully inside me, he remained still, one hand cupping my ass, the other coming up to thread through my wet hair. "You okay?"

"Yeah." I smiled at him, breathing through the stretch and allowing my body time to adjust to the feeling of being completely filled. "Just...just go slow until I get used to it."

"I'll go as slow as you need me to." He kissed me again. "You're so fucking tight around my dick. So good."

"Fuck, baby." I ran my tongue over his plush lips and then sucked his bottom lip between my own. "You taste so sweet. You feel so good inside me."

We began to move together, slowly and leisurely, like we had all the time in the world. Jordan didn't stop kissing and touching me, mouthing at my skin, little moans and cries falling from his lips as he fucked up into me, and I rode him, buoyed by the water, clinging onto his strong body.

"I—I tried to take it slow. Wanted it to last. But I—I—" Jordan shuddered, gripping me tightly as he thrust up, his head falling forwards to rest against mine. Panting hard, he wrapped his hand around my cock. Days of us experimenting with each other meant that he knew exactly how to bring me to the edge, and I came, so hard that I couldn't breathe, my vision whiting out for a second.

When I came back to awareness, I stared in horror as a tear fell from Jordan's lashes, streaking down his cheek. His lip trembled, and he sniffed hard. "S—sorry."

"*Baby*. What's the matter?" I kissed his tear away and then kissed his trembling lip, something inside me breaking apart, seeing him so upset.

"I—it's all going to be over tomorrow. I—I don't know what's going to happen when we get home. I want everything to be okay, and I'm worried I—I've made things even worse."

Oh, Jordan. I eased myself off him, taking care of the condom before leading him out of the pool. Wrapping him up in one of the villa's huge, fluffy towels, I took him into my arms, pressing kisses to his head and face.

"You haven't made anything worse. It's going to be okay,

I promise." I hoped so badly that my words would prove to be true.

He blinked at me with wet lashes, his eyes so wide and sad. "I'm gonna miss you—uh, this. Being here."

I'm going to miss you, too. I never could have envisioned any of this before the island, but in the time we'd been here, he'd become my rock, and I'd become his. It was such a departure from our previous relationship, and I wondered how we could have ever been so toxic with one another when he now felt like such an important part of my life.

"I'll miss it, too. But everything will be okay when we get back. We're friends now, aren't we? We'll get to preseason training with the rest of the team, and they'll be blown away by how well we work together."

His lips curved up at the corners, and the knot inside me eased. "Yeah. We'll blow their minds with our skills. You're right. I...I don't know why I'm getting weird about it. I guess it's just end-of-holiday blues, you know?"

"I know."

We dried off and made our way inside. When we reached the bedroom, there wasn't even a question of us sleeping apart. I pulled him down onto my bed with me and did my best to make him forget about his worries, prepping us both and then fucking him down into the mattress, covering him with my body while I whispered words against his skin, telling him how good he felt, how sexy he was, and how much I loved being inside him.

When he was finally asleep and I was still awake, I pulled him closer to me so that I was spooning him. Pressing a soft kiss to his hair, I swallowed around the lump in my throat.

After tomorrow, I'd be spending my nights alone again.

PART 3

TWENTY-EIGHT

JORDAN

Slumped on my sofa, my legs kicked up on my coffee table, I scrolled listlessly through Netflix. Giving up, I threw the remote down next to me and then began scrolling through my phone. I hadn't even posted to my social media since I'd received my phone back, but I couldn't muster up any enthusiasm. Post-holiday blues were a thing. Even though we'd been sent to the island for therapy, it had ended up being a retreat, a hideaway from the world with the man that had gone from being my enemy to my friend.

Two days ago—or was it three? The ridiculously long flights and jet lag were messing with my head—I'd been in bed with my teammate. Now I was back at home, surrounded by my own things, and it almost felt like the past few weeks had been a dream. An incredibly vivid dream involving things I'd never actually dreamed of, but even so, it almost didn't feel real.

My phone buzzed in my hand.

REUBEN:
> Are my eyes deceiving me?!!!! The notification I just got said Theo Lewin added Jordan Emery to the chat!!!

AINSLEY:
> WTF? Explain Theo

LARS:
> Theo?

REUBEN:
> THEO!!!
>
> T
>
> H
>
> E
>
> O

GRANT:
> What's happening? My phone's blowing up

THEO:
> What happened is, I added Jordan to our group chat

GRANT:
> Does this mean what I think it means?

I grinned to myself, and only eighty percent of my reason for smiling was seeing Theo's name appear on my screen. None of the guys knew what had happened. The only people who knew the details of our enforced stay on the island were Harvey, our agents, and a couple of the club's legal and medical staff. As the captain, Grant had been made aware that we'd been sent away to learn how to work together, but even he wasn't aware of the specifics.

> ME:
> Hi everyone. Thanks for the add Theo

REUBEN:

HELL HAS FROZEN OVER!!!!

LARS:

You are friends?

Ainsley sent a row of brain exploding emojis, and I laughed to myself, my mood lifting as I tapped out a quick reply.

> ME:
> We are. Turns out he's not so bad after all

GRANT:

Good for you for working through your issues. Proud of you both

REUBEN:

Bring on the new season! We'll be fucking UNSTOPPABLE!

AINSLEY:

EUROPE HEAR WE COME

LARS:

Here, not hear

THEO:

Yes, we're friends

> ME:
> He couldn't resist my natural charm

Climbing to my feet, I wandered into the kitchen, phone in hand. I wondered where Theo was now. I hadn't even been to his house before. Where did he even live?

THEO:
> You have no natural charm

ME:
> Rude!

GRANT:
> I feel as if I'm living in a parallel universe. This calls for a celebration. Theo, it's your birthday next week, isn't it?

REUBEN:
> London baby!!!!!

AINSLEY:
> I vote London

THEO:
> Do I get a say in my own birthday celebrations?

ME:
> Nope

LARS:
> No

GRANT:
> Of course you do

THEO:
> I know you won't stop pestering me until I agree. Fine, we can celebrate in London, if we must

AINSLEY:
> We must

THEO:
> Just us though, please? I don't want to make it into a big deal

He'd let me into his inner circle, and now I was going

to spend his birthday with him. I had fucking butterflies. And this was bad. We were supposed to go back to being teammates and friends, now we were home. I shouldn't be getting this excited about spending time with him again.

Grabbing a glass, I headed over to the fridge to pour myself some orange juice. Thank fuck for Rory, who had made sure my kitchen was stocked with the essentials ready for my return home.

When I picked up my phone again, my stomach flipped, and I clapped my hand over my mouth.

THEO:

I want to be serious for a moment. I need to tell you all something. I've been having therapy for an addiction to sleeping pills

GRANT:

Shit, man. Anything we can do?

REUBEN:

Yeah we're here for you

AINSLEY:

What they said

LARS:

We'll support you

Theo. I wanted to be with him so fucking badly. To hug him and tell him I was there for him. But the last conversation we'd had before we left the island, we'd agreed that we'd keep the lines firmly drawn, and that meant that I couldn't go running to him.

"This is it, then." I leaned back against the villa door, where we were waiting to be picked up by golf cart to be taken to the plane.

"Yeah." Theo's voice was quiet. "Time to go back to our normal lives."

"What are we going to do when we get back?" I met his gaze, and he sighed.

"We'll do what we agreed. Everything that happened between us stays here. We don't take it back with us. We don't want a relationship anyway, do we? If things ever got out, it would be disastrous for our careers."

I blinked rapidly. For fuck's sake. Why did it feel like we were breaking up? We'd had some good times with each other, but neither of us was looking for anything more, and both of us knew the consequences if anyone found out what we'd done together. There were no active players in the Premier League who were out, let alone two teammates. Even if that hadn't been a huge issue, we'd been in the headlines so much, and the last thing Glevum needed was even more drama from us both. We knew the line we had to draw. It was time to go home and concentrate on what was important. Football.

"You're right." It took everything in me to keep my voice from cracking. "Friends?" I held out my hand, and Theo clasped it. His hand was so warm in mine.

"It might...it might be better if we take some time apart when we get back to re-establish our boundaries." He rubbed his thumb over my skin in what was probably meant to be a reassuring gesture, but it hurt.

"O—okay. Yeah. That makes sense." Fuck, I was so close to falling apart. But I had to stay strong. We'd get through this, just as we'd managed to get through everything else. We were doing the right thing. "I'll miss you," I whispered, and

he exhaled shakily and then dropped my hand and pulled me into his arms.

"I'll miss you, too."

Going against every single one of my instincts, which ranged from demanding his address and going to him to calling him so I could at least hear his voice, I added a message to the group chat.

ME:
We're all here for you. You're not alone

It was as much as I dared to say.

THEO:

Thanks, I appreciate it. I felt that it was important to let you know, but please keep it to yourselves. My agent got rid of my pills for me, and I've been seeing a therapist who's helping me work through everything. I'll get through this, but I think I need the support of you guys

GRANT:

You've got it. Whatever you need, we're here for you. I'm sorry I didn't realise that you needed help sooner x

REUBEN:

Yeah you're our teammate and our friend

LARS:

You are not alone

THEO:

@Grant don't apologise. I kept it to myself, and there was no way any of you could have known

AINSLEY:

Don't keep that shit to yourself anymore. We're a team and we deal with things together

THEO:

Thanks, everyone. I do appreciate it. Now, can we change the subject?

The talk moved on to other subjects, and I could imagine Theo's relief. It was so fucking brave of him to admit his problem to his teammates, and despite promising I'd keep my distance, I *had* to send him a message, separate to our group conversation.

ME:

I'm so fucking proud of you x

THEO:

Thanks. I struggled, but someone I know told me that my teammates liked and respected me, and I hoped they were right

ME:

They sound very clever and amazing. You should listen to them

THEO:

I did. Hence the conversation in the group chat, where I exposed my shameful secret

ME:

It's not shameful. No one thinks that. They just want to support you

THEO:

Thanks. I think I've been holding everyone at arm's length for so long, and I didn't know how to let anyone in. Until the island

ME:

Yeah I get that. I really am so proud of you

THEO:

Thanks

ME:

Anytime. I meant what I said. I'm here for you and you're not alone x

I waited for a while, but he didn't respond. Taking my original seat on my sofa, I began the tedious process of scrolling through Netflix again. I needed to lose myself in something, anything that would take my mind off my teammate.

I shot upright, rubbing at my eyes. There was a ringing sound and a robotic voice informing me that someone was at the door. Shit, I must've fallen asleep. Bloody jet lag.

Yawning, I flung the door open without bothering to check who it was and found Rory standing outside. He gave me a once-over, handed me a steaming cup of takeaway coffee, and then pushed his way inside, taking a seat on my sofa.

"Make yourself at home." I was aiming for sarcasm, but I was caught by a yawn midway through.

"Jet-lagged?" He raised a brow.

I took a large gulp of the coffee. Mmm, a perfectly frothy latte. "What do you think? I flew halfway around the world. I don't even know what day or time it is."

Collapsing down next to him, I threw my legs up on my coffee table and took another huge gulp of my latte. "Speaking of, can we talk about carbon offsetting my flights? I don't even wanna know what my carbon footprint is right now."

"Already done," he informed me. "The airline has a carbon offset scheme. We just had to add an additional fee on top of your flight costs."

"Good." I turned to face him. "So what's new with you?"

His expression turned serious. "Nothing. I want to talk about you. Cal tells me that you were physically fighting with Theo. That's not what I wanted to hear."

Cal...who was Cal? Wait a minute... "Cal? That guy we met on the island? The one with the American actor, Jett? Ah, fuck, I never got to see Jett again. I wanted to take a selfie with him."

Rory's brows rose. "I have no idea what you're talking about. Cal's my Cambridge uni friend—the one who made your trip possible. I asked him to keep an eye out for you and, if he saw you, to report back to me."

"You asked him to spy on me? How could you?" I widened my eyes, giving him my most betrayed look.

"Enough with the dramatics. It wasn't like that. I simply asked him to let me know if he saw you. And he did, and what he told me concerned me."

"Well, there's no need to be concerned. Your plan worked. Yeah, we fought a bit at the beginning, but me and Theo are friends now. Proper friends."

"Are you serious?" He stared at me, hope and disbelief warring in his gaze.

"Yeah, I'm serious. We sorted our shit out, and now we're friends. You can stop worrying about me fucking things up. It's all good between us."

He eyed me carefully and then smiled, accepting my words. "I'm glad to hear it. It was my one and only idea to get you two on the same side, so I'm pleased—no, relieved— to hear that everything worked out. I spoke with Harvey a couple of times while you were away. Knowles has officially retired, and Harvey's willing to extend your contract on the proviso that you'll both be on your best behaviour. He's going to give it three months, and if all is well, we'll have a new contract drafted up."

Tension I hadn't even known I was carrying drained out of me at his words. "That sounds great. Thanks for everything. You're the best." I stood, crossing the room to the bag I'd left lying against the wall, and rummaged around inside. Straightening up, I returned to Rory. "Here. This is for you."

When I handed him the large bottle of vodka, he smiled, surprised. "You didn't have to get me anything."

"Yeah, well, I wanted to. I couldn't exactly go souvenir shopping while I was in rehab, but I got you that in the duty-free. I know it's not much, but I know you deal with a lot of shit from me, so, yeah."

"C'mere, you." He hugged me with one arm, patting my back. "I'm proud of you."

"Thanks."

When he released me, he waved the bottle at me. "I'm officially off the clock, so why don't we sample some of this, and you can tell me what you got up to while you were away? Whatever won't break your NDA, of course. I've heard a little about the resort from Cal, but I'd like to hear it from you. What do you say?"

Already on my feet and heading in the direction of the kitchen, I nodded. I could do this. All I had to do was avoid mentioning Theo. "You're a man after my own heart, Rory. I've had three weeks of abstaining from alcohol—" *Except for the night I licked champagne off my teammate's body, on a deserted beach under the stars.* "—and I could use a drink. As for the gossip, I'll tell you all the boring details. Did you know that I spent hours clearing debris from the beach? Oh, and the day Cal saw me, I got caught in a tropical thunderstorm..."

TWENTY-NINE

THEO

Lying on my back in my bed, I rubbed at my eyes, gritty from the lack of sleep. Another night of sleeplessness. I'd spoken to Dr. Ross twice since I'd been back, and we'd arranged a weekly therapy session via video call. He kept reiterating to me that there was no instant fix, and while I knew that was true, I was so fucking tired. The jet lag hadn't helped—I'd become used to being on a different time zone, and now I was wide awake when I should be sleeping.

But that wasn't even the worst part. The second I'd arrived home from the airport and the door to my flat had closed behind me, the loneliness hit me. It was even worse at night. I'd grown used to sharing a room with another person, their soft breaths a comfort in the dead of night when I was struggling to sleep, and more recently, the comfort of a warm body next to mine.

Not just any person. The truth was I missed Jordan.

I was lonely. So lonely.

Picking up my phone, I began scrolling through my photos. I'd transferred them from the temporary phone I'd been given on the island, and when we were on the plane home, Jordan and I had also exchanged pictures we'd taken during our stay.

I smiled at one of Jordan's selfies, a close-up of his grinning face as he pointed at a brightly coloured tropical bird perched in the tree next to our pool deck. The next image was one I'd taken—him on the beach with an armful of debris he'd collected, his brows raised and an expectant look on his face. I remembered him berating me for making him carry everything himself, and my smile widened.

I skipped past the three photos that made my heart pound in my chest. My bare back, taken from above, when Jordan was about to massage me. A picture I'd sneaked of Jordan, asleep on his stomach, his upper body exposed, and his face turned towards the camera. And finally, the picture he'd asked me to take. The picture that made me harder than any porn ever could. My cock entering him, that night at the cove.

I couldn't look at them. They were too intimate. They reminded me of something I'd had that I'd never get back.

Stopping on the last two pictures in my camera roll, I flipped back and forth between them. Jordan had taken them on our last night when we'd been in the pool, and he'd asked for a selfie. In the first image, his arm was slung around my shoulders, and both of us were smiling. The second one was an accidental press of the shutter when I'd surprised him by turning to kiss his jaw, and he'd lost his balance and almost gone under. The expression of shock and laughter on his face while I pressed my lips to his skin with a smile made something inside me twist painfully.

I took a deep breath, quickly scrolling back past them, and paused on one of the photos I'd taken of the bioluminescent plankton. The camera had captured the blue glow of the waves against the midnight sky and the blackness of the sea, and it brought memories rushing back. Without stopping to think it through, I opened my social media app and posted the image, captioning it, "Once in a lifetime."

A notification came through almost instantly.

@jordanemery_official liked your photo.

I scrolled to my messages.

@THEOLEWIN_OFFICIAL:
> Can't sleep either?

@JORDANEMERY_OFFICIAL:
> No. Fucking jetlag. I saw the photo

@THEOLEWIN_OFFICIAL:
> I know, I got the notification that you liked it

@JORDANEMERY_OFFICIAL:
> I wanted to comment but thought it prob wasn't a good idea

@THEOLEWIN_OFFICIAL:
> Probably not

@JORDANEMERY_OFFICIAL:
> That was the best night of my life

I groaned aloud. Neither of us needed a reminder of what had happened between us. I shouldn't have even posted the picture in the first place.

Something else I shouldn't be doing was navigating to Jordan's profile, and I'd avoided it up until now, not wanting to torture myself any further. But by the time the sensible part of my brain caught up, my fingers had already made the decision for me.

He'd only posted one picture since he'd arrived back in England. It was a selfie, taken in his mirror—or what I assumed was his mirror, given that he had a large number of other selfies in front of it. He had his tongue out, pulling a cheeky face for the camera, his bare torso on display for the world to see.

My cock responded instantly. I could vividly recall the feel of him beneath my hands, the taste of him on my tongue, tracing over those defined muscles that were now taunting me through the screen.

Reaching down, I adjusted myself with another groan. I wasn't going to allow myself to think of him in that way anymore. He was my teammate and friend, and that was it.

I returned to the photo I'd posted, Jordan's message echoing in my mind.

That was the best night of my life.

It was mine, too.

THIRTY

JORDAN

Preseason training was underway, and when I was surrounded by my teammates, I'd mostly managed to treat Theo the same as everyone else, even though it was killing me inside. He'd done the same to me, too, keeping a cool, calm, professional demeanour at all times. He'd probably managed to get over the thing between us, but even if he hadn't, he gave no sign that being around me affected him. He treated me exactly the same as everyone else. Our teammates were baffled that we were suddenly managing to work together in harmony—other than Grant, Reuben, Ainsley, and Lars, but they were all appreciative of our efforts, and so far, the entire team had been working together like a perfectly oiled machine, as if we'd been doing it for years. The gaffer was happy, or as happy as he could be, and that was all I could ask for.

I had to stay focused now. My career was the most important thing in my life, and finally, I wasn't fucking it up, and Glevum FC might actually have a shot at Europe this upcoming season.

I ignored the ache inside me that refused to go away. I

did my best to stop worrying about the dark circles beneath Theo's eyes because every time I'd mentioned them, he insisted he was okay.

I did my best to put everything behind me and move on, but it was so fucking hard.

I'd arrived at Sanctuary early in order to get my shit together and remind myself to act normal during Theo's birthday celebrations, so I bypassed the VIP area with our reserved booth, slipping into the room I'd hidden in the last time I'd been here, when Theo and I had been at each other's throats.

"Welcome to Sanctuary— Oh, it's you." A guy dressed in nothing but a pair of miniscule gold shorts and a pair of gold knee-high boots gave me a once-over. "You know you shouldn't be back here."

Memories slammed into place. He wasn't sparkly tonight, but there was a subtle shimmer to his skin that made him almost glow in the sweeping lights that penetrated this dark space. "Uhhh...JJ?"

The dancer flashed his bright white teeth at me, not quite a smile. "Hi, Jordan Emery. What are you doing back here? Got someone to hide from? Some friends who are planning to piss me off with their homophobic comments?"

I folded my arms across my chest. "No. I'm sorry about what happened last time. I'm actually here to celebrate my teammate's birthday tonight. I just wanted somewhere quiet to get my head together before everyone else showed up."

JJ's wary look faded. "In that case, can I get you a drink?"

"What's your most expensive champagne?"

"Hmm." Tapping his finger on his lips, he studied me. "You don't want it, trust me. It's *very* overrated. How about a JJ special? A French 75. Gin, sugar, lemon, and champagne. It's fucking divine. Like heaven in your mouth." He smacked his lips together.

"As long as it tastes good, I'm in. Can you make enough for six of us?" I followed him to the bar, trying and failing not to notice the shift of his muscles and the rounded curve of his ass as he walked. It was like Theo had unlocked something inside me, something that I'd never been aware of before.

But despite my appreciation of JJ's looks, my heart rate remained steady, my dick was resolutely unaffected, and my mind was fixated on one person only.

As JJ got busy preparing our drinks, I glanced back towards the doorway. I had those fucking butterflies again.

"Why did you need somewhere quiet to get your head together?" JJ glanced up at me as he poured gin into a cocktail shaker.

"It's complicated. My teammate, he..." I trailed off. How could I explain? I shouldn't be saying anything aloud, anything that could implicate me, or Theo, or both of us.

JJ propped an elbow on the bar, cocking his head as he studied me. His eyes widened, and he put the shaker down, leaning across the bar and lowering his voice.

"I wondered last time, but then I thought I might have been mistaken... My gaydar is rarely wrong, though. The sexual tension between the two of you was fucking hot." He fanned himself.

"What?" I recoiled from him, my gaze darting around me, hoping and praying that no one could hear our conversation. I could feel my cheeks heating.

"What?" One arched brow, and that was all it took to make me crack. Confiding in a stranger—a stranger who I knew was gay, because he'd told me last time I was here, was so tempting. And something told me he wouldn't judge me.

This club took their secrecy as seriously as Black Diamond Resort, with or without the NDAs.

"You won't say anything?"

He immediately shook his head. "Babe, no. Never. Believe me, Sanctuary's manager wouldn't stand for any of that shit from any of his staff, and as for his business partner, you don't want to cross him." Sliding out from behind the bar with a tray with a brimming jug and six glasses, he inclined his head towards the door. "Come on. Let's get these drinks to your booth, and then you can tell me who's putting that sad puppy look on your face."

He swept away, ignoring my outrage. Sad fucking puppy? What the fuck?

None of the others were in our reserved booth, which wasn't surprising since it was still over twenty minutes before everyone else was due to arrive. I slumped back against the plush leather backrest with a sigh. "I don't know why I'm telling you, but I need to tell someone. It turns out that I'm not as straight as I thought I was, and I might have, uh, messed around with someone, but we both knew it couldn't go anywhere. I need to get him out of my head."

"*Oh.*" JJ sank into the booth next to me. "Is this the first time you've been interested in a man? You don't have to tell me."

"Yeah. I didn't...I've never been attracted to men before him, but yeah, I guess I'm not straight anymore. It doesn't matter, though. I'm a Premier League footballer. I can't be anything but straight. Not openly."

JJ's hand landed on my arm, squeezing lightly. "I don't know much about football, but I do know something about the pressures that athletes are under from talking to other people in the community. Football sounds...difficult. I've heard about the homophobic fans."

I nodded. "Well, yeah. That's part of it, I guess. But it's not even just that because so many of the fans are fucking incredible. I know there would be support, even though there'd be shit from the bigots. But it's the whole football culture. All that pressure to be a certain way. Everyone involved in the game that have been brought up to think one way and can't imagine anything else. And then there are the international problems, like we saw at that fucking World Cup. It's not just the English league that we have to think of. Things are even worse in some other parts of the world."

JJ's eyes darkened. "Yeah. Some of the things I've heard...I can't even imagine what it must be like to live somewhere where it's illegal to be gay. It's fucked up."

"It is. Seriously fucked up. So, yeah. That's another thing. It's also... There's no precedent in the Premier League. No active players who are out. The pressure would be fucking insane."

"I can't even imagine." His mouth curved downwards, his shoulders slumping. "Was he worth it, though?"

Memories flashed through my mind.

"He was worth everything."

My conversation with Grant and Reuben faded into obscurity as I watched the final member of our gathering ascend the stairs. My eyes drank him in greedily. Polished black loafers, black trousers that clung to the muscles of his legs, a leather belt, a black shirt that showcased his fucking hot body, with the top two buttons undone and the sleeves rolled up to his elbows, and a shiny Patek Philippe watch on his wrist. Then there was his face. He'd shaved, so his jaw was all smooth, soft skin, and his raven hair was perfectly styled, sweeping across his forehead.

Fucking hell. Men had never made my dick hard before him, but Theo was really doing it for me. He was so fucking sexy, and I couldn't breathe as he drew nearer, my dick straining against my trousers and my heart racing as fast as an Olympic sprinter. Since we'd arrived home, this was the first time I'd seen him outside of a team situation, and I was rapidly falling apart.

I couldn't pull myself together. Soon, everyone was going to know just how into him I was, melting into a fucking helpless puddle onto the floor.

"Jordan. It's ready if you want to come and see."

I tore my gaze away from Theo with an effort, meeting JJ's eyes. I blinked. "Wh—what?"

"It's ready." He closed his fingers around my arm in an iron grip, dragging me away from Theo.

When we were alone, in a shadowy corner of the VIP area, the pulsing club lights sweeping around us, I turned on him. "What the fuck?"

"I'm doing you a favour. If you don't want your friends to find out, you need to stop being so obvious."

I stared at him in horror. "I was being that obvious?"

His mouth twisted. "Yeah, babe, you really were. You were looking at him like he was your last meal."

Shit. I slumped against the wall, my head in my hands. "Did anyone notice?"

"I don't think so, but you might want to tone down the eye fucking. I nearly combusted."

Fucking brilliant.

"I—"

"Jordan."

My breath caught in my throat at the sound of the new

voice. JJ melted away, and I was left alone in this dark corner, with only the wall at my back holding me upright.

He was right in front of me, strong and solid and smelling good enough to eat, and I was completely fucking helpless. My cock was pounding, and my heart was beating so fast I was probably going to be in need of medical attention at any second.

Planting his hand on the wall next to my head, he leaned in, trailing his nose up my throat.

My body trembled. I fisted my hands at my sides, wanting to touch him with everything I had but knowing that I couldn't. Knowing that he was out of my reach.

"You smell so fucking good," he murmured against my throat. His words vibrated across my skin. Raising his head, he met my gaze, his voice turning hard. "What are you doing here in the dark? What were you doing with that dancer?"

THIRTY-ONE

THEO

There was one thing I'd been looking forward to when my birthday plans had been arranged, One thing that I wasn't supposed to be looking forward to. One thing that I wasn't supposed to want.

As soon as I'd seen Jordan, reclined in the booth with his dark, tousled hair and a heavy-lidded gaze and the tightest shirt known to man stretched over his muscles, in a deep sapphire colour that brought out the blue in his eyes, I was lost.

Every single one of my plans was forgotten as I followed him through the VIP section, raging with jealousy as I watched the gorgeous member of staff put his hands on what was mine.

The guy caught my glare, smirking before he disappeared into the shadows, leaving me alone with Jordan for the first time since the island.

Stepping right up to him, I met his gaze. His body was solid against mine, and I could feel his erection against my thigh. My own cock was pressing against my trousers, hard for him, but I had to ignore the effect he had on me. We were in public, and nothing could happen between us.

Even knowing the danger we were in, I found myself placing my hand on the wall, the beat of the music thrumming against my palm as I angled my head forwards and breathed him in. "You smell so fucking good."

He shuddered against me, his chest rising and falling rapidly. Fuck. I wanted to taste him so badly, but I couldn't. I lifted my head. "What are you doing here in the dark? What were you doing with that dancer?"

I winced at the bite in my tone. I had no right to question him like a jealous boyfriend.

Jordan's lips curved into a wry smile. "Apparently, I was blatantly eye fucking you. JJ brought me over here before anyone could notice."

My brows rose, and I tried to bite back my own smile, without success. "Is that so?"

"No need to sound so happy about it." He scowled at me, and the need to kiss that scowl from his lips was like a physical ache.

Taking my hand off the wall, I stepped back, putting some much-needed distance between us before I did something we'd both regret. Rubbing my hand over my face, I shook my head. "I can't think straight around you."

He smirked. "Yeah, I know."

I laughed, some of my tension easing. "Come on. Let's get back to the others before they notice we're missing."

"Wait." Curling his fingers around my bicep, he held me in place. "Happy birthday. I got you a present."

He pressed something into my hands, and I glanced down. "What's this?"

A shy, sweet smile curved over his lips. "It's nothing,

really. Just a key ring from the airport. I didn't think...I didn't know if anything more would be appropriate."

I examined the key ring—a silver palm tree—and then slid it into my pocket. The fact he'd given me anything at all was completely unexpected, and even though it was a cheap trinket, I knew what it meant.

It was a reminder of our time together on the island.

Swallowing hard, I met his gaze again. "Thank you. How are you doing?"

He shrugged. "Okay. You? Are you sleeping any better?"

"Getting there." I found myself leaning in again. I wanted to kiss him, to feel his lips on mine. I couldn't even remember what it was like to not want him. How had we ever hated each other so much?

"Theo!"

We both spun around at the shout to our left, exchanging wide-eyed glances as we saw Reuben waving at us.

I turned towards the booth, but Jordan placed a hand on my arm. Dipping his head to my ear, he spoke softly.

"Look. I know it...it's your birthday, and I have no right to say anything anyway. But if you're gonna go home with someone tonight, please can you wait until I've left?"

What? Go home with someone? "I'm staying in a hotel."

"Yeah." He twisted away from me. "Okay. Have a good night. Happy birthday."

Before I could clarify that I only meant that I was staying in a hotel and I had no plans of taking anyone back with me, he was gone.

An hour into the celebrations, and the night had taken a turn for the worse. After obligatory birthday shots and selfies—suggested by Jordan, of course—my well-meaning friends, knowing nothing of Jordan's and my situation, had invited several women to join us. Beautiful women. Grant and Ainsley, the two of my teammates who weren't single, were alternating between dancing in front of the glass balustrade of the VIP area, which looked down onto the main club dance floor, and playing some convoluted drinking game with Lars, Reuben, and some of the women. I had no desire to participate because I needed to keep my wits about me.

A hot spike of jealousy and hurt lanced through me as across the booth, one of the girls slid towards Jordan and then cuddled up to him, almost in his lap. Clenching my jaw, I gripped my glass so tightly I wouldn't have been surprised if it had shattered. I couldn't look away. I needed to look away.

Jordan dipped his head, saying something into her ear, and then flashed her an easy smile. He slid out of the booth, walking over to the glass balustrade. Leaning his forearms on the edge, he stared down over the dance floor. His sleeves were rolled up, and during the time we'd been here, he'd undone four of the buttons of his shirt, giving me a tantalising view of his smooth, tanned skin.

I mumbled an excuse to the woman on my left that I'd barely spoken two words to, sliding past her and out of the booth, joining my teammate.

"She's pretty."

His gaze remained on the people dancing below us. "Very. She invited me for a threesome with her friend."

The jealousy and pain I'd felt earlier was insignificant compared to the hot wave that came crashing over me at his words. I moistened my lips, managing to croak out a single word. "Oh."

"I turned her down."

My heart stuttered. "Why?"

"Why haven't you spoken to the girl you were sitting next to? She's been trying to get your attention all evening. From what I've heard, she's just your type."

"Fuck, Jordan." I closed my eyes.

"We agreed that what happened between us was over once we left the island. We should be trying to move on." His tone was flat, but when I opened my eyes again and glanced over at him, I could see the muscle ticking in his jaw, the way his brows were pulled together, his body stiff and tense.

"We did, and we should."

At my words, he sucked in a shaky breath, biting down on his lip.

I moved closer so the fabric of my shirt was brushing against his. "We should," I repeated. "But not tonight."

Finally, he looked at me.

"Not tonight," he said.

THIRTY-TWO

JORDAN

Lifting my hand, I knocked at the hotel room door. This was reckless and irresponsible of me. If any of the hotel staff or guests caught me going into Theo's room… That was how rumours started, wasn't it? Although I was fairly sure that the speculation would be more along the lines of me challenging him to a fight or something, given our previous press coverage. There was no way anyone would guess that I was here to—

The door flew open, and I pushed inside, slamming it shut behind me. When I turned to face Theo, he had his arms folded across his chest, and his brow was raised in that haughty way that made me want to crack his cool demeanour.

"What are you doing here, Jordan? We shouldn't be doing this."

"I know. I'm not here for that. I…I wanted to wish you a happy birthday."

He sighed. "You already did that in the club. You can't be here, as much as I want you to be."

I held out the small box I'd been concealing behind my

back. "I have birthday cake. Fresh from the hotel kitchen. Come on, Theo. Let me celebrate with you. We can behave. We're professional athletes. We have willpower."

"I'm not sure I have much willpower when it comes to you," he muttered but turned on his heel, heading over to the small seating area in front of the window, the London skyline stretched out before us, glittering in the night. When we were both seated on chairs perpendicular to one another, I opened the box, taking out the two salted caramel cupcakes I'd managed to procure downstairs with the help of an autograph for the chef. Being a semi-famous footballer had its perks.

I definitely didn't watch the way Theo's throat worked as he swallowed, and he definitely didn't watch me licking caramel buttercream from my fingers. It was all perfectly innocent, just two friends alone in a room together. Two friends who were definitely not angling their bodies closer, staring at each other's mouths like they wanted to kiss...

Fuck. I abruptly leaned back in my seat, sending it wobbling onto two legs, almost tipping it over. When I'd recovered from my near-death experience, I cleared my throat. "So, uh. Did you have a good birthday?"

The atmosphere instantly changed as Theo's mouth twisted. "My parents didn't wish me a happy birthday. I suppose...I told you we were more or less estranged. I shouldn't have been expecting to hear from them." His voice grew quiet, laced with hurt. "There was a part of me that hoped... Never mind."

All thoughts of keeping my distance were gone as I flew out of my chair, pulling him upright and wrapping my arms around him. "They're fucking stupid if they can't see how amazing you are, Theo. They don't deserve a second of your time."

His arms came around me, and he buried his face in the crook of my neck with a sigh. "Thanks. I know, or I know that should be the case. It's something I've been working on in therapy. But it still doesn't stop it hurting when they don't even acknowledge my birthday."

I kissed the side of his head. "I know, baby. But I'll be here to tell you just how fucking incredible you are, okay?" I paused. "Not too often, though. We don't want you to get even more arrogant than you already are."

"Brat," he said, lifting his head to grin at me. "You're the arrogant, cocky one."

"Takes one to know one." I grinned back at him.

"Jordan." His smile disappeared.

"Theo." Had his face always been this close to mine?

At the same time, we both sprang apart, clearing our throats. Throwing myself back into my chair, I noticed Theo discreetly adjusting himself before he began to pace the room. I pulled my phone from my pocket in an attempt to distract myself from my own inconvenient boner, scrolling through the photos I'd taken in the club earlier.

"Theo?"

"Yeah?" The little rasp in his voice was so fucking sexy.

For fuck's sake. My body and my brain were both betraying me, and I was trying so hard to be on my best behaviour.

"Uh, do you mind if I post this?" I held up my phone so he could see the screen. He stopped his pacing, leaning down to view the image.

"You want to post a photo with me in it?"

Why did he sound so surprised? Probably because I'd never posted a photo of the two of us before. Not that it was a photo of the two of us—Grant, Reuben, and Ainsley were all in the picture. But this would be the first time I'd ever shared an image of him to my social media.

"Yeah, if you don't mind."

He shrugged casually, but there was a small, pleased smile on his face, and it made me feel warm inside. "If you want to."

"I do." In case he changed his mind, I quickly shared the image, captioning it "Happy birthday @theolewin_official" and tagged him and our teammates. "It's done."

"Thank you. For..." He shook his head, leaving the sentence unfinished. "I can't put it into words."

My gaze fixed on his gorgeous face, and my heart skipped a beat.

"Okay." I climbed to my feet, pocketing my phone. "You know how I said we had willpower? Mine's running out, so I'm gonna go back to my own room. Unless...unless you want me to stay."

"You know I want you to stay," he said in a low voice. "But we can't do this."

"I know." Forcing my feet to move, I backed away from him, towards the door. My fingers closed around the handle. "Happy birthday, Theo."

"Thanks. Goodnight, Jordan."

I opened the door. "Night."

It took every bit of my remaining willpower to close the door behind me and walk away.

THIRTY-THREE

JORDAN

"Thanks for meeting me today. I know you've been busy."

"Never too busy for you." Rory smiled at me over the top of his laptop screen. "What's up? Nothing that's going to give me grey hairs, I hope. Your conduct has been exemplary lately."

He was right. It had. The new season was underway, and so far, we'd won three games and drawn one. I'd managed to keep out of the headlines and had made a point of posting more team photos to my social media. They were mostly behind-the-scenes pictures from our training sessions or images of me hanging out with my teammates, but I made sure that a significant portion of them included Theo. Everyone needed to know that we were now friends.

"It's not to do with my conduct, but it might give you grey hairs." I threw out the words flippantly, but although I tried to stop my feelings from showing, I was terrified beyond belief. It was killing me to keep everything inside, though, and after a long video call with Dr. Weaver, I'd decided that I wanted someone in my life to confide in.

Someone who was close to me, who I was eighty to ninety percent sure wouldn't judge me.

Closing his laptop, Rory gave me his full attention. "I'm listening."

"So…uh…I'm bi. Bisexual."

Shock flashed in his eyes, but to his credit, he kept a neutral expression on his face. "Alright," he said carefully. "What do you need from me?"

"I—I don't know." Fuck, my hands were shaking, and now my voice was giving me away. "I need—I need—"

"Breathe, Jordan." Rory pushed away from his desk and came around to the front. He crouched down next to me, clasping my arm. "It's going to be okay."

"Okay." I did as instructed, sucking in a deep breath and then another. "Okay," I said again more calmly. "I wanted to tell you because I'm tired of keeping it all inside. I'm not… It probably wouldn't be a good idea for me to come out publicly, would it? I think I might want to, but I don't want to cause any more problems for Glevum, and I don't want people to hate me."

"Oh, Jordan." Rubbing his hand across his jaw, he sighed. "That's not a decision I can make for you. There's some precedent in some of the other leagues, but if you were to make a statement as a Premier League player, we'd need to prepare for the fallout. The media, the fans, other players and staff members, the sponsors. You've already been making headlines, and this… I'd do what I could for you, of course, but I can't protect you from everything."

He wasn't saying anything to me that I didn't already know, but my heart sank anyway. Why did it have to be so fucking hard? It shouldn't matter who you wanted to love.

Not that love was part of the equation. This was about the fact that I'd discovered this new side of me, and

I didn't want to hide it away. I knew there were plenty of good reasons to keep it to myself, especially being a professional sportsperson, but at the same time, I knew that keeping it hidden wasn't something I could personally do. But how far I wanted to take it, how many people I wanted to know…that was the part I was unsure about.

"I know. I've already thought about that. I don't want to make things harder, but at the same time, maybe it would be good if I did make a public statement. At least I wouldn't have to hide if, uh, if I wanted to be with a man in the future or something. And what if there are other people like me? Wouldn't it be good for them to know they're not alone?"

Rory stared at me for a long moment, and then he gave my arm a reassuring squeeze. "How about you take some time to think about what you want, weigh up the pros and cons. I can discreetly gather some information on what the process of coming out publicly might look like, and we can take it from there. Perhaps we could put some feelers out with Harvey. Get his opinion on things. He's your manager—a lot of the responsibility will fall on his shoulders should you choose to take this path."

"Okay, yeah. That sounds like a good plan." I attempted a shaky smile. "Fuck, this is the scariest thing I've ever done."

"I'm proud of you, Jord. Thank you for telling me." Rory climbed to his feet. "I've always got your back, I promise. We'll get through this. You're not alone."

"I know. Thanks." When he returned to his seat, I leaned back in my chair, some of the weight lifting from my shoulders. Now that I'd shared my bisexuality with him and he'd given me his support, I could breathe easier. "There was one other thing I wanted to talk to you about.

Don't worry, it's nothing big. I just have a few ideas about how we can make your office more environmentally friendly."

Rory groaned. "If this is about me printing everything, I've already explained that to you."

I ignored his comment for now, but we'd be revisiting that argument again sometime because the man was single-handedly keeping printer paper companies in business. "First of all, you need some plants in here. You really need to think about the quality of the air you're breathing in."

"How nice of you to be so concerned for my lungs," he said dryly. "Go on, then. What else?"

"Have you thought about setting up a composting station in here?"

"No, Jordan, I have not thought about setting up a composting station."

I grinned at him. "Don't worry, I'll get it all sorted out for you."

He lowered his head to his desk with another groan. "I don't get paid enough for this."

Standing outside the red-brick terraced house that had been my childhood home, I took a deep breath, clasping the envelope in my trembling hand. All I had to do was push it through the letterbox, and then I could go.

Lifting the metal flap, I pushed the envelope through the slot and backed down the front path.

I wasn't quick enough. The door swung open, revealing my dad. Everyone said he looked like an older version of me, but he was broader and taller than I was, with a lined face, silvery hair and beard, and blue eyes rather than grey.

"Alright, Jord? What you doing hanging around on the doorstep? Come in. I was just about to make a cuppa."

"Uh, yeah, okay. I guess I've got time for one." I crossed my fingers that he didn't see the envelope lying on the hallway carpet.

Unfortunately, my luck had run out because he swiped it from the floor. "What's this?"

My mouth was dry. I cleared my throat. "Don't open it until I'm gone."

His brows lifted, but he just shook his head, turning in the direction of the kitchen. I followed him down the hallway, casting around for a subject that would keep his attention from the letter.

"Are you sure you don't want to move out of here?" Taking a seat at the kitchen table—the same dented and scratched pine one that had been here all my life—I glanced up at him. "You know I can help."

"I've told you already, I'm happy here. I've got my mates down the road, the local pub, and now they've built that new Tesco, I don't even need to drive anywhere for food."

Stubborn bastard. I'd offered to buy him a new place when I'd received my signing bonus and again at the beginning of the new season. Both times, he'd shut me down straight away, insisting that he would never move.

"Fine." I sighed. "What about a new car? Yours is more rust than metal at this point. I could get you a really nice hybrid."

"Those electric cars are more hassle than they're worth. Two Jugs John says you can't charge 'em anywhere."

"Two Jugs John knows nothing," I stated. My dad shouldn't be taking advice from a man who got his nickname from downing two giant jugs of snakebite, one after the other, and then got so drunk he trashed the local pub, causing hundreds of pounds' worth of damage. "There's three charging points at the new Tesco, and anyway, I'm talking about a hybrid that charges itself. You still have to put petrol in it."

"I suppose that might be okay," he allowed, and I caught the amused smile he was trying to hold back. Rolling my eyes at him, I folded my arms on the tabletop. I knew he was trying to wind me up, and it was working, damn him.

"It's a deal. It can be your birthday present. I'll even let you choose the make and model."

"From your pre-approved list?"

"Obviously."

We grinned at each other, and then he turned away to pull mugs from the cupboard, dropping teabags inside them.

While he was busy making the tea, I took the chance to pull up my group chat. Some of my teammates were coming over to my house tonight to play poker. I'd purposely organised it because I knew I wouldn't want to be alone with my thoughts after today, and my friends would provide a helpful distraction.

I was in the middle of replying to Reuben, telling him to bring Chilli Heatwave Doritos because they were the only acceptable savoury poker snack, in my opinion, when I heard a sound that filled me with horror.

The rip of an envelope being opened.

My blood turned to ice.

"Jord...what's this?" My dad spoke slowly.

Oh, fuck. My phone dropped to the table as I buried my head in my arms. "I told you not to open it until I was gone."

The blood was rushing in my ears, but over it, I heard the crinkle of paper, my dad muttering something under his breath, and then the clinking of a teaspoon against ceramic.

There was a soft thud in front of me. My dad cleared his throat. "Drink your tea, son."

Gritting my teeth, I lifted my head from my arms. To begin with, I only focused on my mug, a curl of steam coming from the top.

When I dared to raise my eyes to my dad, he was staring down at his own mug.

"It's always been you and me. Walking you to school in the mornings before I had to be on the building site, up until you started senior school. Our weekends at Barnwood Park, cheering Glevum on. Going to the chippy on the way home." He exhaled heavily. "I've always been so proud of you, you know. When you got a place at the youth academy, I told everyone. Everyone at work. All the lads at the pub. Then you got the contract with Forest Green Rovers. It hit me then."

Picking up his mug, he sipped his tea. I followed suit, managing to gulp down some of the soothing liquid, despite my trembling hands and tightness in my throat.

"You were my son, but you were suddenly an adult. You had a career doing something you loved, something you were passionate about. Something that so few of us get to experience. You always lit up when you played football, Jord. It was clear to me that this was your path."

His voice cracked, and I watched the stoic man I knew as my dad cast around for words. "Let me make one thing clear. This letter. I don't care who or what you're into. The only thing that matters to me is that you keep playing football for as long as you can, because that—that lights you up like nothing else."

I couldn't breathe. "You...you don't care if I'm into men as well as women?" I managed to choke out.

His eyes met mine, and he gave a small shake of his

head. "Not gonna lie, it'll be an adjustment for me. It's just...you've never given me any indication before, but that doesn't mean I don't support you. Just give me a minute to get my head around it all, okay?"

"Okay."

"Drink your tea," he commanded, and I lifted my mug to my lips.

THIRTY-FOUR

THEO

"I'll be back." I left Grant shuffling the deck of cards while Ainsley, Lars, and Reuben continued their ongoing debate about their favourite flavour of crisps, and followed Jordan into his kitchen. He'd been quiet tonight, and I was worried. He hadn't even made any of his usual teasing remarks to me. We'd settled into a friendship, and as his friend, I was concerned for him.

Friendship. I was getting good at lying to myself. What I felt for him wasn't friendship. It was far, far more than that, but we'd made an agreement, and I was doing everything in my power to stick to it. It was easier when other people were around, of course, but in the evenings, when we were lying on our respective beds and texting each other about anything and everything, I missed him with a physical ache.

My teammate was standing with his back to me, his hands braced on the counter, his head bowed and his posture radiating tension. Something was wrong, and I couldn't bear to see him like this. Even though I knew that I shouldn't, I came up behind him, wrapping my arms around his waist. "Jordan."

He jumped but then sighed, melting into me. I pressed my lips to the side of his head. "What's the matter, baby?"

His hands flexed on the counter. "You can't call me that when we're not together."

He was right. I'd said it unthinkingly. It felt natural. Right. Fuck, I was making things so much harder. "I'm sorry. What's wrong?"

"You shouldn't be doing this. Any one of our friends could walk in here and see us."

"Tell me to go and I will."

"I don't want you to go." Letting go of the counter, he turned in my embrace, wrapping his arms around me and resting his head on my shoulder. "Nothing's wrong, really. It's been an emotionally draining day, I guess." He suddenly stiffened, a gasp flying from his mouth, and tore himself out of my hold.

Grant stood in the doorway, watching us. His face betrayed nothing, but all I could think of was the fact that he'd just seen two of his teammates wrapped up in each other, in a completely out-of-character display.

Fuck.

"It's, uh, it's not—" Jordan was lost for words for a minute, and then he gathered himself, squaring his shoulders and taking a deep breath. "Grant. Can I talk to you for a minute?" He shot me a pleading look, and I nodded, heading towards the doorway, brushing past Grant, who stood aside to let me leave. I couldn't bring myself to go far, though, in case Jordan needed me, and so I leaned against the wall next to the kitchen door, waiting.

From my vantage point, I could hear Jordan's words when he began to speak. "I wanted to talk to you. About what you saw just then. I've had a bit of a, uh, a draining day, and Theo was comforting me."

"It's none of my business," Grant responded.

"Yeah, okay. But the reason I've had a draining day kind of is your business."

I heard the squeak of Grant's trainers on the kitchen tiles, and when he spoke again, his voice was soft. "What's up, man?"

"You're my captain, and so I—I wanted to tell you." Jordan exhaled sharply. "I'm bi. I hope—I hope it doesn't change anything. It's not gonna affect my ability to play, and I'm not sure if I'll go public or whatever, but I wanted you to know."

Fucking hell. Of all the things he could have said, I'd never imagined he'd come out. I'd thought...I'd thought it was a case of keeping that side of him on the island.

Then again, why shouldn't he tell people if he wanted to?

Why shouldn't you tell people, Theo?

"You know...I did wonder." Grant's voice was thoughtful. "I thought you might have had a bit of a thing for Theo last season."

"You *what*? I hated him!" The indignation in Jordan's tone made me smile before Grant's words sunk in. Jordan and I had hated each other before. How could he have seen things that weren't there?

"No one has such strong reactions to another person unless there are deep feelings there." There was a dull thud, a muffled curse, and then a bark of laughter from Grant. "Alright, alright, no need to hit me."

"Whatever. I hated him, and now he's my friend. But that's irrelevant right now. I just want to know if it's gonna cause any problems for you." Jordan gave a defeated sigh. "I don't want to be a problem."

"Okay. Me, personally? No problems, man. You've got

my support, one hundred percent. I can't speak for the rest of the team, though. If you do go public, then...yeah. There could be issues." Grant swore under his breath. "Don't let that stop you, though. Fuck it. Fuck whoever has a problem with it."

"Thanks." That one word was so soft and vulnerable that it broke me. I clenched my fists at my sides, forcing myself to stay where I was instead of going to him like every part of me wanted to.

"Who else knows?"

"I told my agent and my dad today. And now you. I want to tell Harvey, but I thought I should tell you first."

"Alright. Let me know what you need. I'll come with you when you tell Harvey if you want."

"Okay. Thanks. I think...fuck it. I'm gonna tell the others right now." Jordan came barrelling past me into the lounge, skidding to a halt in front of Ainsley, Lars, and Reuben. "I'm bi. Uh. Bisexual."

There was a stunned silence, during which the guys exchanged glances. From behind me, Grant cleared his throat, stepping into the room. "Does anyone have a problem with that?"

The three of them shook their heads. Then Reuben slowly raised his hand.

Grant rolled his eyes. "What? You don't have to raise your hand to talk. We're not in school."

"I just wanted to know if that means we can put up a rainbow flag in the dressing room. It needs some colour."

"Isn't there a bi flag?" Lars spoke up.

"I'll google it." Ainsley's fingers flew over his phone screen. "Nah, bro. We can't have that! Pink, purple, and blue. That's gonna clash with our team colours."

Jordan stared at me, wide-eyed, and I shrugged. I had no idea what was happening right now.

"Yeah, no, I vote for the rainbow one." Reuben gave a decisive nod.

"Forget the flag. Are you guys seriously okay with this?" Jordan's voice was firm, but I noticed his hands were trembling.

"'Course we are." Climbing to his feet, Reuben clapped him on the back. "You telling the rest of the team?"

"I haven't decided yet."

"If Walker gives you shit, I will fuck him up," he promised darkly.

"Uh, thanks."

"*I'll* deal with anyone who gives Jordan any shit," Grant said, shooting Reuben a warning look. "Not you."

Reuben grinned. "If he trips and falls onto my fist, it's not my fault. Just saying."

"Behave." Lars cuffed Reuben on the arm and then turned to Jordan. "We will support you."

The words came tumbling out of me, a torrent that I couldn't hold back. If I didn't say it now, would I ever have the courage?

"While we're all here, I am, too."

Everyone's gazes swung to me. I could feel my face heating, but I kept up my cool, calm façade. I didn't dare to look at Jordan. But he was so fucking brave; how could I stay quiet, knowing what I knew about him? About myself?

"You're bi? *You?*" Ainsley gaped at me, and I frowned at him.

"Why is that any more surprising than Jordan being bi?"

"Iuh." He tapped his lips. "I dunno, actually."

Grant raised his brows at me, surprise clear on his face.

Stepping over to me, he squeezed my arm. "You've got my support, too," he said in a low voice.

"I appreciate it."

Releasing my arm, he cleared his throat. "Alright. Before we get back to our poker game, does anyone else have anything they want to share?"

Reuben raised his hand again. "Me. When I was sixteen, I broke into—"

"No." Grant muffled the rest of Reuben's words with his palm. "No confessing of crimes. If none of you have anything important to share, I suggest we get back to the game."

As soon as I sat down, after receiving words of encouragement and support, my hands began to shake as what I'd just done hit me. My friends knew I was bi. They accepted me. My own family hadn't accepted me for who I was, and yet these guys had, without question.

For the first time, I felt as if I truly belonged.

When everyone had left, I hung back. As soon as the door had closed behind Grant, Jordan was there, standing right in front of me. "Fuck. We just did that," he breathed.

"Yeah. We did." I still couldn't believe it.

Moving back, he gave me a searching look. "Did you plan on telling them?"

I shook my head. "No, but you were being so brave and owning it. How could I hide the truth?"

"Do your parents know? I told Rory and my dad today."

"No. Why should I tell them? They don't accept me for who I am. I don't want to give them more excuses to tear me down. I owe them nothing."

"Good." He leaned forwards, placing a kiss to the tip of my nose, and then instantly recoiled. "*Shit*. Sorry. Sometimes I forget we're not on the island anymore."

"Me too. Sometimes I just want—" My mouth brushed over his. "—to kiss you," I finished, sliding my lips against his in a soft, slow caress.

"Don't do this to me. I told you before that my willpower was running out." Jordan backed me up against his front door, kissing me again. "It's so fucking hard to treat you like everyone else after all we've been through. I need to get over you."

"I know. Me too. If anyone found out—" My words were cut off by his thigh sliding between mine, his hands going down to my ass and yanking me closer.

"Theo. Fuck." He kissed down my throat as my head fell back against the door, a groan falling from my lips.

The doorbell rang.

Jordan screeched into my neck as my body jerked at the sudden loud noise.

"Fucking hell." Tearing himself away from me, he rubbed his hand over his jaw, then dragged his hand through his hair. "Fuck."

The doorbell rang again. My heart pounding, I opened it because Jordan was making no move to.

Grant stood on the step. His gaze landed on me and then flicked to Jordan.

His eyes widened.

"Forgot my phone," he said eventually. I stood aside to let him in. My heart was racing, and across from me, Jordan looked as if he was about to pass out.

When he returned to the door, Grant stared between us again, and then he sighed. "Don't look so worried. I didn't see anything." He paused. "Unless there's something else you want to share."

"Nope. Nothing at all. Bye, Grant. Bye, Theo. See you at training." Jordan pushed us both through the door. "Bye." He shut it in our faces.

I glanced over at Grant, who was smirking. When he caught my eye, he laughed. "You two are going to cause us so much trouble. Good job I like you both." He strode over to his SUV, whistling.

I slumped against my Aston Martin with a groan, closing my eyes.

Tonight, we'd set things in motion that couldn't be stopped. I just hoped that we were prepared for the fallout.

A thought hit me then. If this had happened last season, I would have been relying on sleeping pills to get me through the night. But now, I was going to drive home, do my bedtime ritual—warm shower, cup of herbal tea, and a book—and then fall asleep without the use of artificial aids.

Jordan's signing to my football team had set off a chain of events that I could never have imagined, but there was one thing I couldn't deny.

My life was far better now.

THIRTY-FIVE

JORDAN

"You were fucking amazing!" Reuben grabbed me around the waist, spinning me. "That goal!"

"Put me down." I smacked him on the back, and he laughed, depositing me on the floor. My teammates surrounded us, full of congratulations for me scoring the only goal of the match—the goal that had led to us beating Liverpool FC, 1-0. We'd gone into the game as the underdogs, playing at Liverpool's iconic Anfield stadium, packed with thousands of home fans to our tiny fan contingent of twelve hundred—which included my dad and five of his mates. None of us had been expecting a win, and yet, somehow, we'd done it, and I'd scored the only goal, booting it between two of their defenders and into the back of the net before the goalie could reach it.

I was so high I felt like I was floating on air. This win had sealed our position of seventh in the league, and getting into Europe was no longer just a dream—it was within our grasp.

From the other side of the away team dressing room,

Theo caught my eye. *Good job*, he mouthed, and my heart skipped a beat.

I looked at him then. Really looked at him. His hair was all mussed from running around the pitch for ninety-four minutes, he was sweating and breathless, and there were grass stains on his football shirt.

It had been months since we'd been together on the island, but in that moment, I knew that there was no getting over him.

I wanted him.

Only him.

Theo Lewin. My rival. My teammate. My friend. The man who gave me fucking butterflies and made my heart race.

There was no one else for me.

But it wasn't only my decision. Two high-profile football players in a relationship would be a huge deal. Even if I got lucky and Theo somehow felt the same, even if he was prepared to take the risk and be with me, it would affect not only us but so many other people.

Sometimes, I wished life could be simple. Boy meets boy. They get together. They live happily ever after. The end.

That wasn't my reality.

Taking a seat on one of the benches, I began to unlace my football boots. When I glanced up, Theo was watching me, an intense, serious look on his face. I had no idea what his problem was, but he needed to stop looking at me like that because I was going to get a boner, and then everyone would notice.

I dropped my gaze back to my boots, but I couldn't help shooting Theo another quick glance. He was still watching me, unsmiling.

I didn't know what that expression on his face meant, but I wanted to find out.

A hand shot out and grabbed my arm. I yelped as I was yanked through a doorway into a darkened room, the only light coming from the bottom corner of a partially opened blind. A slam sounded behind me, and then someone's palm clamped down over my mouth as I was manhandled onto a tabletop.

A hard, heavy body held me in place as the hand covering my mouth lowered to curl around my throat. "Do you have any fucking idea?"

That voice.

"About what?" I tried to arch upwards, but I was pinned in place. I lifted my hand, gripping his throat, his pulse wild beneath my hold, matching my own.

Hot breath skimmed across my lips. "How hard it's been to forget you. How I tried to move on, to tell myself that what happened between us was only a holiday fling. Then you kept turning up, kept chipping away at my defences. We're supposed to be friends, but it feels impossible. Watching you on the pitch today...fuck, Jordan. You were in your element, and I realised something. Seeing the way you control the ball turns me on." The last words were ground out, like he resented me for making him feel this way.

"Yeah? Well, I never stopped wanting you, Theo." I squeezed his throat, feeling him swallow around my grip. "I thought I could forget everything that happened on the island, but guess what? Being your friend is a fucking lost cause because you still make my fucking dick hard."

"*Jordan.*"

"Fucking shut up." I was irrationally angry at him, and I had no reason to be. He hadn't led me on, any more than I'd led him on. "Guess what's worse than that? You're the only person that really knows me. Half the shit I told you, I've never told anyone else. You're in my fucking head and in my heart."

His mouth landed on mine, hard and vicious, a biting punishment as he pressed his body down into mine. "We agreed this would stay on the island. This was only a holiday fling."

"Yeah, I know. Except it wasn't, was it?" I twisted my body, sending him flying onto the desk. I landed on top of him, bracing myself to keep him in place.

"Fuck you, Jordan." Theo struggled beneath me, bucking me off, sending me staggering backwards. He came for me, slamming me up against the wall. Our lips met, wild and so fucking hungry, our moans combining, his tongue stroking against mine.

"Fucking...want...you," I panted, yanking his joggers down. He groaned into my mouth, tugging mine down, too, and then our bare cocks were against each other, and it was *so fucking good*.

He spun me, and I fell backwards, landing on the table with a thud. He came with me, and I wrapped my legs around him to hold him in place, my hips arching upwards, the drag of his cock against mine a fucking delicious friction that had me tugging his head down to mine, my mouth connecting with his throat, feeling his pulse hammering against my lips as I sunk my teeth into his skin.

I thrust up as he ground his hips down, both of us reduced to grunts and pants, chasing our release.

When I came, it felt as if I was on fire. My entire body

jerked, my cock pulsing between us as the sensations stole the breath from my lungs. I was completely overstimulated by the time Theo came, and I moaned, the pleasure-pain coursing through me as I collapsed back onto the smooth, solid surface of the table.

"I think I need therapy to get over you," I whispered breathlessly, my arms closing around him, holding him in place.

"You said it wasn't a holiday fling." Panting hard, he dropped his head to my shoulder. "Do you—"

"What the fuck!" A slice of bright light shattered the darkness. My head shot up, and I blinked rapidly, allowing my eyes to adjust. When I saw the figure silhouetted in the doorway, I groaned.

"Hi, Reuben."

"My eyes! I can't unsee that!"

The door slammed shut.

"I guess he knows about us." I stroked my hand down Theo's back. It was so good to be able to touch him properly after abstaining for so long.

"It seems that way." Theo placed a kiss to the hollow of my throat. He sounded remarkably unconcerned for someone who'd been discovered in a compromising position with his teammate.

"You're not bothered?"

"I am, but...Jordan. Everything I said was true."

The shake in his voice made me raise my head, meeting his gaze. "It was true for me, too."

His hand reached out, his fingers tracing across my jaw. "I can't lie to myself any longer. I thought that when we returned to our normal lives, this would cease to be an issue. For months, I've tried."

"Me too. I thought it would go away. I didn't…I didn't know you felt the same way."

His fingers closed around my jaw, tilting my head up so our lips were aligned. "I do."

"So what do you want to do about it? Do you want us to be together? Because I want that, so fucking badly."

"Yes," he said. "Yes. I want you to be mine."

THIRTY-SIX

THEO

Jordan lay sprawled across his sofa, his head in my lap while I absentmindedly threaded my fingers through his hair, my other hand clutching my phone. He brought his hand up to stroke over my jaw. "You need a shave."

I raised a brow. "Do I? I thought you liked my stubble."

"I do...it looks fucking hot. But you're giving me stubble rash. People are gonna notice."

"How many people are looking between your legs?"

"Fuck off." He flicked at the underside of my chin. "You know I don't mean there. I mean on my face."

"Stop that, brat." I grabbed his hand, pulling it away from my face. "Why do you keep choosing violence?"

Tugging his hand from my grip, he gave me a soft, sweet smile. "I'm only giving you what you deserve."

"I'll give you what you fucking deserve if you don't behave."

"Ha. I'd like to see you try." Grinning up at me, he placed his hand back on my jaw. "Seriously, though, I like you however much stubble you do or don't have. You're hotter than the sun, either way."

"I suppose you're not too bad to look at, either."

"My 1.1 million followers definitely agree." His smile dropped. "Theo? Speaking of people noticing my stubble rash, what are we gonna do about Reuben? Should we say something to him?"

Cupping his chin, which did not show even a hint of stubble rash, I curled my body over so I could press a kiss to the tip of his nose. "Mmm. I've been thinking about that." I resumed stroking through his hair, the movements calming me. "Grant has his suspicions, too. I think I'd like to tell them, if you're okay with that."

"Are you sure you want to?" Jordan gave me a searching look. "I...I'm good with our friends knowing. They wouldn't say anything. But if you're not ready or whatever, I'm happy to keep things between us. As long as we get to be together, I don't care who does or doesn't know. As far as the rest of the world is concerned, we're best friends. They don't need to know what happens behind closed doors."

"I'm sure. Reuben saw us, and like I said, we both know that Grant has his suspicions. I trust them. Ainsley and Lars, too."

"Yeah." He smiled up at me. "Okay. How do you want to do this? Drop it in the group chat? Or tell them in person?"

Lifting my phone, I scrolled to our group chat. "Some things are easier to say over text."

Jordan grabbed his own phone. "Let's do this."

ME:

@Grant @Ainsley @Lars @Reuben we have something important to tell you in confidence

> JORDAN:
> It HAS to stay between us

Ainsley immediately sent a string of eyeball emojis, making Jordan laugh.

> REUBEN:
> You know you can trust us
>
> GRANT:
> We've got your backs and we'd never betray your confidence
>
> AINSLEY:
> Why do I feel like everyone knows something I don't? Unfair
>
> LARS:
> @Ainsley I don't know @Theo @Jordan we are here for you

I exhaled sharply. "Okay. This is it." My hand shook as I tapped out the message, but Jordan was right there, his head a warm weight on my thighs, his hand reaching up to gently stroke up my side, keeping me grounded.

> ME:
> I'm in a relationship with @Jordan
>
> AINSLEY:
> THE FUCK? Did everyone know about this?
>
> Sorry happy for you both but FUCK ME I didn't see that coming
>
> REUBEN:
> I saw them coming. MY EYES!!!!
>
> JORDAN:
> Liar. We already came

AINSLEY:

WHAT THE FUCK IS HAPPENING! Reuben why were you watching our teammates fucking?!!! That's fucked up bro

REUBEN:

It was an accident!!! They didn't even lock the door! Guess where they were? Anfield! ANFIELD! My eyes will never recover!

GRANT:

Anfield?! I have no words. As for the two of you being in a relationship, I guessed that something was happening between you. I'm happy for you both, and you know none of us will say anything

LARS:

I can see it. You are both suited. Stubborn and hot tempered

AINSLEY:

My bro Lars speaks the truth. You two belong together

ME:

None of you have a problem with us being together?

GRANT:

NO

LARS:

Of course not

AINSLEY:

No

REUBEN:

No!

JORDAN:

Thanks everyone x

He shot me a small smile. "Okay. Now our friends know. Is there anyone else you want to tell?"

"I think I'd like to tell my agent...and Harvey, in case any rumours come out. And I think...I think I'd like to come out publicly."

Lifting his head from my legs, he sat upright on the sofa, facing me. "That's a big decision."

"I know. But I also know that you want to come out publicly, and I don't want you to have to go through that alone, knowing that I'm also bi, and not only that, you're my boyfriend."

"You shouldn't come out for me," he whispered. "You should do it for yourself."

"I know, and I am." Pulling him into me, I kissed him softly. "It's only part of the reason. I feel...like I want to do this. I want people to know who I am."

Straddling me, he wrapped his arms around my neck. "We're gonna get a lot of shit for this."

"I know. But we'll get through it. One day at a time."

"Yeah." Reaching for his phone, he scrolled through his contacts. "Okay, then. If we're doing this, we'd better make some calls."

The conference room was a hive of activity and noise. Around me, people were barking into phones, tapping furiously at laptop keyboards, and talking over one another.

"Bloody hell, it feels like we're preparing for battle or something." Jordan slipped into the seat next to me, instinctively reaching out for my hand. I slid my fingers between his, the knot of anxiety in my stomach loosening as his warm palm pressed against mine.

"I suppose we are, in a way." I glanced over at him, and he bit down on his lip.

"Any regrets?" His voice was uncertain, and I immediately wanted to reassure him.

"None, baby." I stroked over his skin with my thumb. "Believe me, I've thought about this long and hard. I'm fully prepared to see this through."

He exhaled a relieved breath. "Good. Me too."

"Alright!" Harvey slammed his fists down on the table, making both me and Jordan jump. The room instantly fell silent. "Let's get this started."

The large conference table filled up as everyone took their seats. Harvey was at the head of the table, and joining him in today's strategy session were Rory, Amir, Grant, Reuben, Ainsley, and Lars. Six people who could be counted on to support us, whatever life threw at us.

The others sitting around the table were mostly unknown to me, although I was aware of who they were. Members of our PR and legal teams, two people from the Professional Footballers' Association, aka the PFA, and Daniel Dawson, the owner of Glevum FC. It was an intimidating combination of people, and I was so glad I didn't have to face this alone.

"PR have drawn up a plan." Harvey met my eyes, then Jordan's. "None of this is set in stone, and I want you to speak up if there's something you don't agree with. This affects us all, but you two are at the centre. You get the final say."

He clicked his mouse, and the large screen at the front of the room lit up, and then we began.

Harvey spoke about the fact that he would prefer to delay our coming out statements to the end of the season in order for the focus to remain on our performance in the league and the team's aim of getting into Europe. In addition to that, our PR team hoped that it would make it easier for us because we wouldn't have to deal with fan pressure at the most crucial time of the season. Coinciding our statements with the beginning of the summer break would give us a generous cushion of time for everything to die down before the next season began.

The two PFA members ran through the things we might experience when we made our statements, citing the homophobic abuse that we would probably have to deal with, particularly online. They assured us that they were here to provide us with day-to-day support, as well as a network of trained professionals to help us through the process.

Apparently, our social media accounts would be temporarily taken over by our PR team to help protect us from any abuse. Jordan was unhappy about this until Rory promised him that he would personally ensure that Jordan's selfies were posted regularly to his accounts.

By the time everyone had their input, over two hours had passed. But we'd come up with a plan.

Three days after the end of the football season, a pre-prepared statement would be jointly shared by Glevum FC and Jordan's social media accounts. The same statement would be sent to news outlets. The club would encourage players to reshare the statement or provide messages of support. Harvey would discuss this with the team before the statement was made, to give everyone a heads-up and to let them know that homophobia would not be tolerated, and anyone caught making homophobic remarks would face heavy penalties. In addition to the team discussion, our sponsors would be contacted in advance to give them time to prepare accordingly, should they wish to publicly comment.

A week later, my own statement would be shared. There was some disagreement about the timing—whether it was better to share both statements at once or whether we should wait even longer. Most had agreed that it would be better to wait, even as long as a full season, but there was no way on earth I would let my boyfriend go through the process of publicly coming out alone. A week was the maximum I was prepared to wait.

As for our relationship—we'd been strongly advised to keep it hidden for now. Speculation would be rife as it was, with us both being on the same team, but it was decided that we needed time for the public to get used to the idea that two Premier League footballers could be anything other than straight. We would have another meeting a few weeks into the season, when we had more of an idea of how our coming out was being handled by the media and fans.

"So that's it, then," Jordan said when everyone else had left. "There's no turning back now."

"No turning back. Only forwards. One step at a time. One day at a time." I leaned my head on his shoulder. "Whatever happens, I'm so glad we have each other."

"Me too. You don't have to go through anything hard alone anymore, Theo. You've got me now."

"I know." Whatever came next, we'd face it together.

THIRTY-SEVEN

JORDAN

Why did it always come down to the final game of the season? If we won this, we'd be home and dry. We'd finish in sixth position, and we'd earn a place in the Europa League.

Our fans were hungry for it. We were hungry for it. It wouldn't be an easy game, though. We were playing away, with a record away fan attendance. Our opponents were Chelsea, who were a much bigger team than Glevum and who were also vying for a place in the Europa League. This was the day of reckoning for both teams.

The pressure was immense, but we were ready for it. And the bonus was it was helping both me and Theo keep our minds off what was coming once the season was over.

From the first touch of the ball, I was unstoppable. All of us were. The hours and hours we'd spent strategising, poring over footage of Chelsea's games, were paying off. We went ahead when Reuben got a fucking beautiful goal from the halfway line, and although Chelsea equalised, thanks to a fumbled own goal from James Walker, we were dominating the play.

The second half kicked off, and amidst the noise from the Chelsea fans, I could hear our contingent of fans chanting for us, singing, and cheering us on, and it made me even more determined to do them proud. When Scott Gordon, one of our attacking midfielders, booted the ball to me, I saw my chance. Not wasting a second, I crossed it to Theo, who sent it into the top corner of the goal.

I ran to him, celebrating with my teammates and our fans, all of us exhilarated and caught up in the high of the moment. We were so close to achieving our place in Europe we could almost taste it.

Chelsea weren't going down without a fight, though. They got control of the ball, sending it down the other end of the pitch and into the box. Lars was ready, poised for a save, but Ainsley kicked the ball out of play before it could reach him.

With under a minute left on the clock, Chelsea had a corner kick. Players in blue swarmed our defence. We couldn't let them score, not this close to the end.

The ball sailed towards us, curving in the direction of the goal, the Chelsea players ready to help hit it home. But Grant got to it first with a powerful header, changing the ball's trajectory and sending it flying towards me.

My foot connected with the ball, and I kicked it down the pitch as hard as I could. All that mattered was getting it away from our goal.

My lungs burned as I ran, Chelsea's defenders chasing after me. Their goalie came racing out of the goal, booting it back down the other end of the pitch, but it was too late.

The ref blew his whistle, and it was all over.

We'd done it. We'd finished in sixth position in the Premier League and guaranteed ourselves a place in the Europa League next season.

This was the best moment in my career.

I spotted my dad in the crowd, going wild with his friends, jumping around and celebrating, and I laughed out loud. Reuben jumped on me, and then Ainsley jumped on him, sending us all to the grass, laughing with happiness and relief and pure fucking euphoria. Theo came running over, and I jumped to my feet, throwing my arms around him. Other players and the management team piled in, the two of us at the centre of a team hug.

"We fucking did it!" I shouted.

"Yes, we fucking did!" Theo's smile was so wide, and he looked so fucking gorgeous that I couldn't wait to get him alone for some personal celebrations.

But for now, we had some celebrating to do as a team.

We'd earned it.

I grinned down at the text from my dad. He'd gone home with the rest of the travelling fans, and the celebrations were continuing in his local pub. Two Jugs John had volunteered him to buy a round of drinks for the whole pub since his son was one of the players. Tapping out a response, I let him know that I was going to transfer some money to his bank account to cover it, and he'd better accept it. I wanted to tell him about me and Theo, too, but now wasn't the time. I'd made arrangements to go over to his house when I got back home so that I could tell him then. He knew about my upcoming statement, and he supported me, and I was pretty sure he'd be okay with me being in a relationship with one of his favourite players. I hoped. It wasn't something I wanted to hide from him.

"Okay. Done." Pocketing my phone, I turned to Theo. "Ready?"

He gave the peeling pub sign a dubious glance but shrugged. "Ready."

I opened the door for him, and we went inside. When I'd planned this, I'd tried to find a place that was in easy reach of our hotel, that served alcohol, and, most importantly, wasn't the kind of place rich footballers would be expected to hang out. So we were at a dive called the Rose and Crown, which had a rating of 3.2 on Google. Apparently, they had a local indie band called the 2Bit Princes playing tonight, which was good because it meant that most of the patrons would be focused on that rather than the people around them. Just to be on the safe side, Theo and I were both dressed down in dark hoodies and jeans, and I was wearing a backwards cap. Even if someone did recognise us, they'd hopefully just think we were lookalikes.

Taking a seat in a high-backed booth, resting my elbows on the sticky table surface, I read the poster advertising the band night while I waited for Theo's return. I'd promised him that tonight was just about the two of us, so my phone would be staying on silent in my pocket, and when he returned, he'd be getting one hundred percent of my attention.

I didn't have to wait for long. Just a couple of minutes later, Theo slid into the booth next to me and handed me one of the pints he was holding. "I think the guy helping the band set up might have recognised me. He did a double take when he saw me."

"Where is he now?" I scanned the crowd, most of them beginning to move towards the stage area where the band were doing a soundcheck.

"Not sure. He went off to the side of the stage somewhere."

The pub lights dimmed as the band began to play. "I don't think it matters. We're practically in the dark here, and no one's paying us any attention. I bet I can get away with holding your hand under the table and everything."

Theo smiled, his hand finding mine. "Yeah. I like this."

We sipped our pints as we discussed the match against Chelsea and our chances against some of Europe's top-tier teams in the Europa League. When we'd thoroughly analysed our chances and were halfway through our third pints, we began a debate about whether Marvel was superior to DC or if it just had better marketing. Conversation flowed so easily with Theo, and that was one of the reasons he was my best friend as well as my boyfriend. I could talk to him about anything and everything and never run out of things to say.

I could also stare at him all day, every day. He was so fucking hot. I was a lucky, lucky man.

By the time the band had finished playing and the bell had rung for last orders, I was so fucking happy I felt like my heart would burst.

"Jordan? Are you ready to go?" Theo looked at me with a little smile on his face, and I felt so giddy and high and warm and full of all these emotions I couldn't even contain — Oh. *Oh.*

Love.

I loved Theo. I loved him so much.

He needed to know. Right now. Even if he didn't say it back. I couldn't not tell him.

"Yeah. Let's go." I practically dragged him out of the pub, making him laugh, and the sound just made me even giddier. I was a fucking mess. I was walking on clouds.

Glancing around me, I spotted an alleyway just past a kebab shop. That would do nicely. Also, we could get kebabs afterwards. Romantic as fuck.

"Come over here a minute." I led him past the kebab shop to the alleyway entrance. He raised a brow.

"You want me to go down a dark alleyway in this part of London? We could get stabbed."

"If we survive, I might stab you with my sword later."

He smirked at me. "Now there's an offer I can't refuse."

I opened my mouth to deliver a comeback but then closed it again. This wasn't the time. I needed to be serious, to let him know that I meant every word I was about to tell him.

Pulling him into the alley, close enough to the entrance for the streetlights to illuminate our faces, I backed him up against the wall, lifting my hand to his jaw. His smile dropped as my thumb stroked across his skin, and his beautiful blue eyes studied me intently.

"Theo?"

"Yeah?"

"I—I want to tell you something, and I want you to know that I mean every word." I licked my lips and then took a deep breath. This was it. "I love you, Theo. I think I've loved you for a long time."

He stared at me in stunned disbelief, and then his hand curved around the back of my neck, yanking me into him. His voice was choked up when he replied, his lips skimming over mine. "Oh, Jordan. I love you so much. It's the same for me. I'd been falling for you for so long, and then you were mine, and I let myself fall all the way."

"Fuck. Theo. Fuck." I couldn't think, couldn't breathe. I kissed him, frantic. "My chest hurts. What I feel for you is so much. I think my heart's going to explode."

"Breathe, baby." He caressed my face, kissing me slowly and softly until I could breathe again. "I love you. I'm so happy you're mine."

"I'm so happy you're mine. You're everything to me. I want to, I don't know, carve your name into my heart or something."

"That's quite disturbing." He kissed me again.

"Yeah. Probably."

"No probably about it. Can we leave this dark alleyway now so I can get you back to the hotel and show you how much I love you?"

I grinned. "It's like you can read my mind. But we're getting celebratory kebabs first."

Neither of us noticed the figure at the bus stop on the other side of the road, holding up a phone.

THIRTY-EIGHT

THEO

When I blinked my eyes open, the first thing I registered was the head of brown hair resting on my shoulder and the arm slung around my waist. I smiled, wrapping my own arm around my sleeping boyfriend, stroking down the smooth skin of his back and pressing a kiss to his head. I fumbled for my phone to check the time, knocking over the half-empty bottle of lube that I'd left out on the side, and it dropped to the table with a loud clatter. Freezing in place, I peered down at Jordan, but he didn't stir. Good. He needed his sleep. It had been a long day yesterday and an even longer night, and both of us were sore and tired and very, very satisfied.

I blinked. And then blinked again.

Eighteen missed calls.

Quickly thumbing my phone open, I scrolled through the list. Amir, Grant, and Harvey had all tried calling me. Instead of wasting time listening to the voicemails, I hit the button to return the most recent missed call, which was from Grant, two minutes earlier.

"Grant? What's happening?"

He told me.

The hotel conference room we'd commandeered was filled with the Glevum staff and teammates who had stayed overnight in London rather than returning to Gloucestershire. The PR and legal teams had joined us via video call, along with a representative of the PFA. Rory and Amir were thankfully both in London, and their presence calmed the raging storm inside me just enough that I could breathe through it.

But it was the hardest thing I'd ever had to do. Jordan and I had planned to come out on our own terms, and now that had been ripped away from us. We had a whole fucking plan, and it had been cruelly snatched away by the anonymous asshole who thought they had the right to out us and our relationship to the world.

Whoever had taken the pictures had a clear shot of us in the alleyway, as well as out on the street. Me, laughing as Jordan pulled me out of the pub. The two of us walking along the pavement next to each other, our arms and hands brushing. Me, up against the brick wall of the alley, staring into Jordan's eyes while he cupped my cheek, our bodies pressed close together.

We might have been able to come up with something to explain the pictures, but the asshole had also posted a video. Me and Jordan, kissing, completely lost in one another, oblivious to the rest of the world.

Everything had been posted to Reddit, and it had spread like wildfire. Our PR department was already being hounded by the media, and we had to come up with a new plan right now. A new statement that would both get our original message across and condemn the actions of this person who thought they had the right to take away something that should have been ours to share.

Jordan turned to me. His eyes were red-rimmed, making them look greener than usual, and his lip was trembling. He was barely holding it together. I wasn't much better, but the overwhelming need to comfort my boyfriend overtook my own worries.

"H—how could they do that? That was ours. I—I told you I loved you." A tear spilled from his lashes, tracking down his cheek. "They stole the most special moment of my life, and for fucking what? Attention? Why would someone be so cruel? Why?"

I gave zero fucks about anyone else in this room. The love of my life was hurting, and it was tearing me apart. "Baby, come here." Pulling him into me, I wrapped my arms around him, kissing his tear away. "We're going to get through this, okay? It's you and me. We've got each other. We're strong enough to deal with whatever life throws at us."

He sniffed, giving me a tiny nod. "Promise?"

"I promise."

It was then that I noticed the room had fallen silent, and I looked up to see all eyes were on us. Fucking great. Jordan burrowed into me, and I stroked my hands up and down his back while I concentrated on breathing in and out evenly, doing everything I could to hold it together.

"This is serious between the two of you, isn't it?" Rory spoke softly.

Jordan raised his head, meeting his agent's gaze. "Yeah. Very. I—I love him."

My arms tightened around him as I dipped my head to

his ear, speaking too low for anyone else to hear. "I love you, too."

Rory nodded. "When the two of you told us you were in a relationship, I could see it. It made sense to me because of the way you always used to obsess over him."

"I did not obsess over him." Some of Jordan's fire returned as he glared at his agent, and it eased something inside me.

A small smile appeared on Rory's face. "Anyway, what I was going to say was I didn't realise just how much you meant to each other. I should have. The fact you were both prepared to make your relationship public at some point should've given me a clue. But seeing you both together now…I think it's clear to everyone in this room that you're in love."

On the big screen, I noticed one of the members of our PR team was dabbing at her eyes with a tissue, and when I glanced over at our team captain, his eyes were suspiciously shiny.

"We won yesterday, and we're going to win against this fucker!" Reuben suddenly shouted, waving his fist in the air. "Love fucking wins!"

Jordan let out a surprised laugh, and the sombre atmosphere lightened.

Harvey clapped his hands together. "Let's come up with a new plan."

THIRTY-NINE

THEO

"Look at this." Jordan rolled over on the bed, holding up his phone. "Rory says my sponsors want to renegotiate my contract and do another couple of shoots, specifically for the gay market."

I smiled at him, tugging him into a kiss. "That's good news."

"Yeah. We could do with some of that."

We'd been holed up in Jordan's house for the past week because it was in a private development, and therefore, the media couldn't come near us. We weren't specifically hiding, but we both needed time to adjust to our new reality and the huge amount of media attention we were getting. Our team had received their fair share of attention, too. Our teammates had been hounded for interviews and sound bites, and the club's email, post, and phone lines had been swamped—although, thankfully, that seemed to be dying down from the initial frenzy. Everyone had an opinion, and they wanted to let us know.

The identity of the Reddit poster had been found,

thanks to a call to action from Glevum. It was nothing more than a thoughtless wanker of a teenager, looking for online kudos, and Harvey had assured us he was dealing with it. In a way, they'd almost done us a favour because their actions had been widely condemned, and almost all the British press coverage had been sympathetic towards us. It was miraculous. Even the tabloid coverage had been better than either of us could have hoped for. The tabloids mostly seemed to be in shock that their favourite scandalous party boy player was in a relationship with the person he'd been aggravating for months. Speculation was rife that our animosity was a cover for our "torrid affair," as one tabloid put it.

Social media was...mixed. We'd received a flood of supportive messages, not only from our teammates and other footballers but complete strangers, too. But among the support was the vitriol, the hateful messages and comments. Everyone had done their best to shield us from the worst of it, but it was impossible to avoid it entirely. Some of the things we'd read had been filled with such venom both of us had been brought to tears on more than one occasion.

"It's my dad," Jordan announced when his phone began ringing. He answered it, hitting the speaker button. "Hi, Dad."

"Alright, Jord? How're you and Theo holding up? Need me to have words with anyone? Two Jugs John punched a man down the local last night when he dared to talk shit about you, so if you need some muscle, he's our man."

"Aww. That's nice of him. Tell him I said thanks." Jordan smiled, and I shook my head. *Always choosing violence*, I mouthed at him, so he kicked me in the shin. I gave him an icy glare, and he smirked as he returned to the conversation. "We're doing okay. The first few days were the worst. It'll probably go on for a while longer, then people will get bored and move on to something else. I dunno what it'll be like when the games start up again. Harvey's put out an announcement that any fans who make homophobic comments will be ejected from the stadium and their season pass revoked, if they have one. I hope it's enough. I don't know what'll happen with the fans from other teams."

"Leeds and Wolves both got fined last season for homophobic chants from their fans. Something like a hundred and fifty k each, Gary said. The lads are gonna keep an ear out at the games, and if the fans say anything, their clubs will have to pay." He grunted. "I don't know if it'll help, but it might be a bit of a deterrent."

"I love you, Dad," Jordan suddenly said. "Thanks for supporting me."

The sound of a throat clearing came through the phone. "Love you, too, son. That's what I'm here for. I'm here for you both, alright? Speaking of the both of you, when are you gonna bring Theo round? I need to give him the dad talk." He cracked his knuckles. "I've got a shovel in the shed that's just right for digging someone's grave."

My eyes widened, and Jordan laughed. "No, Dad, you're not going to try and scare off my boyfriend. I'd like to keep him, thanks."

"Ah, I'm just messing with you. Come round next week, okay? Or I'll come to you if you're worried about the paps."

"We'll come."

They spoke for a few more minutes before ending the call. When Jordan had placed his phone on his bedside table, he crawled over to me, straddling my body. Stroking my hair back from my face, he stared down at me, concern in his eyes. "What's that face for?"

I sighed. I was hoping he wouldn't notice, but he could read me too well. "It's nothing, really. I had an email from my uncle. A distant uncle, but even so." Opening up my email app, I handed my phone to Jordan.

His expression darkened as he read the message. "Fuck him, and fuck your parents. They have no right to judge who you want to be with. So fucking what if I'm not a lawyer or a politician or I can't give you biological kids? I'm doing my dream job, and I'm very fucking good at it, and there are plenty of ways we can have kids." He paused. "Y'know, in the future. If we wanted to. The point is I'm a fucking *catch*."

"There's that modesty I love so much." How did he always manage to brighten my world when I was feeling low?

"You know it's true, baby." Flashing me a grin, he lowered himself on top of me, planting his hands on either side of my head. "But do you know what else is true? *You're* a fucking catch, and I'm the luckiest person in the entire fucking galaxy because I have you. You're my favourite person in the universe, Theo Lewin."

I couldn't speak for a minute, too overwhelmed by everything I felt for this man who was looking down at me with so much love in his eyes. When I'd recovered enough, I cleared my throat. "I think I want to block him. My parents, too. We haven't spoken in a long, long time, and I—I…"

"You don't need to come up with any reasons to justify blocking them. Do it now."

"Okay." My hands shook slightly as I navigated through the screens on my phone, deleting and blocking, removing all traces of toxicity from my life. When I was done, I closed my eyes and exhaled. "I feel...better."

"I'm so proud of you." Jordan placed a kiss to the tip of my nose. "Let's make you feel even better. Imagine this—you and me getting called up for the England team."

I blinked my eyes open, staring up at him. "You think there's a chance of that happening?"

He shrugged. "It's possible. Look at the facts. When we released our statement telling everyone we were bi and in a relationship with each other, the official England team reposted it. Not only that, the England manager *and* the captain, plus some of the other players, posted and commented. We're on their radar now, I guarantee. They're probably watching footage of us as we speak. You know how good we are together."

I tugged him down to me, rolling us over so I was pressing him into the mattress. "I love you so much. We are good together, and not only on the pitch. I don't know about the England team, but I'm happy. I have a career I love, and next season, we get to play in the Europa League. But most importantly, I've got you. You're all the family I need."

When I lowered my head for a kiss, Jordan slid his hand in between our mouths. "Wait a minute. You've got family who support you. Your cousin, the one who interviewed me for *Offside* magazine...what was his name...Dean?"

Dean Lewin. We barely knew each other because his branch of the family wasn't upper class enough for my parents' tastes, and he lived somewhere in London, so we'd only interacted a couple of times in my life.

But maybe... "I'll send him an email."

Jordan removed his hand. "Later, though. First, I want to re-enact our island massage, but without the cockblocking oil."

"Mmm. Sounds good to me." I threaded my fingers through his hair as he smiled down at me. "Before that, I want a kiss."

"Whatever my lord commands."

"Brat," I whispered against his lips, and after that, there was no more talking.

FORTY

JORDAN

"Thanks for meeting with me." Dean Lewin, *Offside* magazine's digital editor, shook Theo's hand and then mine. "You remember my colleague Adam?"

Adam cleared his throat, holding out his hand. "Nice to see you both again."

Dean gave him a soft, private smile, and the pieces fell into place.

When Theo had decided to email his cousin, he'd discovered that Dean had already emailed him, offering his support. He'd mentioned that he was gay in the email, and when he'd informed Theo that he didn't have anything to do with Theo's side of the family because of his chosen profession and sexual orientation, Theo had found a kindred spirit. They'd been emailing back and forth for a couple of weeks, and now, here we were to do an interview.

My boyfriend was a fucking superstar, and I was so proud of him. This interview wasn't only about football. Theo wanted to open up, to talk about his experiences with his sleeping pill addiction and how therapy had helped him, as well as his relationship with me and the highs and lows of us being the first out players in the Premier League.

The digital version of the article would be dropping the day before our first game of the season, and the expanded print version would be available in the following month's issue. Finally, people would hear our side of the story, in our own words.

We seated ourselves on the comfortable sofas in the private room Dean had booked in a local hotel, and a member of staff came over to take our tea and coffee orders.

Dean placed a small recording device on the table between us. "If it's okay with you both, I'd like to make this as natural as possible rather than me throwing questions at you. I'll direct the conversation here and there, but mostly, I'd like you to just share your experiences. Afterwards, I'll get the article written up, and then you and your legal team will receive copies to approve before we go to print. Does that sound okay?"

We both nodded, and he smiled. "Before we start, I just want to say thank you for trusting us with this. It means a lot."

"You're family," Theo said, and I couldn't help leaning over and pressing a quick kiss to his cheek. I was so fucking happy that he'd connected with his cousin.

Adam hit the Record button, and we began.

"I'd like to start with you giving us some of the history of your relationship. Good and bad."

Theo looked at me, a smirk curving over his lips. "When I was thirteen, the most aggravating, cocky boy I'd ever met walked into my life. Or perhaps 'tripped' into my life is more appropriate."

I punched him on the arm, lightly, of course, because he

was the love of my life, and I didn't get off on causing him physical pain. Most of the time.

He laughed, loud and bright, and it made me warm inside.

"We were both attending the same football youth academy…"

After we'd both been through our history and subsequent animosity when I'd joined the team, Dean asked Theo about his sleeping pill addiction. We'd agreed beforehand that there would be no mention of his parents, so he simply stated that he'd struggled with sleeping issues for a long time. He described how both the medical and mental health support had helped him through the withdrawal process and how he still continued with his therapy sessions. I spoke a bit about my own experiences with therapy and how I believed that it could help so many people if they were willing to give it a try.

"Thank you for sharing that with us. Now, returning to your relationship, can you tell us when things changed between the two of you?"

Because we were bound by Black Diamond's NDA, we'd decided to treat the therapy as if it had happened separately from our time on the island. Our official story was that we'd been sent away on a team-building break to teach us how to work together.

"I began to see Jordan in a different light. I'm not sure I could pinpoint when it happened, exactly, but the fact that we were forced to spend most of our waking hours together meant that we had to learn to get along, otherwise we would have both been miserable."

"We'd probably have killed each other," I interjected. "In fact, we had a near brush with death. We were hiking to a waterfall, and we got caught in a tropical storm…"

Between the two of us, we spoke about how our relationship had changed during our time away, and although we were both interested in being more than friends, we'd mutually agreed not to cross the line because of the pressures that we would face. And not only us but everyone at Glevum FC and our friends and families.

"What changed? What made you decide to take that step?" Dean leaned forwards in his seat, his elbows on his arms.

I met my boyfriend's gaze. "Honestly? I tried to get over him, and time kept passing, but I still wanted him. I knew that I wanted a relationship with him. We'd both come out to several people. They'd taken it well, and it felt like...like maybe it wasn't so impossible, after all. The day we beat Liverpool 1–0, I wanted to tell Theo that I wanted to be with him."

Theo covered my hand with his. "For me, it was the same day. Jordan scored an amazing goal during the match. I looked across the pitch and saw him, and I just knew."

My heart stuttered. "You knew what?"

"I knew that I loved you."

"You did?" I croaked out, my eyes wide as I stared at him.

He smiled. "Yeah, I did. I knew that you were it for me."

"You did?" I repeated. "*Fuck.* I love you so much." Throwing myself at him, I planted kisses all over his face until a pointed throat clearing reminded me that we weren't alone. "Oh, shit, sorry. Sorry. I—I didn't, uh, I didn't mean to do that." I sat up straight, feeling my cheeks burning.

"You're so fucking cute when you get all flustered," Theo murmured into my ear. I shot him a half-hearted glare, which turned into a grin when I noticed the way he was all mussed up where I'd basically attacked him. He was so fucking gorgeous.

"Sorry," I said again. "I don't usually attack him in front of other people."

Adam smirked. "No need to be sorry. It was entertaining. Why can't all our interviews be like this?"

Dean swiftly moved us on, and we discussed the fact that the choice of how and when we came out was taken away from us. I could see that he was struggling to remain an impartial journalist, as was Adam, as evidenced by his sudden outburst.

"How fucking dare they take that away from you?"

"Adam," Dean cautioned with a hand to his knee but then added, "He's right, though. It makes me so angry."

"Us too. We've had a lot of support since it happened, though, haven't we?" I glanced over at Theo, and he nodded.

"We've had the backing of the people closest to us. Most of our teammates have been both publicly and privately supportive. We're lucky that we're surrounded by a strong network of people. Glevum and the PFA have gone out of their way to ease the process as much as possible, too, and they're providing us with ongoing support and counselling."

"What about the reaction from the public?"

"We've been overwhelmed by the messages of support we've received from fans and the general public and the LGBTQ community. We've even spoken to some other professional players and youth players who maybe aren't ready to come out, but they say we've given them hope. That's been incredible to hear." Theo paused. "There's been negativity, too. The good has outweighed the bad so far, but some of the things we've seen have been quite upsetting. We tried to prepare for the negative side, but there's no way that anyone can be properly prepared for that kind of thing, especially with there being no precedent in the Premier League."

We spoke for a few minutes longer about some of the comments and messages we'd received, good and bad, and after that, it was time to wrap up the interview.

Dean shook our hands again. "Thanks again for meeting us today. I'll get the article over to you ASAP. Good luck with the opening game of the season. As the fortune cookie I had yesterday said, love will triumph over hate. Go out there and hold your head high. Be proud of who you are, and know that by doing this, you're making a difference in so many people's lives. You're giving them hope."

"Yeah. You're right. Let's go out there and show them that nothing will keep us down." I jumped to my feet. "We're Jordan and Theo, and we rise to the fucking top because we the fucking G.O.A.T., baby!"

Theo stood, wrapping his arm around my waist. He rolled his eyes, but he couldn't hide the grin that was tugging at his lips. "What am I going to do with you?"

"Hmm. I can probably come up with a few ideas."

Back at my house, in one of my favourite places with my favourite person—my bed and Theo—I pinned him beneath me. "Today has been a hard day, and I think we need some balance. Something fun to take our minds off everything."

"Yeah? What did you have in mind?"

I lowered my head, skimming my mouth over his ear. "I'm not sure if you can handle it."

"I can handle fucking anything you give me." His low

promise made me shiver, my cock already lengthening against him, which he was going to be aware of any second since we were naked.

"You say that, but can you handle this?" Rolling off him, enjoying the way his gaze went straight to my rapidly hardening dick, I reached for the item I wanted. My fingers grasped the curved, smooth plastic, which vibrated under my touch as I turned it on.

I held it up, and his brows rose. "That's what you have in mind?"

With a nod, I threw the PlayStation controller in his direction and then grabbed another for myself. "FIFA. One match. Me against you. Winner gets to choose who tops and who bottoms tonight. What do you say?"

He pulled himself upright, widening his legs and patting the space between them. I swallowed hard at the sight of his erection, so fucking thick and delicious. My mouth watered.

No. I wouldn't let him distract me.

"What are you scared of, baby?" He stroked the duvet cover between his legs. "Come and sit here while we play."

I shot him a glare but crawled in between his legs and settled myself with my back to him. His cock was pressing up against my ass.

Fuck my stupidly sexy boyfriend and his stupidly gorgeous dick. And fuck him even more for making mine hard. He was about to get a rude awakening, though, because when I was focused on something, nothing else would distract me.

I chose my team, or tried to, except my hand slipped when I was scrolling through the list because the bastard I was pressed up against accidentally-on-purpose brushed my dick with his arm when I was choosing. Manchester

United? Seriously? The team that had thrashed us 5–0 last season? Fuck those assholes. For payback, I waited until it was Theo's turn and then rolled my head to the side, dragging my teeth down his neck as I arched back against him.

"Fuck you, Jordan," he growled when my moves made his body jerk and select Accrington Stanley, a League Two side. I smirked as the match loaded.

"Payback is sweet. Serves you right for making me pick Man United."

He retaliated by biting my throat when I was making my player tackle his, close to his goal. I lost the ball, and he laughed. "What were you saying about payback?"

This fucker was going down. All the fucking way down. Deep underground.

It was time to play dirty. I waited until his player had the ball, and then, just as he was about to try for a goal, I removed one hand from my controller and quickly thrust my arm behind me, wrapping my fingers around his erection.

He gasped, the controller falling from his grip, and suddenly, everything was a blur of heat and skin sliding against mine and a mouth spouting a string of curses into my ear. We rolled on the bed, twisting at the last second and narrowly avoiding one of the controllers, which was way too close to my ass for comfort. I swiped my arm out, sending it to the floor, and then continued in my mission to subdue Theo.

"Give up," he rasped against my throat, pinning me with the length of his body. His hands wrapped around my wrists, holding me in place.

"I never give up," I snarled, wrenching my wrists free of

his grasp. Scraping my nails down his back, I thrust upwards, and we both moaned at the sensation.

My grip on him softened, my arms wrapping around his broad back. He sighed, placing a kiss to my throat. "Do you give up, baby? Are you going to let me choose who does who tonight?"

"Mmmm. Theo." I trailed my lips up the side of his face as I ran my hand up the length of his spine. "Love of my life. Man of my dreams. When will you learn?"

"Learn what?" His head rose, and he stared down at me.

I saw the realisation dawn in his eyes at the same time I spoke the words. "I. Never. Give. Up."

Then I twisted my body, getting out from underneath him, and threw myself onto his back. His ass was so fucking sexy that I couldn't help thrusting against it. He groaned, burying his face in the pillow. "Fine, you win, you infuriating, stubborn bastard."

"I knew you'd see sense." I pressed a kiss to the back of his neck. "Since I'm here, I think I should go on top tonight. Any problems with that?"

"Fuck, no. Fuck me now."

That was what I liked to hear. I left him there for a few seconds while I grabbed the lube, and then I took a moment to appreciate the sight of my boyfriend's gorgeous body, spread out for me like a fucking buffet.

"I'm so glad we had those tests. I love fucking you without a condom," I groaned, circling his hole with a lubed finger.

He pushed back against me as my finger slid inside him. "Yeah. Me too. Feels so good. Give me another."

I obediently complied with his demand and then added another, stroking over his prostate, making him moan and jerk and leak all over the bed. Fucking hell, my dick was going to explode if I didn't get inside him right now.

Withdrawing my fingers, I lined myself up. He moaned, and I took that to mean he was ready, so I pushed forwards, entering him in one long, slow movement. When I was buried inside him, I paused, pressing my lips to the side of his throat. "Fucking love you so much. You feel so good around my dick."

"Love you, too. Move, baby. Don't hold back. Make me feel it."

I shuddered at his words. And then, because I'd do anything for this man, I did exactly as he said. I thrust hard, fucking him into the mattress, pounding him as he ground his dick into the sheets. He moaned and gasped and writhed beneath me, and it took everything I had to keep up the same pace. It was so. Fucking. Good. "Fuck, Theo," I panted, so close to the edge. "I'm gonna fill your fucking ass with my cum."

He stiffened beneath me, and then he jerked, my name falling from his lips as he came. Riding on the knife edge of an orgasm, it took seconds for me to follow him over. I collapsed against his back, my chest heaving.

"Theo?"

"Hmm?"

"I think fucking you bare might be better than getting into the Europa League."

"What?" He manoeuvred himself so that my softening dick slid out of him. Rolling onto his side, he grimaced as he landed in his own cum, and I smirked at him.

My smirk died away when he dragged me into it, smearing cum up my leg. "Theo! What the fuck?"

"Serves you right. What were you saying about the Europa League?"

"I said, I think fucking you bare might be better than getting into the Europa League."

"Yeah? Maybe I need to test this hypothesis, with me fucking you." He rolled us over again. Our chests pressed together as he kissed me, so softly it gave me butterflies. "What do you say?"

There was only one acceptable answer. "I say yes."

FORTY-ONE

JORDAN

"Theodore Lewin, I presume?" My dad raised a brow at my boyfriend.

"Shut up, Dad. You know exactly who he is." I elbowed him as I pushed past him into the house, and he laughed.

"Sorry, sorry. Theo. Welcome. Does anyone fancy a cuppa?"

"I'd love one if you're making one," Theo said politely, following me into the hallway. My dad ushered us into the kitchen, and I noticed Theo staring around curiously. When my dad began preparing the tea, he turned to me. "I really like this. It feels...welcoming. It's a proper home."

He was right. It did, and it was. It wasn't anything special to look at, just a small two-bedroom terrace, but it was where I'd grown up, and to me, it would always feel like home. Maybe one day in the not-too-distant future, Theo and I would have our own place that we could make into a home of our own.

"I'd show you my old room, but there's nothing left to see. Dad turned it into his home gym. I feel so betrayed."

My dad cuffed me around the head. "Shut it, you. I

seem to remember you telling me I needed to do something for my health, and it was you that bought and assembled all the gym equipment."

"Excuse me for caring about your health, old man."

He pointedly ignored me, turning to Theo instead. "Milk? Sugar?"

"A dash of milk, no sugar, please. Thank you."

Aww, my boyfriend had such good manners. *Suck-up*, I mouthed to him, and he glanced over at my dad to make sure he wasn't looking before showing me his middle finger.

Did I say my boyfriend had good manners? I was wrong. He was so fucking *rude*.

Wait. Had he picked up his bad habits from me? Nah. The blame had to lie with Reuben or Ainsley, surely. They were such bad influences.

"The weather's nice today. Might as well sit outside," my dad suggested, and we followed him into the garden, which was bathed in the rays of the morning sun. He indicated for us to sit at the ancient wooden patio table that creaked and groaned at the slightest hint of a breeze.

Despite the dubious quality of the furniture, the garden was nice. Even though my dad worked full-time in the building trade, he spent a lot of his free time tending the garden. There was greenery everywhere, all kinds of flowers and herbs and bushes filling the small space. The patio area we were seated on had grown smaller and smaller every year as my dad reclaimed the soil beneath for his plants, and I was ninety-nine percent sure that one day, I'd walk out here and the whole thing would be swallowed up by shrubbery.

Picking up my mug, I took my first sip of tea. Delicious. Why did my dad always make the best tea? It never tasted quite the same when I made it.

My dad drummed his fingers on the table, making it wobble, sending tea sloshing out of all our mugs. "Are you boys ready for the match against Brighton later? The lads are prepared for all eventualities. We've been running over scenarios at the pub."

"I'm not sure how much we can prepare. We're going into the unknown. We have the support from Glevum, but we have no idea how the fans will react." Theo's brows pulled together, and I reached out, gently squeezing his arm in reassurance. I had no idea what would happen during our first match of the season, but I was trying to be strong for him. This could prove to be our biggest test as a couple. It was the first game. Everyone knew about us. The *Offside* article had come out yesterday, and we'd both avoided the internet since then, not wanting to add to the pressure of what was already the highest-stakes match we'd ever played.

"Me and Two Jugs John have been mobilising the troops. Don't you worry."

I stared at my dad. I *really* didn't like the sound of this. "Mobilising the troops? Dad, this isn't a war."

"It might be, and if it is, we're ready," he muttered darkly. "They don't call us the Glevum Gladiators for nothing. Just concentrate on the game, and we'll handle the fans."

What could one group of less than ten people do against thousands of others?

I had to hope that it didn't come to that.

For all my talk, I was a nervous wreck as I waited in the tunnel with the rest of my team. My gaze dropped to my feet, and despite my nerves, a small smile tugged at my lips.

Every single member of Glevum FC wore rainbow laces today, thanks to the club collaborating with an LGBTQ+ charity to promote inclusiveness in sport.

"D'you think we can wear these every week?" Reuben came up next to me, twisting his foot as he examined the bright colours threaded through his boots.

"I think it's a one-off."

"Yeah, you're probably right." He grinned at me. "That flag I put in the dressing room is here to stay, though."

"That was you?"

"I told you we needed more colour." With a shrug, he turned to face the entrance to the pitch, bouncing lightly on the balls of his feet. "You ready for this?"

It was an echo of the question my dad had asked me this morning, and I didn't have a proper answer. How could I ever be ready for this? How could I prepare for the unknown?

"I hope so."

My gaze sought Theo's, and when I found him, I inclined my head. He came to me straight away. "Is everything okay?"

"Just having an attack of nerves," I told him honestly.

"Me too." Stepping closer, he lowered his voice. "But whatever happens out there, just remember, it's you and me." He repeated the words he'd spoken to me on the day we'd been outed, when everything was falling apart.

"You and me." I curled my finger around his, squeezing for a moment before I let him go. "Okay. Let's do this."

We filed out onto the pitch. Everything was a blur of colour and noise, the roar of the crowds echoing in my ears as we emerged into the open. I blinked, and blinked again, spots dancing in front of my eyes. I would not lose my fucking composure out here in front of everyone. I was a professional.

"Jordan." Theo's voice was urgent. "*Jordan*. Look."

The stadium finally came into focus, and I. Fucking. Lost. It.

I sank to my knees, right there in the centre of the pitch, tears blurring my vision. From every corner of our stadium, home and away fans were calling our names. Mine and Theo's. And there were rainbow flags among the crowds, bright bursts of colour, waving and dancing, a visual representation of support, an acceptance, an acknowledgement that love is fucking love.

There were boos and jeers, but they were completely fucking drowned out by the wave of support pouring down on us, the cheers echoing around Barnwood Park stadium, joined by the players, both Glevum and Brighton, clapping us, encouraging the fans to lift us up with even more noise. I'd never, ever experienced anything like it in my life, never even dreamed that anything close to this would ever happen, and all I could do was kneel there on the grass, letting it wash over me, breaking apart and being pieced back together, all at the same time.

A hand reached out to me, and I took it, letting Theo lift me to my feet. He looked deep into my eyes, his own filled with tears.

"Remember what Dean said? Love will triumph over hate."

I wiped my tears away. "He's right. Love wins."

Theo nodded. "Love wins."

Our team surrounded us.

"Love wins," Grant said. "Love fucking wins. And you know what? Today, we win. Let's do this."

FORTY-TWO

JORDAN

"Not so bland and soulless now, is it?" I grinned at Theo, who was still standing in the exact same spot as he had when he'd entered the lounge five minutes earlier.

"Wh— How? When?"

Seeing my boyfriend so gobsmacked made me grin even harder. "I've been paying attention. As soon as we agreed that you'd move in here, I started my research. Look."

I scrolled through my phone until I found the right folder and then held it up so he could see it.

"Your favourite colours. The décor you seemed to like in your flat. Notes from conversations we've had." I paused. "But we can change whatever you want. I want it to be our home, not mine, and that means that you get an equal say. This is the only room I had decorated because we spend a lot of time relaxing in here, and I wanted you to be comfortable when you moved in. We can redo it if you want, and we'll choose the décor for all the other rooms together."

My formerly boring lounge with no personality whatsoever, all plain white walls and beige carpet, had been transformed. Thanks to my research, I knew Theo liked soft, darker colours and lots of warm wood. So the walls were now painted a rich, inky blue, and I had plenty of wood accents everywhere, including a giant coffee table made of reclaimed wood, sanded and stained in a warm cedar colour. The carpet had gone, replaced by wooden floorboards, and a huge rug in blues and greys and creams covered the centre of the room. A large standing lamp in the corner next to a vintage wingback chair I'd commandeered from Theo's house provided a glow of warm yellow light. There was also a Tiffany lamp, again, stolen from Theo's former flat, illuminating the opposite corner of the room. I'd placed it on top of a wooden sideboard in the same colour as the coffee table, and I'd printed and framed various photos of us, arranging them next to the lamp. I'd left the walls bare so that he could choose whatever art was to his taste.

Theo swallowed hard, his throat working. "I don't know what to say."

"Say…Jordan, when your football career is over, you could become an award-winning interior designer."

That seemed to snap him out of his frozen state, and he met my gaze for the first time since he'd stepped into the lounge. Stepping closer, he wrapped his arms around me, trailing soft kisses up my jaw to my ear. "Jordan."

"Yeah?"

"When your football career is over, I have no doubt that you'll succeed in whatever you choose to do. And I'll be here supporting you, every step of the way."

Oh. The teasing smile dropped from my face, and I cupped his jaw, kissing him slow and deep. "I fucking love you, you know."

"I know. I love you too." He brushed another kiss across

my lips before releasing me with a sigh. "As much as I'd love to keep kissing you, we need to get ready for our guests."

"Before we do that, I have something for you." I dug the piece of metal from my pocket and pressed it into his palm. "You already have all my security codes, and this is the only thing left to give you."

He stared down at the shiny new key I'd had cut for him, a slow smile spreading across his face. Digging his hand into his own pocket, he pulled out the key ring I'd given him on his birthday and added the new key.

"It's official. I now pronounce you lord of my manor."

"Don't fucking start, brat. You'll pay for that comment later."

"I look forward to it, my lord." I shot him a bright grin. He growled and launched himself at me, but I sidestepped him, laughing.

Our fun was interrupted by the sound of the doorbell, and within the space of ten minutes, our house and garden were both full to bursting with most of the football team, some with partners and kids in tow. Rory, Amir, and Amir's wife showed up soon after, and I managed to talk them into helping with the food prep in the kitchen because feeding that many people was not an easy task. We were keeping it simple with a barbecue, and Grant took over manning the grill, chasing away anyone who tried to help him.

The doorbell rang again, and by the time I'd pushed through the crowds to get to the door, someone had already opened it.

"Oi oi!" Two Jugs John came into view, hoisting a twenty-four pack of lager over his shoulder. Then my dad's grinning face appeared, followed by two of his other friends, Buzz and Gary. As a good host, I welcomed them in, accepting the slaps on the back that was their way of showing their friendly support.

My dad pulled me aside with a hand to my arm as Theo showed the others into the kitchen. "Theo settled in, then?"

"He only officially moved in about twenty minutes ago, but yeah. I guess he's been unofficially living here for a while. Some people will probably think it's too fast, but we didn't want to waste any more time. We've done enough of that since the island."

My dad nodded. "Makes sense." Lowering his voice, he moved a bit closer. "Has anyone been giving the two of you any trouble?"

"Not really. After the Brighton match...I dunno. It was clear how much support we had, and the media loved it. You probably saw the headlines."

"Yeah. You two are the next Posh and Becks, from what I've heard."

"Posh and Becks? Okay, old man." I smirked as I thought about Theo's reaction if I started calling him "Posh." Although... "Which one of us are they saying is David Beckham? Because I think Theo might actually be the better footballer. Don't tell him I said that."

Arms wrapped around my waist, and a firm body pressed against my back. "I heard that."

"You heard nothing."

My dad laughed, clapping me on the shoulder. "I'll leave you two to it." He disappeared into the kitchen, and I leaned back against Theo.

"How long until everyone leaves? I spent all day waiting for the hot tub to get to the right temperature."

"Hmm." His lips skimmed over my ear, making me shiver. "Are you thinking what I'm thinking?"

"If it involves you and me getting naked in the hot tub,

then yes. Although…we'd better use condoms. I'm not cleaning cum out of it. Unless you're prepared to deal with it."

"I'd rather not." He smiled and then lightly scraped his teeth over my skin, followed by a trail of soft kisses down my throat. "Fuck, you're so gorgeous, Jordan. I wish we were alone. I'm looking forward to making you pay for the comment you made earlier."

Fuck. Why did he have to be so fucking delicious? My cock was already lengthening in my jeans, and any minute, someone was going to notice. "I'd like to see you try."

"I bet you would, baby."

That was *it*. I spun around, grabbing his wrist and dragging him through the kitchen, ignoring my teammates and friends. When I reached the utility room, I yanked the door open, shoved him inside, and slammed the door closed behind us. Without stopping to take a breath, I crowded him up against the wall and slanted my mouth over his.

He opened up for me straight away, his tongue sliding over mine, his lips soft and hot and so fucking perfect. I would never, ever get enough of kissing this man.

"Jordan. Fuck." Theo's mouth went to my jaw, his hands pulling me into him, our dicks grinding together in a way that made me want to get rid of the layers of clothes between us right fucking now. I moaned.

"Theo. Please—"

There was a crash. "No! My eyes! Again!"

I let my head fall forwards to Theo's shoulder. "Hi, Reuben."

"Why is it always me?" he cried. "All I was trying to do was find the tequila. Ainsley said it was in here."

Loud laughter came from outside the door, just as I said, "What tequila?"

Reuben spun around, outrage all over his face. "Ainsley Shaw, you are a dead man!" He took off like a shot, and I heard the sound of shouts and pounding footsteps coming from the kitchen.

"I suppose we'd better rejoin the others." Theo cleared his throat, adjusting himself in his jeans. His eyes met mine, and they were so dark and hot I had to take a pointed step away from him so I didn't do something inadvisable like lock us both in here and fuck his brains out. "But we're continuing where we left off later."

"Yes, we fucking are." I planted a quick, hard kiss on his lips before I stepped back, focusing on breathing in and out deeply until I was mostly under control. "C'mon. Let's go and eat the food our friends prepared for us. We'll have our own private housewarming party later, and no one else is invited."

"Agreed." He slid his fingers between mine, and hand in hand, we went to rejoin our friends.

Out in the garden, sprawled on the grass under the final rays of the summer sun, I looked around me and smiled, so fucking happy that I felt like I could burst. My teammates were mingling with my dad and his friends. Grant was busy with the barbecue, deep in conversation with Rory, Amir, and Lars, while Amir's wife was helping Grant's wife and a couple of the other parents supervise some of the kids that were kicking a football around at the bottom of the garden.

As for me? To my left, on a blanket on the grass, I had a full plate of food and an ice-cold beer. And to my right? I glanced down at the fingers entwined with mine. I had the most important thing of all.

My best friend and the man I loved more than anything in the world.

Theo.

THEO
EPILOGUE

TEN MONTHS LATER

"I keep expecting Dr. Weaver to pop out of the bushes." Jordan glanced suspiciously around us. He caught my eye, grinned, and then sighed. "That feels so long ago now, doesn't it?"

"Yeah. Well, it was just over two years ago." Over two years since we'd been forced together on that island. Over two years since Jordan Emery had become my confidant, my lover, and my best friend. Now, here we were, at another tropical retreat, but this time, we were in Thailand in a private celebrity hideout, and our luxury resort was exactly that—a resort. It was beautiful beyond words, but I knew that both of us would always hold a soft spot for Black Diamond Resort because it was the place where we'd begun to heal, to find ourselves and each other.

"Two years of you and me." Stretching out on the lounger next to our own private plunge pool overlooking the sea, Jordan yawned. "And this past year has been the best year of my life. I got to call you mine in front of the world, you moved in with me, *and* we managed to get to the quarter-finals of the Europa League. I still can't believe we did it. That was insane."

I took a sip of my ice-cold beer, trying and failing to ignore how utterly delicious my boyfriend looked, lying there in a tiny pair of electric-blue swimming shorts, his skin smooth and kissed with gold from his hours of sun worshipping. "We'll make it further next season. I'm sure of it."

"Yeah. We will. And who knows. Maybe we'll get called up for the England team one day, too." His phone beeped, and he rolled onto his side, reaching under the lounger to view the alert. "Hey, look at the group chat."

I picked up my phone, mostly to give my eyes something to focus on that wasn't Jordan's body. We were supposed to be relaxing, and we couldn't do that if we were all over each other like we had been in the four days we'd been here so far.

When I opened the group chat, I smiled to myself.

> AINSLEY:
>
> @Jordan did you know that apparently you're a BISEXUAL ICON according to this online article I just read?
>
> LARS:
>
> What does being a bisexual icon entail?
>
> AINSLEY:
>
> No idea
>
> REUBEN:
>
> @Jordan you're a BICON. Get it?
>
> Does anyone want to see the t-shirts I had made for London Pride?!!!

GRANT:

I can't believe they're letting you march in the parade

REUBEN:

ME? I'm an ally bro!!!

AINSLEY:

Me too

LARS:

I am also

GRANT:

Yeah okay I am too, but all I'm saying is you'd better behave. You're representing our team

REUBEN:

We're all representing our team! All of us were invited. I'll be on my best behaviour!

GRANT:

I'll believe it when I see it

REUBEN:

ANYWAY LOOK AT THESE T-SHIRTS!

He attached a photo of four black T-shirts. The front said "Proud Ally" in rainbow letters, which was fine. But the back said "#THEODAN" with two overlapping football symbols underneath the wording. Jordan and I exchanged glances.

JORDAN:

#theodan?

AINSLEY:

Jordan! How's Thailand?

> **LARS:**
> I thought Theodan was a character in a fantasy series
>
> **REUBEN:**
> It's a ship name thing! You know when they combine two names
>
> **GRANT:**
> I agree with Lars, sounds like the name of a character from a fantasy book
>
> **REUBEN:**
> Fuck off all of you! It's better than JORDEO

> **ME:**
> I'm assuming my opinion is irrelevant, but I vote for neither

> **JORDAN:**
> @Ainsley Thailand is amazing
>
> **AINSLEY:**
> Send us some photos. I need something to look at. I'm fucking dying of boredom at my girlfriend's uncle's house. They don't even have Netflix

> **ME:**
> We don't either

Jordan's fingers hovered over his phone screen, but then he looked over at me. He glanced away and then looked back, dragging his gaze down over my body in a slow caress. "Theo."

"Yeah?"

"I think we need to end this conversation. Now."

Thrusting his phone back underneath his lounger, he climbed to his feet and then sauntered towards the villa doors. When he reached them, he looked back at me and then hooked his fingers into the waistband of his shorts. I watched, my mouth dry as he peeled them off in a glacially slow movement, exposing the gorgeous curves of his ass.

Placing my own phone on the floor, I rose to my feet. My erection made an obscene outline along the front of my swim shorts, and I watched as Jordan's gaze went molten, heavy with want as he palmed his cock while he gave me a slow, thorough once-over.

Prolonging the moment, I kept my shorts on as I prowled towards him. He took a step back, then another, disappearing inside the villa.

"Why are you running from me, baby? You know I'll catch you." I stepped inside, ridding myself of my shorts, and stalked naked through the lounge.

He only had a few places to hide, and I was going to find him and make him pay for running away from me.

A faint noise reached my ears, and I smiled, turning on my heel and heading for the bathroom.

Water.

I entered the bathroom, my gaze immediately going to the huge shower, twice the size of the one at home. When I'd moved in with Jordan, we'd had the bathroom renovated so that there was plenty of room for two of us in the shower at once, but in comparison to this one, ours was miniscule.

Pulling open the shower door, I took a moment to appreciate the beautiful sight in front of me. My hot, wet boyfriend, water cascading down his body, his hair darker than usual and plastered to his head, his thick eyelashes spiky and glistening with droplets of liquid. His eyes were closed, so I took advantage, sneaking up on him, spinning him around and pressing his chest against the tiles, with my hand wrapped around his throat.

Banding my arm around his waist, I dipped my head to

his ear, nipping at the lobe as his body melted into me with a shiver. Fuck. I'd never get used to the effect we had on each other.

"Were you trying to run from me, baby?" I slid my hand up, feeling him swallow against my palm as I gripped him underneath his jaw, tilting his head back.

"N—no." He circled his hips, a hot, wet friction on my cock that threatened the remains of my control. I was already hanging by a thread, just from having my body plastered against his, with him so fucking helpless in my arms.

"Liar." I bit down on his throat, and he jerked against me.

"Theo. *Please.*" He reached back, pulling me closer.

"Please what?"

"Please fuck me."

Releasing my grip on his throat, I slid my hand down, over his chest, stopping right above his heart. I could feel it pounding underneath my palm. I groaned, pressing my cock against his ass, needing to be inside him so badly, but at the same time, wanting to prolong the anticipation.

My other hand slid up onto his chest, and I smoothed my palms over the hard muscles of his pecs, lightly tugging at his nipples because I was addicted to the whimpering noises he made when I touched them. He panted against me, his head falling back, his cock jerking and leaking precum without being touched. It was fucking mesmerising.

I ran my hands down over his abs and traced his v lines with the pads of my fingers, getting closer and closer to his cock but not touching it. Warm water rained down on my back, and in front, I was on fire from Jordan's body heat, both of us instinctively moving against one another, unable to remain still.

"*Please*, Theo." His voice was a broken sob, and I gave in, giving him what he wanted. What we both wanted. I reached for the lube I'd left on the shelf, generously coating my aching erection, and then pressed two fingers inside him. It had only been a couple of hours since we'd last done this, and he opened for me easily. Without wasting any more time, I withdrew my fingers, gently pressed down on his back so he was at a better angle, and then began to push inside.

We both moaned when I was in all the way. I took a second to appreciate the view in front of me—or I planned to, until Jordan thrust his hips back, grinding his ass into my dick.

"Fuck me. Now. Please. Stop fucking teasing me."

Fuck, he was already wrecked. I couldn't afford to waste any more time. I fucked his hot, tight hole hard and fast, both of us panting for breath, steam swirling around us as he braced himself on the tile wall, and I held his hips, my fingers digging into his damp skin as we chased our release. He cried out, the sound echoing around the shower, his cock jerking and shooting jets of cum over the tiled wall.

Hands-free. That was the sexiest thing I'd ever seen in my life. Moaning his name, I flew over the edge, pumping my cum inside him until I was completely and utterly spent.

Both of us were shaking when I withdrew from him. We sank to the floor, and I pulled him into my arms. Water rained down next to us, but I angled us away from the flow. I brushed his wet hair away from his face, kissing his nose.

"Are you okay?"

He nodded slowly. His eyes were glazed, and he was boneless in my grip. "Tired. So fucking good. Hands-free. Fuck. I'm so tired."

"Come on." I tried to lift him, but considering he was almost as heavy as me, it was a lost cause. "Let's get dried off and have a nap."

"Okay." He managed to climb to his feet, swaying slightly, and I wrapped my arm around his waist to hold him steady. After we'd cleaned up, I turned the water off and then led him out of the shower, drying him gently with a towel. We could shower again properly later, but for now, all I wanted to do was to lie in our huge, soft hotel bed with Jordan in my arms.

The beach restaurant had set up a row of small tables on the sand, each with two chairs. The sun was beginning to lower in the sky, and the lights that were strung up in the palm trees were already emitting a soft yellow glow in preparation for the sunset. A singer crooned softly from a little further down the beach, accompanied by a backing track and the sound of the waves lapping at the shore. Sitting across from my boyfriend, cocktails in front of us, I smiled.

He returned my smile instantly with a soft one of his own, his fingers idly playing with the cocktail stirrer. "I can't believe how relaxed I feel. All those orgasms you've given me, the sea air, the naps, being away from everything."

"Me too." I reached for his hand, curling my fingers around his. "I'm so glad I'm here with you."

"It's been worth it, hasn't it? Our journey. Hating each other, then loving each other. Finding a best friend. Coming out. All the support. Even the hate we still get for being together matters less when you look at the big picture. There's so much love. So many people who believe in us."

"It's been worth everything. The bad days. The good days. I'd go through them all again if it meant I'd end up right here with you." Lifting his hand, I pressed a kiss to his knuckles before releasing it to sip my cocktail.

Jordan's smile was so happy, and it meant everything to me. "Want to do something?"

"What?"

Standing, he tugged me to my feet and then dipped down beneath the table. When he straightened up, he had a football tucked under his arm. "What do you say? Want to play a bit of one-on-one?"

"Where did you get that?"

"I have my ways. Okay, I might've seen a couple of the staff members kicking one around this morning when I went for a run, when you were busy being lazy."

Leaning into him, I placed my mouth to his ear. "Lazy? Is that what you're calling it? I've got a lot of stamina, Jordan, but you woke me up at 6:00 a.m., after we'd spent all night fucking. Only one of us had a nice long nap yesterday in between rounds, and it wasn't me. You drained my balls. I needed time to recover."

He smirked at me. "Yeah, yeah. Whatever you need to tell yourself. Come on. Drink the rest of your mojito, and let's go. Unless you're too scared to play me."

"Jordan." I drained the rest of the cocktail, noticing that his glass was already empty. "Do we need to have a talk about your delusions?"

Grabbing my hand, he linked his fingers with mine, leading me down the beach, away from the resort. "They're not delusions. You can admit it, you know. You're intimidated by my god-tier talent."

His hand was warm in mine as we walked down the

beach, the sand soft under our feet. I glanced over at him, shaking my head. "There's that modesty I love so much."

"You love everything about me. I'm an amazing footballer, a model, and now I'm a bi icon, according to Ainsley. Who wouldn't love me?" He shot me a teasing glance.

"You missed humble off that list."

"I'm so humble. The humblest of all men."

"Of course you are." I tugged him into me, kissing him hard. "You're right, though. You know how much I love you."

Nipping at my lip, he ran his hand down my back. "I'm the luckiest man in the world. I'm so fucking lucky to have you. You're the best person I know. Every time I think I can't love you more, my heart just expands." Pulling back from me, he dropped the football to the sand and then spread out his hands. He paused for a second before slamming his palms together, miming an explosion. "I'm genuinely worried it's going to explode one of these days."

"I don't think that's how it works, baby."

His eyes narrowed. "I hope you're right, for your sake."

I pulled him into another kiss. It was my favourite way to stop him talking.

When we drew apart, both of us were breathless. He smiled at me before pressing a soft kiss to my cheek. Scooping up the ball, he took my hand again. "I like being here with you, with no one else around."

"Me too. Here, we're just two anonymous people on the beach. Jordan and Theo. Not the famous footballers. Just us."

"Just us." He grinned at me as we began walking again. "And a football. Come on, let's play while it's still light enough to see."

We kicked off our sliders and stepped onto the hard, packed sand at the water's edge. The waves lapped at my toes, the setting sun still warming my skin. I turned to face Jordan and stopped and stared.

His brow was furrowed in concentration, his eyes fixed on the ball at his feet as he flicked it from one foot to the other. Lit up by the fiery reds and coppers of the fading rays, he was so beautiful he made me lose my breath. Memories flashed through my mind, one after the other. Another beach, another time. I'd thought he was so beautiful even then, but I never could've imagined we'd end up like this. Together.

His head rose, and his eyes widened at the expression on my face. "What?"

"Nothing." I stepped closer to him, catching the ball with the side of my foot and bringing it to a stop. "Just thinking. The first time we played football together on the beach—that was the first time I really felt as if we were teammates. It was the first time I thought that maybe things would work out between us."

"Me too." He curved his hand around the back of my neck, pulling me into the slowest, deepest, softest kiss, his fingers sliding up into my hair as my arms wrapped around his waist. "And they have."

I felt the ball slip out from under my foot a millisecond before Jordan tore away from me, a wide, bright grin on his face.

"Better work on those reflexes, baby."

An answering smile spread across my lips. "You're going to pay for that." I lunged at him, but he darted back, laughing, before spinning around and kicking the ball down the beach.

"Yeah?" he called over his shoulder. "Come and catch me, then."

THE END

THANK YOU

Thank you so much for reading Jordan and Theo's story!

Feel free to send me your thoughts, and reviews are always very appreciated ♥ You can find me in my Facebook group Becca's Book Bar if you want to connect, or sign up to my newsletter to stay up to date with all the latest info. Check out all my links at https://linktr.ee/authorbeccasteele

Want another M/M standalone football (soccer) romance? Check out Savage Rivals, available on Kindle Unlimited at https://mybook.to/savagerivals

If you're interested in Dean and Adam, you can find their ongoing story on my Patreon.

And finally, what about JJ, Sanctuary's sparkly dancer with an affinity for tiny shorts? You can find him in the LSU series in Sidelined, at https://mybook.to/LSUsidelined and his own book, Ignite, is coming soon!

Becca xoxo

A NOTE FROM THE AUTHOR

I wanted to share a little note before I go. At the time of writing Reckless, there are no out players in the English Premier League. No one should ever feel pressured to come out, and if they do, it should always be on their own terms. I spent a long time doing research for this book, and a big part of my research was to look at what the process of coming out might be like, and the pressures and issues that the players might face. Although Reckless is fictional, the issues faced by Jordan and Theo are very real.

The UK LGBTQ+ rights charity Stonewall is partnering with Premier League clubs and other sporting communities to campaign for inclusion in sport, with their Rainbow Laces campaign. To find out more about their work, or to support the campaign, check out their website.

Equally, the mental health issues in this book are very real. Regarding the sleeping pill addiction that Theo struggles with - this is a problem which affects professional footballers at all levels.

Finally, if you've struggled with any of the issues in this book, please know that you're not alone. There is help available. Some resources:

USA:
The Trevor Project - LGBTQ+
National Alliance on Mental Illness (NAMI)
American Foundation for Suicide Prevention (AFSP)
Substance Abuse & Mental Health Services

UK:
MindOut - LGBTQ+
Mind
Taking Action on Addiction
Campaign Against Living Miserably (CALM) - men's mental health charity
Samaritans

International:
Checkpoint - global mental health resources
Samaritans - worldwide links

ACKNOWLEDGMENTS

I'd like to start by thanking you for reading Reckless. It means so much to me, and I'm forever grateful.

To the other authors involved in the Unlucky 13 shared world - I've loved working with you and writing in this world we created!

Thank you to Charli, Terra, and Bethany for your constant messages throughout this writing process. They kept me going, and I appreciate you guys so much! And of course, Claudia and Jenny - where would I be without you both? Love you!

A huge thanks to my betas Jenny, Charli, and Amy. You're awesome! And on that note, I should probably thank my other slightly more reluctant beta, Mr. Steele. You're quite awesome, too, sometimes.

Speaking of Mr. Steele, I have to thank you for all your footballing knowledge. While I took some artistic license here and there, any football-related errors in this book are entirely yours. Or maybe mine. But probably yours, since you're the one with an FA coaching qualification. In addition, I need to thank my son for his enthusiasm for naming players and positions, and coming up with an entire team with me. Although I'm sure he will never read this, he deserves recognition for the work he put in.

Thank you as always to my dream team Sandra and Rumi, for getting this book ready for publication. We are officially #teamchaos and we will never change. And thank you to Kerry for the diamond cover!

Finally, another huge thank you to my amazing MB and ARC teams, my Patrons, readers, bloggers, and everyone who played a role in sharing, promoting, and reading this book. It means a lot.

Becca xoxo

ALSO BY BECCA STEELE

LSU Series

(M/M college romance)

Collided

Blindsided

Sidelined

The Four Series

(M/F college suspense romance)

The Lies We Tell

The Secrets We Hide

The Havoc We Wreak

A Cavendish Christmas (free short story)*

The Fight In Us

The Bonds We Break

The Darkness In You

Alstone High Standalones

(new adult high school romance)

Trick Me Twice (M/F)

Cross the Line (M/M)

In a Week (free short story)* (M/F)

Savage Rivals (M/M)

London Players Series

(M/F rugby romance)

The Offer

London Suits Series

(M/F office romance)

The Deal

The Truce

The Wish (a festive short story)*

Other Standalones

Cirque des Masques (M/M dark circus romance)

Reckless (M/M soccer romance)

Mayhem (M/F Four series dark spinoff)*

Heatwave (M/F summer short story)*

Boneyard Kings Series (with C. Lymari)

(RH/why-choose college suspense romance)

Merciless Kings

Vicious Queen

Ruthless Kingdom

Box Sets

Caiden & Winter trilogy (M/F)

(*The Four series books 1-3*)

*all free short stories and bonus scenes are available from https://authorbeccasteele.com

**Key - M/F = Male/Female romance

M/M = Male/Male romance

RH = Reverse Harem/why-choose (one woman & 3+ men) romance

ABOUT THE AUTHOR

Becca Steele is a USA Today and Wall Street Journal bestselling romance author. She currently lives in the south of England with a whole horde of characters that reside inside her head.

When she's not writing, you can find her reading or watching Netflix, usually with a glass of wine in hand. Failing that, she'll be online hunting for memes or making her 500th Spotify playlist.

Join Becca's Facebook reader group Becca's Book Bar, sign up to her mailing list, check out her Patreon, or find her via the following links:

- facebook.com/authorbeccasteele
- instagram.com/authorbeccasteele
- bookbub.com/profile/becca-steele
- goodreads.com/authorbeccasteele
- patreon.com/authorbeccasteele
- amazon.com/stores/Becca-Steele/author/B07WT6GWB2

Printed by Amazon Italia Logistica S.r.l.
Torrazza Piemonte (TO), Italy